The Pride
of the
Acre

The Pride
of the
Acre

Stephen O'Connor

gatekeeper press™
Tampa, Florida

The Pride of the Acre is a work of fiction. All incidents and dialogue, and all characters with the exception of some well-known or historical figures, are products of the author's imagination and not to be construed as real. Where real life or historical figures appear, the situations and dialogues concerning those persons are fictional and are not intended to depict actual events or to change the fictional nature of the novel. *The Pride of the Acre*, from inception to execution, was entirely the product of a human imagination. AI was never consulted and never will be.

The Pride of the Acre

Published by Gatekeeper Press
7853 Gunn Hwy., Suite 209
Tampa, FL 33626
www.GatekeeperPress.com

Copyright © 2024 by Stephen O'Connor
All rights reserved. Neither this book, nor any parts within it may be sold or reproduced in any form or by any electronic or mechanical means, including information storage and retrieval systems, without permission in writing from the author. The only exception is by a reviewer, who may quote short excerpts in a review.

The editorial work for this book is entirely the product of the author. Gatekeeper Press did not participate in and is not responsible for any aspect of these elements.

ISBN (paperback): 9781662957383
eISBN: 9781662957390

Before me runs a road of toil
With my grave cut across.
Sing, trailing showers and breezy downs —
I know the tragic hearts of towns.

—Alexander Smith, "Glasgow"

Other books by Stephen O'Connor:

Smokestack Lightning, Stories
The Spy in the City of Books
The Witch at Rivermouth
This Is No Time to Quit Drinking
Northwest of Boston, Stories

For more information, visit lowellwriter.com

Cover image: John Boutselis: Facing East Photo

For Jim and Elinor

Day Dawns

Charlie was dreaming of Laila Grant, a woman he had loved, though she was never truly his. It was an extraordinary dream and one from which he would never willingly awaken because, in it, she spoke to him. In general, when she came to him in dreams, it was in a place where her words could not be heard, aboard a boat on a stormy sea, under thunderous skies in a wind-swept wood, or in some hour of clamorous peril. In one dream, she had shouted incomprehensible words to him amid the clashing swords and the shield-shattering blows of a capital overtaken in war. Her shadow was cast over him by what Charlie took to be the burning towers of some citadel. He always struggled through those dreams to protect her, though he knew that it was she who was more likely to protect him somehow.

In the pale hour before this gray dawn, she had not come to him amid threatening seas nor at the climax of some cataclysmic battle, but on a sun-spangled shore under the green boughs of oak where they had once stood when she was alive. In the shallows, a blue heron stood, fixed in the cloud-mirror of the water amid the lily pads of the rushy fen, more motionless than the great tree that spread its gently nodding boughs above them. Laila spoke to him. "Charlie, I miss you."

Tears gathered in his closed eyes and seeped onto his pillow. "Laila, I thought you were gone."

"No," she said. Her dark eyes searched his own. Stepping toward him, she spoke in a voice that was soft and low and playfully insistent "I'm here. With you."

Some troubling sound, a wakeful harbinger from the world of day, told him all this was wrong, but he turned it off and embraced the resurrected woman. How she was living and where she had been were questions, and it was not the time for questions. He stroked her dark hair and kissed her mouth and lived entirely and all in the world of a lost joy when the spell was broken. The water around the heron rippled and then the heron himself seemed to ripple as he spread silent wings and then froze like an image on a celadon vase. Charlie became aware of his empty arms and saw Laila's figure retreating into the dim recesses of the wood.

Voices filtered through the curtain of the dream—like hunters faintly heard approaching through a forest until one called, "Charlie Tumulty!" The scene lost definition and it all came back—or was that a dream too? That today was—yes, today is . . .

"Big day for you, Tumulty!" the sergeant said. "Freedom."

Charlie sat up. The sergeant, in black shirt and cap, the blue chevron of his rank on his shoulder, leaned against the bars of his cell and asked, "Are you ready?"

Chapter 1

1989

Charlie felt weak—a lost child in a crowd of strangers. The November landscape that unfolded as the train rolled along the tracks from North Station in Boston toward the Gallagher Terminal in Lowell was familiar; it was the world itself that was strangely unfamiliar. That morning, he had been released from Walpole after a nine-year stint. An old friend from a boxing gym in Somerville had picked him up, taken him to lunch at Doyle's and then to the station, where he ordered a double shot of Jameson at the Iron Horse and boarded a train for his hometown of Lowell.

A guy at the bar had said to him, "Hey, I know you."

Hardly turning, Charlie said, "Right. Is this where you take a swing at me?"

"I wouldn't mess with you, pal. You're Charlie Tumulty, the boxer."

"I was," Charlie said and squinted as he downed the whiskey the bartender set before him. He didn't even like hard liquor, but he felt he needed something to fortify him against the anxious feeling that had seized his heart in returning to the world beyond the bars and the wire.

"Yeah, I saw you fight on a card in Lawrence, once. One of those unsanctioned bouts. You fought two fights, an hour apart. Won both."

"Long time ago."

The rolling scenery blurred as he focused on the reflection in the train window. An old woman sat diagonally across from him on the other side of the aisle. Her searching eyes were on him, and he wondered what she saw there. A thirty-six-year-old man with an institutional haircut carrying a gym bag. Jeans, a tan jacket, and sneakers. They had handed him a box with these "release clothes" that, thank God, Fitzgibbons had left for him. Otherwise, he'd have had to exchange his orange jump suit for whatever moth-eaten sweatpants and wrinkled tee shirts they pulled from a goodwill container.

When he went into the joint, they had taken his watch, a signet ring, a Celtic cross medal that had belonged to his grandfather, and a few other things. And this morning, the only things that remained in the bag the administrative C.O. handed him were the watch, now dead, and, on a rusted ring, a couple of keys to the front and back doors of what had been Eddie's Piano Bar.

"Where's the rest of my stuff?" he asked.

The C.O. rolled his eyes and said, "That's what's in there. You want to go back in the holding cell while you fill out a missing articles form?"

Charlie shook his head.

The man nodded and handed him his gate money, fifty dollars and a check for the money he had on the books, the five hundred he'd managed to save from his fifteen-dollar-a-week salary working as a line cook in "Culinary." He signed a paper agreeing that if he were arrested for any of a long list of crimes, he would immediately return to prison. Then, the C.O. waved him along without a word of farewell or encouragement. He walked toward a door he had never passed through before. A buzzer sounded, and he paced another corridor toward the final station, where his fingerprints were matched with the prints they had on file for Charles Tumulty. It was determined that he was himself, and he was escorted to the final exit. The door slid open, and the world appeared. *Freedom. Are you ready?*

"Winchester Center! Next stop, Winchester Center!" The metallic voice brought him back to the prison somehow. Metal doors. Metal voices. Only now, as he watched people moving along the platform full of their own direction and purpose, he felt that vague fear they say always haunts the newly released con. *Can I make it out here?* Nearly a decade had passed, and he felt as if he'd been released onto the moon. People walking freely under a vast sky. No walls topped with circular razor wire marring every horizon. No guard towers. No guards. All the colors were brighter. All the sounds bizarre.

He recalled all that he had left behind in that other world that had been his world and that still cast its shadow over his freedom. He had missed the 1980s. Sitting in his cell, day after day, year after year, reading the books Fitzgibbons brought him until his eyes were bleary. The faces of the prisoners passed through his memory as they had in the endless daily succession of cafeteria lines. Their voices clamored and echoed in the corridors of his mind as they had in corridors of steel and stone. In stacked cellblock rows, chins jutting between bars, caged men talking shit to a guy in another cell, or maybe to God, but God wasn't listening. And amid this sad furor, old Hardie Bangs calls out a chess move to Charlie. Both men had chessboards set up in their cells. Hardie, a rock in the rushing stream of madness.

His last day in the kitchen: men, some of whom had become like brothers to him, saying their goodbyes, Alejo Natividad, Wallace Fry, Ganson Balden and the quietly unbroken Hardie Bangs with a face like carved ebony and the deep and velvet voice of a late-night disc jockey, telling him, "I'm afraid you're gonna be back. Charlie." Hardie knew Charlie's story.

That frightened him more than anything. *I can't go back. Not ever.* Yet he knew that if ever he met the man who had taken Laila's life, he would send him to hell and face the consequences. He would go back. Love had to be stronger than fear. Stronger than death.

The sound of doors at the rear of the car sliding open jarred him from this reverie. "Tickets, please." The sense of insecurity grew. He was a child again, tentative, unsure of the rules. He held the ticket tightly in his hand. The dark uniform of the conductor made him uneasy. "Tickets, please." Involuntarily, he bowed his head as he presented his ticket. The conductor punched it and moved on wordlessly, and Charlie felt relief, as if he had survived some dangerous encounter. *This will never do,* he told himself. *Charlie Tumulty, the contender, the tough guy, the Pride of the Acre—afraid of a train conductor? Who the hell am I now? How did I get here?*

Soon the fuzzy metallic voice returned. "Final stop, Lowell. Lowell, Massachusetts ladies and gentlemen." And he remembered that character in *A Tale of Two Cities* freed from the Bastille. Dickens had called the chapter simply, "Recalled to Life."

Chapter 2

1965

Thirteen-year-old Charlie Tumulty shielded his eyes, squinting at the road before him, pausing for a moment to watch the thickly falling snow swirling in the arc of glowing streetlights, and to listen as the wind rushed through the alleys of the Acre, and the snow whispered to the empty streets. He could almost appreciate the beauty of the scene, but he was cold. A gust tore at the visor of his baseball cap, which he caught before it flew; he reversed it on his head. The cold bit his fingers and pried into the split leather of his shoes and ate through worn soles to wrench at his toes and numb his feet, rising through him to smother in a chill wet fog what seemed to be the faintly burning coal that was his young heart. Cold echoed and amplified the other pain that was hunger, an aching block of ice in the pit of his stomach. "Too cold," he murmured, and continued, head bowed, against the eye-stinging snow.

He almost wished he had stayed at home, but Hanley, his mother's boyfriend, and his dumbass pal Skipper came back with subs from Broadway Pizza and didn't bring him anything. Hanley mainly hung around the house and drank. He watched Julia Child, but he never cooked anything. He had gotten hurt in a scaffold accident on a construction site, and he intended to stay on disability as long as he could, though he had taken a couple of framing jobs under the table. He limped a bit, but he wasn't really hurt.

Charlie had found nothing in the refrigerator but some beer and a half bottle of milk. He had eaten what remained of the Cheerios for breakfast. The men were playing cards and smoking and drinking in the kitchen. Charlie stayed on the couch trying to get his mind off the hunger by rereading his *Superman* comics, but the emptiness in his stomach grew into a void that threatened to encompass him. Near nine o'clock, Hanley and his sidekick were getting loud, and Charlie was too hungry to think about Lex Luthor's villainy or Lois Lane's allure.

His mother Grace worked as a waitress at the Pineview. If he could make it down there, she would get him something to eat. He grabbed his jacket and baseball cap. "Where the hell you think *you're* going?" Hanley asked, as if he were a real father.

"Fuck you, Hanley."

"Hey! You little shit!" The other man laughed at Hanley's lackluster attempt at paternal discipline, but Charlie knew he was too drunk to try to stop him and certainly wouldn't chase him through the storm. The truth was he couldn't care less.

So now it was the grail of the Pineview menu that drove him onward, his bare hands pulled into his sleeves and pressed against benumbed ears. An orange strobe tinted the falling snow as a plow approached, its grating blade drowning the silken murmur of settling flakes. Charlie stepped into the deeper drifts of the sidewalk to let the plow pass, but it stopped. The driver leaned over and cranked the window down enough to yell, "What are you doing kid? Why don't you go home?"

"Eddie?"

"Jesus, Charlie! You're gonna freeze!"

"I'm locked out. I gotta get the key from my mother." He shielded his eyes and looked up at the driver, staggering in a sudden blast of snow-laden wind.

"Hop in." It was his Uncle Eddie, his father's brother and the owner of Eddie's Piano Bar. He made extra money plowing for the city. "Is she still working at the . . ."

"Pineview," Charlie said as he climbed into the high cab.

"I'll drop you there. They'll find you frozen for Christ's sake, like poor Ira Hayes." He eyed him critically. "You ain't dressed for this kinda weather, kid!"

The cab of the truck was warm, but Eddie pushed a lever, and the boy heard the heat fan shift and blow harder. He held his hands low under the dashboard where the heat flowed over them. Uncle Eddie was a big man; he wore a fur-lined aviator hat that, Charlie thought, gave him a comical air, especially when he added, in the voice of W.C. Fields, "It ain't a fit night out for man nor beast." He cast another sidelong glance at Charlie and said, "How you gettin' back?"

"I can walk."

Eddie shook his head. "That's crazy. Get the key and I'll wait for you."

"My mother will want to get me something to eat while I'm there."

Eddie nodded, peering into the swirling snow as the truck trundled over the S Bridge and down onto Middlesex Street. "I'll come back in a half hour. Your mother won't be thrilled to see me."

"Why don't she like you, Eddie?"

"Oh, it's an old story, now. I can't keep my mouth shut when I see something I don't like. Your father isn't always crazy about me, either."

"I hardly see him. All he cares about is getting drunk."

"It was the war, Charlie. It was all the war. Made most of us a little crazy." A few minutes later, he pulled off Princeton Boulevard into the parking lot of the Pineview. There was a cruiser and a few other cars whose contours were losing their definition under snow. "It's 9:15," Eddie said. "Look for me around 9:55. Somethin' like that, before 10:00."

"Thanks, Eddie." The orange light of the plow dimmed as the truck receded into the curtain of white and Charlie ducked around back and banged on a metal door beside the dumpster. A skinny guy with a blue bandana around his head opened the door. "What the hell you want?"

"I need to see Grace Tumulty."

"You her kid?"

"Yeah."

"All right. Come inside, you're freezin' the place out." Charlie stepped over the threshold as the man went off, shivering. He took off his cap and shook the snow to the floor and stamped his feet, looking around at the brightly lit kitchen with its stainless-steel counters and brick-red tile floors. Fry baskets, pans, and various pots hung above fryolators and ovens. Beside the sink, a boy in checked pants and a white tunic noisily unloaded a dishwasher. Beneath the smells of cleaner, Charlie inhaled the smokey scent of fried meat, and his stomach ached.

His mother rushed in, tucking a pencil behind her ear, a swinging door in her wake. "Where is he?" She spotted him. "Charlie?" She raised her hands, at a loss. "What happened? What are you doing here? It's snowin' to beat the band."

"Ma." He hesitated because the dishwasher had paused in his work and was observing the scene. He was embarrassed and took a step to his left so that his mother blocked the boy's view of him. "I'm hungry, mom! There's nothin' to eat at home. Hanley and stupid Skipper went to Broadway Pizza, but they didn't bring me back anything."

"Useless son of a bitch. I'm sorry, Charlie. I'm a terrible mother."

"No, you're not Ma, but I'm hungry. I just had Cheerios this morning and a slice of pizza at school."

Her shoulders sagged, and she bit her lower lip and shook her head. "Alex, can you make the kid a burger? Make him a burger."

"No problem. You like fries, kid? Of course you do."

Grace tilted her blonde head, and in the fluorescent light, Charlie noticed a few gray hairs. Her blue eyes grew round, and her lips pressed into a pout. "I am a shit mother, I know. I just didn't plan for you, Charlie. That's all right. You come from a line of tough people, and you're gonna have to be tough, too. You'll be all right."

He hugged his mother and inhaled her scent: flowers and tobacco smoke. "I love you, Ma."

"Oh, you're damp and freezing. Not much in tips tonight, Honey. Just a couple of cops and some people who live close to here. I'd better go check on 'em. Come with me."

She took him out of the brightly lit kitchen into the dimness of the restaurant. "O Holy Night" was playing on some speaker, and she sat him in a booth near the door and got him a Sprite. "Ma, a guy is gonna give me a ride home, so I gotta eat fast."

"What guy is waitin' around for you in the storm?"

"A guy doin' some plowin' for the city."

She drew back, still watching him, as if he had insulted her. "What guy?"

"Okay, it's Uncle Eddie."

She made a guttural sound of disgust. "Can't he stay out of our business?"

"He just gave me a ride."

"Is he waitin'?"

"No, he's comin' back."

A customer signaled Grace as if he were scribbling in the air, and she produced her check pad and went off. The cops were leaving and the place was nearly empty. A few minutes later she brought a hamburger with lettuce and tomato and fries, and Charlie ate greedily. His mother went and leaned over the bar to talk to another woman who was mixing a drink. Charlie watched the guy who got his check count some money out on his table and stand up. He pulled a knit hat over his balding head, and as he passed by his mother said, "Good night," and slapped her ass.

"Gus!" she said, turning. "Cut the shit!" The man laughed and started to pull on his gloves. As he passed Charlie's table on his way to the door, Charlie called out, "Asshole!"

The man stopped and said, "What's zat you said?"

"Don't slap my mother's ass, dickhead!"

"Okay, Charlie. It's all right," his mother said. "I'll take care of it."

"It's friendly," the guy said. "We're friends. So settle down, little man."

"You slap all your friends on the ass, dickhead?"

"You're gonna get your face slapped you little shit!"

Charlie slid out of the booth, fists clenched, staring up at the customer. He was angry, and inwardly he cursed his age and his size. *Little man. Little shit.* The words rankled. *Oh, if I were a man, I'd kick your ass!* As things stood, he'd take the hopeless fight. He'd just try to make it difficult enough for the guy to embarrass him. Maybe get in one good shot. He'd been doing wrestling after school at the Boys Club, and he wished he could get the guy in a suicide cradle, but he was way too big.

"Charlie, stop it!" his mother shouted.

"You wanna slap, you little shit? Teach you some manners!" He stepped toward the boy, who raised his fists.

"No! Gus!"

"Nobody's gonna slap anybody," a voice declared. Charlie turned to see Uncle Eddie in the doorway, looking like a war pilot in his fur-lined leather headgear. "It's the Christmas season, Mac. I don't know what he did, but he's a kid. Let it go."

"I'm not gonna take shit from any little punk," the man growled, pointing in Charlie's face.

The smile on Eddie's face faded; the friendly eyes turned hard, and the boy saw it all replaced by a sort of dangerous stillness. "Merry Christmas," he said. And after a pause, "Now screw."

The other man sensed the danger, too. The insolence melted and he stalked out, muttering.

"All right, Charlie," Eddie said when the man had left. "You got your key?"

"Oh yeah, I got it." The phone at the bar was ringing.

"What key?" his mother asked.

"He said he was locked out."

"I got the key," Charlie said.

The bartender called out, "Grace, that was Nick. He said to close up and get home."

"Let's go!" Eddie said.

"Come with us, Ma," Charlie said, wrapping the remainder of the burger and the rest of the fries in a napkin and stuffing it all into his pocket.

She turned her back to him and began to run a damp rag over the recently deserted table. "I'm all set, Charlie. I'll see you at home," she said dryly. "We'll make a snowman tomorrow." She glanced over her shoulder at Eddie. "I'll call a cab, or I'll walk."

"Come on, Grace," Eddie said, but it was useless. Charlie knew that if there was one thing his mother was good at, it was holding a grudge, even an imaginary one. She stalked off toward the kitchen without another word.

With the plow blade up, Eddie drove along Middlesex to Broadway and swung onto Adams Street. A weather report on the radio said snow was expected to end by mid-morning the following day. "You won't have school tomorrow, Charlie," Eddie said.

The boy pulled a french fry from his pocket. "Great. I get to hang around with freakin' Hanley all day."

Charlie recalled his mother's words. "We'll make a snowman." He had said nothing, not wanting to humiliate his mother in front of Eddie, but he certainly had no desire to build a snowman with bare hands, wearing battered shoes, a spring jacket and a baseball cap. In the fall, she always talked about going to some inn up in the White Mountains where they would hike past waterfalls and view the foliage. The snowman was another New England dream from Grace's store of fantasies, none of which resembled anything like their lives.

"Thanks for the ride, Uncle Eddie," Charlie said. "Hope I didn't mess up your schedule."

"No problem kiddo. You're there on the right, the yellow house? Hard to see."

Charlie peered upward through the snow sweep and said, somewhat sadly, "Top floor."

"All right, then." The truck jolted to a stop under the streetlight. "Mind if I tell you something, man to man?"

"Go ahead."

One arm hanging over the steering wheel, the snow swirling in the truck's lights, Eddie Tumulty began, "Listen Charlie. If that guy was a kid anywhere near your own size, I wouldn't have stepped in. Just a word of warning. I like that you're a tough kid, but you can be too tough. Like your grandfather used to say, 'It's often that a man's mouth breaks his nose.'"

"That guy insulted my mother. He just slapped her ass like he was . . ."

"Okay, I understand. Mothers are another category. I would never blame any man, or boy, for defending his mother. Sure. You have to defend your mother. Always. Or your family, or someday your wife. Short of that, just be careful, Charlie. Don't let your mouth break your nose, or maybe worse, for no good reason. I feel some responsibility for you, even though I'm not welcome in your house. I probably have no right to . . ." He paused, wondering if he were transgressing into personal matters. The streetlight, shining through the swirling snow and the ice melting on the windshield, made wild shadows crawl around the cab of the truck. "Sounds like you don't care for this Harley guy."

"Hanley. My mother's boyfriend. Dumb drunken loser. Like my father."

"That's too bad. I hate to hear that. Don't judge your father too harshly. He was different before the war. All that killin' can mess a man up. Messed up a lot of guys. Some wounds you can see, like that long scar on his chest. Some wounds you can't see. Has he ever talked to you about the war at all?"

"Nah. He never really talks to me about anything."

"Anyway, I'm in the phone book. My home phone and the bar, too. Any time you need me, you give me a call, all right? Only if you do go picking fights, don't look for me to help you. If you start 'em, you finish 'em. Now I better get back to work."

"Okay. Thanks, Uncle Eddie."

"Hey kid—what size shoes you wear?"

"Nine. Why?"

"Why do you think? This here is New England. You need some boots, kiddo, and some winter clothes."

"Thanks, Eddie, but Grace will probably be pissed if you bring 'em," Charlie said. He jumped down out of the cab and waded across the snow-covered sidewalks, finishing the rest of the hamburger before he got to the stairs. As he climbed to the third floor, he heard raucous laughter coming from his apartment. The sisters who lived downstairs, the ones his mother called "the floosies," were drinking with Hanley and Skipper.

Hanley growled something as Charlie passed, and he said once more, "Fuck you, Hanley," and the sisters laughed some more.

His room was cold, and he spread what blankets he had over the bedspread and stuffed a towel against the drafty window sill. Finally, he heard his mother coming in. Hurricane Grace, and she swept them all before her. Charlie peered out from his bedroom and saw the sisters and Skipper hurrying to the door clutching their coats and drinks, while Grace shouted, "I'm workin' my ass off so you can sit there getting wasted with your loser buddy and them floosies? And you put on the oven to heat the kitchen? Are you gonna pay the goddamn bill?"

Charlie heard Hanley defend himself weakly. He wasn't smart enough to mount a good defense. "You're a party pooper, Grace."

"And you're a lazy-ass piece of shit!"

There was a shifting of chairs, mumbled threats and a creaking of the floor under Hanley's limping gait. Hanley took to the couch, mumbling an incoherent recitation of his grievances. His mother sat at the table in the lit kitchen drinking a beer and smoking a cigarette. From time to time, she rubbed her forehead with her fingertips or shook her head or blew a hopeless cloud of smoke toward the ceiling. Just another sad page in the story of Grace's life. Charlie wished there was something he could say to her to make her feel better, but he couldn't think of anything and went back to bed.

Hanley was gone two days later. He didn't leave anything from his disability check to help pay the rent.

Chapter 3

After Hanley moved out, Grace and her friend Penny started hitting the Market Street bars and drinking hard. New men began to arrive, usually after midnight. Charlie would hear loud laughter, senseless arguments, clinking glasses and music—sometimes with dancing that jarred the furniture, and occasionally Grace's voice saying, "Shhhh! The boy's sleepin'!" This quieted things down for about thirty seconds, but drunks don't quiet down until they pass out. The worst sounds were the ones he heard later, when his mother went to her room with some new friend from the White Eagle or the Cosmo, and Charlie pulled his pillow over his head and tried not to hear.

One Saturday morning, he found Penny on the couch and two men passed out on the living room floor. The coffee table was littered with empty Schlitz cans, a nearly empty bottle of tequila and a lot of dixie cups. A bag of chips lay open on the floor by the couch; some had spilled and been ground into the rug. He had thought life was bad with Hanley, but this was worse.

He found a loaf of Wonder Bread and a jar of peanut butter and made himself a sandwich. He put on his coat, went out on "the porch" that was really just a landing. He sat on the top step of the narrow stairs, eating and reading the book he'd taken from the school library, *A Light in the Forest*. It was the story of John Butler, a white boy who had been kidnapped by Lenni Lenape Indians back in the 1700s. He was adopted by Cuyloga, who renamed him True Son, and he learned the Indian ways and their language. When the Indians signed a treaty with the British, captives had to be returned. But the boy didn't want to be John Butler anymore; he wanted to be True Son. The Indian village is where he knew he belonged, but Cuyloga told him he had to go back.

Charlie looked up from the book and out over the neighborhood from his third-floor perch. It was quiet as all Saturday mornings were quiet. Smoke rose from chimneys. A few crows traversed the sky, and squirrels leapt among the naked trees, shaking sunlit snow-dust from the branches. Someone was cooking bacon; maybe there was a nice family breakfast in one of the kitchens nearby. Life could be good with a family like the ones you saw on TV. Why couldn't he have had a father like Uncle Eddie?

Charlie thought he was a lot like True Son. He didn't belong anywhere. Not with his mother, really, and certainly not with his father. There was one nice guy his mother had seen for a while. His name was Phil and he had taken him to a Red Sox game. Charlie loved baseball. When you were watching a game, you didn't think about anything else. It was nice being with Phil at a game or playing catch in the yard. They played barehanded with a rubber ball, but Phil mentioned he was going to get Charlie a glove and a baseball. He never did, though. He and Grace started arguing, and he left, like all the others.

    The two guys finally stumbled out—they were big guys with beards who looked like Hells Angels. Charlie lowered the book and slid it under his leg because some guys think you're not tough if they see you reading a book. The men stopped to light cigarettes and said, "Hi." They zipped their leather jackets. One of them pulled a bandana from his pocket and tied it around his head. The other clapped on some sunglasses. "You Grace's kid?"

    "Yeah."

    "Hope we didn't keep you up, kid." He had a bout of coughing and said, "Ah, shit." He spit over the railing and the two men descended the stairs, and Charlie heard a car start out front. He heard Penny and his mother in the kitchen. Their voices sounded defeated. Looking through the window, he saw them drinking coffee and smoking cigarettes. It hurt him to admit it, but he wished he had another life. Another mother.

The next day, Sunday morning, there was a knock on the door. Charlie opened it and saw a tall man with white hair and kindly eyes. He was carrying two bags, and spoke in a low and discreet voice, "I'm from the St. Vincent de Paul Society. Your name was submitted by someone in the parish as a family that might need a bit of help at this difficult time. We put together some things the parishioner mentioned that you could probably use." Charlie took one bag and the man set the other down just inside.

"Who is it?" his mother called.

"A guy from the . . ."

"St. Vincent de Paul Society. We're making a few deliveries in the parish."

Grace came into the kitchen with wet hair and an unlit cigarette dangling from her mouth as Charlie was pulling from the bag a winter coat that looked about his size. She was wearing her waitress uniform, white shirt and black pants, but was still in bare feet on the cold linoleum floor. The man pulled off his cap and said, "Morning, Mrs. Tumulty. I'm Bob Gilman from St. Vincent de Paul. A parishioner put a note in our box with a donation . . ."

"What parishioner?"

"It wasn't signed. The person suggested you could use a few things. Like a lot of people in the parish."

Grace looked from the bags to the man, as if she would like to muster her pride and tell him to take the things away, but she saw Charlie stepping into a good pair of winter boots and surrendered. She sighed, "Yeah. Thanks." She grabbed a lighter off the stove and left the room.

In addition to the coat and boots, there were gloves, two sweaters, a scarf and a forty-dollar gift certificate to

Demoulas Market. Charlie laced up the boots, put on the jacket and walked along Broadway, stopping as always to look in the windows of Fitzgibbons' junk shop, and returned home laden with bulging bags. Milk, eggs, a pound of ham, bread, beans, peas, chocolate bars and a chicken. For once they would be well-stocked, and there was still twenty-one dollars on the gift certificate.

Charlie's father Jack came by the following Saturday, eager to gloat over the departure of Grace's new guy. He leaned back as he sat at the kitchen table, pale blue eyes in a weathered face, one arm hooked behind his chair, still slim, the copper-colored hair that Charlie had inherited combed back, looking remarkably well for a hard-drinking man. "Hanley couldn't take it, finally, eh?" he asked no one in particular, then he turned to Charlie. "Ever hear of Boston Blackie?" he asked.

"Yeah, I heard of him, but I don't know him," Charlie said.

His old man laughed. "He was a safe cracker. Think you could crack a safe, Charlie?"

"Uhm, no."

"Crack a safe!" Grace said, shaking her head. "Don't pay any attention to him, Charlie." She shot a scornful look at her ex-husband. "What, do you want your son to be a criminal?"

He shrugged and said, "He gotta learn *some* trade."

"That ain't a *trade*! Jesus Christ. You want coffee?" she asked, grudgingly. "I just made it."

"Nah," he said, "you make lousy coffee anyway, Gracie." He leaned back, turned to the boy and said, "Charlie, go get my cigarettes in the truck."

Charlie stepped into his new boots, and bent to lace them, but his mother said, "You don't have to do anything for him. He don't do anything for you. Let him get his own cigarettes."

Charlie stood between the two, frozen, caught in the great wheel of love, hate, duty; trying to keep the fragile peace, wanting to respect both parents, though he suspected the old man didn't deserve a lot of respect. But it was his mother who took care of him, in her way, and it was her eyes that commanded. He didn't move, but he finished tying his laces because he had a feeling he'd want to leave soon. Jack Tumulty smiled, delighted to be tearing them all apart. "Come on Charlie boy," he says, "run out to my truck and . . ."

"Don't go anywhere!" his mother countermanded.

"Wait a minute," his father said, "Hold everything, Charlie. I still have a couple here." He pulled a wrinkled pack of Chesterfields from his shirt pocket, smiling contentedly. Charlie started to hate that handsome, smiling face. "I got something to show you," he said, flicking a flame from his US Army lighter with the five-pointed star on the side and lighting the cigarette clamped between his teeth. He rolled up his right shirt sleeve and thrust out his forearm. "It's a tattoo. A new one." Charlie looked at his father's outstretched arm and saw a blue skull-and-crossbones with one word written in gothic script below it. A word that tore his heart in two: GRACE.

"That's a cocker, ain't it?" he asked, enjoying himself, as always, at their expense.

Grace didn't laugh. No one laughed, except the old man. His mother glared at him. "Son of a bitch!" she cried, pulling the coffee carafe off the hot plate. Jack ducked and it dashed against the wall, leaving scattered shards of glass and coffee splattered over the curtains and table and running down the wall to puddle on the linoleum. "Whoa Grace!" Jack cried. "I guess you don't like my tattoo!" He was laughing at the sport he had provided himself, but he added, "If you'd hit me with that, you'd be riding in an ambulance shortly."

"Dad! Stop it!"

"You think you scare me?" she shouted. "Remember the last time you hit me? Was it worth it, tough guy? You hit me again, you'd better kill me or sleep with a fuckin' gun for the rest of your life!"

He stood. "Temper! Temper! You still got my gun. I never got it back you crazy bitch!"

"An' I got it handy if anybody ever comes in here uninvited. Including you."

With sudden innocence, he said, "Listen, I just came by to give you some money." He pulled a green wad from his pocket.

She stretched out a hand. "Give me the money and beat it."

"That's not very polite. Say *please*!"

She lunged for the money, but his father pulled it away over his head, stumbling against the table, which shuddered and was knocked back with a grating sound until it thudded against the wall.

"Well, do you want it or not?" She lunged again, muttering curses, and they struggled for possession of the money. Charlie grabbed his coat and ran out the door and down the three flights to the street. He saw his father's rusting truck with the ladders piled high on racks, the bed cluttered with buckets of tar, bent drainpipes and broken slate. He stopped and kicked the truck, but if he made a dent, it hardly mattered. He ran up to the S Bridge and along Middlesex Street for a while until he cut through a car dealership and jumped a fence, which was easy because the plow had pushed a snowbank up against it. He was glad his gloves and hat were in the coat pockets as he crunched along the frozen path under bare trees toward the piece of wilderness tucked into this corner of the city, hidden from every street—Black Brook.

Chapter 4

The edges of the "brook," which was really a large swampy pond, were frozen. But true to its name, the pond itself was a black mirror which held the bare trees. Charlie saw Danny Redding, known as "Squiggles," on the other side. He had got saddled with that name because Miss Flynn at the Bartlett School said his writing "Looks like a lot of squiggles!" They waved, but there was no way for Charlie to get across here. The rafts they used in summer were frozen among the bracken of the shore. He traced the edge of the icy pond until he came to the brook that fed it. He crossed there, jumping between small islands of marsh grass, rocks, and fallen trees.

Charlie came up on Squiggles, who had set up an old tire against a tree and was throwing snowballs through its center. He lived on Burnside Street, so a path into Black Brook was nearly in his backyard. "I'm practicing for spring baseball. Goin' out for pitcher. They need pitchers," he said.

Charlie watched for a while and Squiggles invited him to try. He threw three hard snowballs through the center, and the other boy said, "You're pretty good. You could be a pitcher. The guys from last year graduated. They need more than one."

Charlie didn't recall anyone ever having told him he could be good at anything. He had never been on a team, though he had played some friendly games at the North Common when he could share a glove with a guy on the other side. He hardly noticed the time pass as they threw at the tire and Squiggles explained all about the finer points of pitching. "You got a glove?" he asked.

"No."

"You can use my brother's old one. You'd better start practicing throwing and catching a baseball if you want to go out for the school team." And Charlie decided if he was any good at it, he would go out for the school team.

David "Foxy" McRae lived on the first floor. He was already fourteen, but his mother made him go to St. Patrick's School, where he was in eighth grade. He had shaggy blond hair, wore an oversized army coat and smoked pot in the garage with two kids Charlie had seen hanging out at the Red Bridge in the summer. They had painted their names up there and jumped off the top span. That took stones. Bigger stones than Charlie had. Foxy used to ask Charlie if he wanted to smoke a joint with him and the bridge jumpers, but Charlie wasn't interested in that. Seemed like all the losers he knew were into getting drunk and doing drugs, and the smart people weren't. Maybe that's why they called it "dope." He was curious about what alcohol did to a person, and he thought he'd like to try it once to find out. In the long run, he suspected that the road to a better life went around those things. He'd rather do wrestling at the Boys Club, and he hoped, play baseball.

Near Christmas, he saw Uncle Eddie on a ladder hanging a string of Christmas lights across the eaves of the Piano Bar. His uncle spotted him and climbed down the ladder. "How are you, Charlie boy?"

"I'm pretty good." He gazed upward. "Nice lights. But isn't it a little late to be hanging lights?"

"One of the strings went out—I'm just replacing it. What are you up to? Doin' any sledding?"

"I been up to Mount Pleasant," Charlie said, "and practicin' baseball."

"Baseball? In the snow?"

"My friend Squiggles lets me use his brother's glove. Still, it kinda stings when your hands are cold."

"I should think so."

"I think I'm gonna be a pitcher."

Eddie nodded and smiled and gave him a rough hug. "You know what you want, and you work for it, I'm pretty sure it will happen. Just stay away from booze and drugs and work hard. You'll be all right, Charlie, believe me."

"I do, Eddie." A couple of holiday shoppers passed them with bags from Bon Marche and Eddie said, "Merry Christmas, ladies." They returned the greeting, but Charlie was quiet. "What happened with my father in the war?" he asked.

The smile dissolved, and Eddie shook his head and took a deep breath. "Those are not my stories to tell, Charlie. Maybe someday your dad will tell you about it. It was pretty tough for him. Pretty tough." He pulled his glove back from his wrist and looked at his watch. Then, he took off the glove, reached into his pocket and pulled out some wrinkled bills. "I have to finish this Charlie, but go over to the Palmer Street and get a hot chocolate and a muffin."

"Thanks, Eddie."

"Be good, Charlie boy."

Charlie started to walk toward the coffee shop, but stopped and said, "Eddie, you had a wife, right?"

"Yeah, I had a wife. A nice Greek lady. Daphne. But I wasn't right after the war, either. Combat fatigue is a real thing. God, I used to sleep with a rifle in a sleeping bag on the floor. Can you believe that? 'Hyper-vigilance' they call it. In the Army they used to say, 'Stay alert. Stay alive.' Problem is you stay alert all the time. You can't turn it off, even when you're back. And you drink to relax. Anyway, she left and I don't blame her. Married another guy smarter than I was, and luckier too."

"How did you get better?"

"There's a priest who's a veteran at St. Patrick's, Father Walsh, and he helped me a lot. And I think, banging the piano a bit in my amateurish way, and listening to good pianists. You know how I decided to have a piano bar, Charlie? Our company ended up one day in a bombed-out school in France during the war. There was a piano there, and one of the guys took off his helmet and put down his rifle and started playing the Maple Leaf Rag. It changed the day. We all felt better for a while. Music is therapy, and the piano is the queen of all the instruments. Time and Father Walsh and music helped me. Hey, if I could have pulled myself together sooner, Daphne would've stayed. You'd have a nice aunt. Some mistakes you don't recover from, Charlie. You figure it out too late." He tapped the side of his head. "That's why you have to think—you can't let your troubles keep you down, Charlie."

"You're pulled together now, right?"

"Like I said, it was after the war . . ."

"I wish you were my father, Eddie." It was what Charlie had thought since he'd first met his uncle, but he felt embarrassed to have said it.

"Why, that's the nicest thing anyone's ever said to me, Charlie. I would have been proud to be your dad. You call me if you need me."

Charlie turned quickly and ran toward the Palmer Street Restaurant.

There was nothing much under the Christmas tree for Charlie. A box with a flannel shirt, three comic books, and a paperback of Ripley's *Believe it or Not!* but Charlie didn't mind. He knew his mother was always broke, and she had to pay the rent. She'd gone to a Christmas party at the Cosmo and was in bed with a hangover. He was lying on the couch reading one of the comic books when he heard a knock at the back door in the kitchen and footsteps descending the stairs.

He opened the door and saw a gift-wrapped box beside a baseball bat with a bow on it. "Louisville Slugger" was printed across the smooth grain of the wood. He picked up the bat and the box and went inside. "To Charlie," the card read, "from Santa." He tore the wrapping away and opened the box. The rich smell of leather filled his head. A baseball glove, and in its webbing, a gleaming white baseball sewn with brilliant red thread. At the bottom were two books, *The Science of Hitting*, by Ted Williams, and *Maybe I'll Pitch Forever*, by Satchel Paige.

"Who was that?" his mother called from her bedroom.

"That was Santa Claus," he said. "He brought me a baseball bat and a glove. For Christmas."

"Santa Claus, right." She was silent for a moment and then asked, "You like baseball?"

"Yeah," he said. "I'm gonna be a pitcher."

January was cold, but there was not much snow. It came on heavy in February. With his new boots and gloves, Charlie went shoveling. He got Foxy McRae to come along. Foxy was a strange kid—strange in a good way. He hung out with kids behind the Bartlett, kids Charlie didn't particularly like, smoking weed, but he went to St. Patrick's. He not only went to church on Sundays, but served as an altar boy. Charlie had seen his own birth certificate—parents' religion: Catholic, but that was the end of it. They had never brought him to church.

"What do you like about church, Foxy?" he asked as they trudged up the hill of Wilder Street with their shovels over their shoulders.

"It's kinda like goin' back in time, all the high ceilings and the stained-glass windows and that rumble of the organ that makes your insides vibrate and the choirs and the sound of the Latin. I don't know. Makes you think God really is there."

"Maybe. Who knows?"

The two of them knocked on doors in the Highlands, where they had an idea people had more money than they did in the Acre. At one house on Florence Ave., an old woman asked how much to shovel her driveway and walkway. "Eight dollars," Charlie said.

"Don't be ridiculous, young man. I'll give you four."

"How about six?"

"Five," she said.

When they were done, she handed the money to Charlie and said, "Now don't buy dope with that!"

"Tell him!" Charlie said, pointing at Foxy.

"He's only kiddin'," Foxy assured her, and whispered to Charlie as they turned, "I'm gonna get at least a nickel bag."

By the end of the day, they were exhausted, but had $105. "Just give me fifty," Foxy said, "You shoveled more than me." Charlie kept the five and gave his mother fifty. "Put that toward the rent, Ma."

"Ah, you're a good boy, Charlie," she said. He felt proud to have contributed something to the financial struggle, maybe make things a little easier for his mother, but the next morning when was putting out the trash, he found a torn receipt from a bookie for the Daily Double at Suffolk Downs. She had put the fifty dollars on a couple of losers. She had never known the real odds on anything.

Chapter 5

1966

Pitching practice picked up after that. Charlie and Squiggles found a way into an abandoned mill building that sat astride the river beyond the Aiken Street Bridge. There, in the vast empty echoing space, they could take turns, one pitching and the other crouching like a catcher. They were protected from snow and wind, and with the new glove, the ball was easy to catch in the leather webbing and Charlie's fingers never stung. As March went off like a lamb, they took to the soggy fields to practice hitting after school or played a game with anyone who showed up. And Charlie read *The Science of Hitting*. Ted Williams quoted some player named Hornsby, "A great hitter isn't born, he's made. He's made out of practice, fault correction and confidence."

Spring took hold, and they could finally play baseball outside at Highland Park or the Bartlett or over at Hadley Field. Charlie and Squiggles both made the school team as pitchers.

Mr. Fitzgibbons had what Charlie's mother called a "junk store" on Broadway. It was full of books, clocks, dishes, second-hand furniture, jewelry, records, lamps, photographs, signs, radios, some clothes, old everything. Old prints and paintings hung everywhere. Every inch was stacked and lined with old things. They sat with their secrets under glass cases and filled porcelain bowls on cluttered tables. On sunny days, some of the contents of the shop spilled out onto the sidewalk. Though he couldn't say why, Charlie loved the junk store. Fitzgibbons didn't call it a junk store, of course. The sign over the door said, "Vintage Furniture & Antiquities." You could go there every day and always see something you had not noticed before.

One Saturday morning he went in to look around. Fitzgibbons raised his eyes from the book he was reading and peered at Charlie over the glasses perched on his prominent nose. His hair was ash-colored and unkempt. He needed a shave. The grizzled stubble, Charlie thought, added character to his face. He wore a dark sweater vest over a red plaid shirt. Cigarette smoke rose in curling columns around him. To Charlie, he was another antiquity of the place, at home among all these things that had belonged to people who now resided in Edson or St. Patrick's Cemetery or who-knows-what grave. Like a stern boss, he tapped his cigarette over an ashtray. "You keep comin' in here. What do you want, kid?"

"You got any comic books?"

Fitzgibbons got up. He was slim and moved nimbly about the maze. He pointed to a bookcase. "There are some comic books in that crate on the bottom shelf, nickel apiece. If I catch you stealin' anything..."

"I ain't a thief."

"Well, good for you. What the hell you want comic books for? Here!" He went to another bookcase and began to pull books off the shelf. "*King Solomon's Mines*. H. Rider Haggard. That's what a kid your age should be reading." Charlie looked at the cover and shook his head. He rifled through other titles. "Wait. Here's a good one. *The Light in the Forest*. Take that one, kid. You like science fiction? Here's a great one: *Daybreak: 2250 AD*. Gimme twenty cents for those two. Never mind those stupid comic books."

Charlie handed him two dimes and took the books.

As he was leaving, Fitzgibbons called out, "Hey, what's your name, so I don't have to keep calling you 'kid'?"

"Charlie Tumulty."

"Another harp, eh? I'm Mr. Fitzgibbons."

"I know."

"How do you know?"

"My friend Truck Mahoney—his mother got him a mattress here. She said you pretend to be a bastard, but you're really a nice guy."

"Well, don't spread that around, Tumulty."

Charlie hadn't told Fitzgibbons that he had already read *The Light in the Forest* because he wanted to read it again.

The copy he'd read belonged to the school, and he wanted his own copy. He took the books and read nightly until his eyelids grew heavy. Sometimes he woke up in the middle of the night to find the book still open on his chest.

Before the month was out, Charlie had finished the books and was back to the junk store. "Did you like the books?" Fitzgibbons asked.

"I really liked *Daybreak, 2250 AD*. I'd love to have a cat the size of a mountain lion that I could communicate with through, you know, using telepathy . . ."

"A cat that you could communicate with telepathically."

"Yeah. That was really cool. But *The Light in the Forest* was the best."

"The better. There were only two."

"The better," he repeated, remembering that Miss Walker was a stickler on that sort of thing.

"The young white boy, John Butler, he was kidnapped by the Indians and . . ."

"I know the story, Charlie. Better than a comic book, isn't it? You don't need anyone to draw cartoon pictures." He tapped his head. "The pictures are up here."

"Yeah. I guess so. There were Indians around here, right?"

"Hell, yes. Why do you think they call them the Pawtucket Falls?" Fitzgibbons knew all about that and about everything. He understood the way things used to be because he'd studied the old maps and drawings and photos and had read a lot of history. He told Charlie that the Pawtucket Indians had their village right on the spot where the Pawtucket Congregational Church stands now, overlooking the Pawtucket Falls.

"And why do they call the Acre 'the Acre'?"

"Well, according to a guy named O'Dwyer who wrote a book back in 1920 called *The Irish Catholic Genesis of Lowell*, if I remember correctly, he said that Kirk Boott, the mill owner, asked his Irish housekeeper why her countrymen were always fighting with the Yankees and drinking and causing trouble. She told him that they would continue to cause trouble until they had a church and a priest to control them, and she said it must be one who speaks 'the old tongue.' The Irish language. And so, Boott got a priest, a Father O'Brien, and donated an acre of land on which the Irish could build a church. It's much bigger than an Acre now, and it's certainly not all Irish anymore, but it's still called 'the Acre.'"

Charlie loved listening to the history. Fitzgibbons told him that there used to be a twenty-seven-mile barge canal that connected the Merrimack River in Lowell with the port of Boston and that Black Brook had been part of it. A lot of it had been filled in since that time. Fitzgibbons opened a portable record player and put on some music with piano and saxophone. "John Coltrane," he said, lighting a cigarette. "Genius," he said. "A Love Supreme." He snapped the lighter closed.

"How do you know so much about everything?"

"I read, Charlie. If you don't read, you don't know." He exhaled a blue-gray cloud of smoke and asked, "Hey, how'd you like to make a few bucks?"

"Doin' what?"

"Nothing illegal. Sometimes I have to clean out an estate." He saw Charlie's puzzled expression. "In other words, somebody dies, and I buy the contents of the house. I have to do that Saturday. You got a friend? I'll give you both, let me see, two bucks an hour, and if you do a good job I'll throw in a little extra."

"Okay."

Charlie and Foxy went to work for Fitzgibbons, helping to load his truck and empty it into a big old barn he had behind his house. Once, they cleared nearly three thousand books out of an estate in Belvidere. Sometimes, he and Foxy went up with him to Hollis, New Hampshire, and worked as "porters." They helped Fitzgibbons set up his table at the flea market, carried stuff for him and the other dealers from their cars to their tables, and helped customers lug purchases to their cars. Those days they worked for tips. The dealers tipped them a quarter or fifty cents here and there. Charlie loved to listen to Fitzgibbons talking to the customers that came to his table. He learned something about rare books, antiques, and history. And of course, the old collector gave Charlie books to read, *The Stories of Edgar Allen Poe*, *The Call of the Wild*, *A Farewell to Arms* and *The Grapes of Wrath*.

Charlie and Foxy rode their bikes to Fitzgibbons' shop just before he closed for the Fourth of July. Charlie unwrapped the chain wound under the seat and locked the bikes to the Broadway street sign.

They didn't want to call it a junk shop anymore, since they were now employees. But even Fitzgibbons didn't call it a "Vintage Furniture and Antiquities Shop." Sometimes he called it "The Old Curiosity Shop" or "Memory Lane," and sometimes by other strange names he made up like "The House of Forgotten Dreams," or "Dead Man's Lost and Found,' which was kind of spooky because it really was full of stuff that had belonged to dead people.

Fitzgibbons was wearing sunglasses over his reading glasses as he sat at a small table by the plate glass window, smoking as usual, and reading a battered blue volume in the sun. There was usually some saxophone or a symphony turning on the record player behind the counter, but that day he was listening to an old song.

Barbara Allen was buried in the old churchyard
Sweet William was buried beside her,
Out of sweet William's heart, there grew a rose
Out of Barbara Allen's, a briar.

He got up, took off the two pairs of glasses and squashed his cigarette in a butt-littered tin dish. They followed him through the maze of bedposts, dressers, desks, lamps, and tables laden with overstuffed boxes back to a glass display case and counter. He stepped behind it and opened a small white refrigerator, from which he drew two bottles of Moxie. He opened them and put them on the counter. "For my Broadway Irregulars," he said.

The boys thanked him and tilted them back. Moxie had a distinctive taste. Either you loved it or you hated it. The boys loved it. Fitzgibbons told them that it had originated in Lowell and that the key ingredient was something called "gentian root," which he told them, E. B. White had claimed was "the path to a good life." They didn't know E.B. White, but Ted Williams drank it, and what better endorsement could you have?

There was a collection of old photos in a box on the counter, couples in the clothing of another century, the men in long coats with watch chains crossing their vests, the women in ruffled blouses and skirts that hung all the way down to their laced boots. They all looked serious. There was only one photo in which a woman was smiling. She seemed to be playacting, with her hands on her hips, peering slightly backward over a raised shoulder, where a young man knelt, a cap in one outstretched hand, the other over his heart.

"Who were these people?" Foxy asked. "Did they live here?"

"They did," Fitzgibbons said, donning his reading glasses, "that photo was taken in Lowell, at Carroll's Photography, which was at 212 Merrimack Street from after the Civil War in the late 1860s until about 1885. No one will ever know more than that. That's why I sometimes refer to this place as 'The House of Lost Stories.'" Charlie smiled. Another name.

"You see, everything in this place was connected with the lives of people who have vanished, like the Pawtucket Indians—gone. Now all memory of them is lost, leaving only the artifacts they knew and loved in life. I spend my days here, daydreaming amid those artifacts: a rocking chair in which some old dame once recalled her long-lost lover as she nodded by the glowing coals, framed needlepoints young women made to show their skill to prospective husbands, print lithographs of Irish martyrs on the scaffold that reminded some immigrant of a heritage of defiance, worn implements maybe from the days when all of Lowell was the farmland of East Chelmsford, and of course, the old books where the dead speak to us. Look here." He lifted the blue volume he had been reading when the boys entered.

From within its pages, he drew some dried flowers. "I found these pressed between the pages. I looked them up in my *Wildflowers of New England*. They're Wood Lily. *Lilium philadelphicum*. See?" He held the star-shaped flowers before them; the petals still held hints of orangey red. "Women used to press flowers in books. Over the years, the image of the flowers has been transposed onto the printed page, right over the poem like the image of Christ on the Shroud of Turin; under the flowers' stolen shadow you can read the poem this ghost once marked with the flowers of the forest." He put his glasses back on and read:

O heart, how fares it with thee now,
That thou should'st fail from thy desire,
Who scarcely darest to inquire,
'What is it makes me beat so low?'

Something it is which thou hast lost,
Some pleasure from thine early years.
Break, thou deep vase of chilling tears,
That grief hath shaken into frost!

Such clouds of nameless trouble cross
All night below the darken'd eyes;
With morning wakes the will, and cries,
'Thou shalt not be the fool of loss'.

His words sank into the dim and dusty silence of the packed rooms. "Sounds nice, but I don't get it," Foxy said, shaking his head and throwing his leg up on a crate as he leaned back to sip his Moxie.

Fitzgibbons smiled, showing tobacco-stained teeth. "The dead speak. You have to keep listening until you understand."

Charlie took in those words and looked up at a dark oil painting of a cottage on a lakeshore backed my mountains whose summits were lost in mists. "How old is the world, Mr. Fitz?"

"I once read a Scottish writer, 19th century. He said the world began for each of us when we were born, and ends when we die. So it's no older than any of us. Something to think about, there."

They heard the door open. "That must be Mr. Barton. He's coming to show me a collection of 78 rpm records." They ambled back to the front where one of Fitzgibbons' antique-dealing cronies was setting a box down on a chair. The various collectors and dealers who were his friends were a curious lot—many of them seemed to have passed through some time warp like the ones Charlie had read about in *Superman* comics. Their conversations convinced him that they would have been more comfortable in some distant past when the books, music and art they loved had been popular.

Charlie and Foxy greeted Barton, a tall man with wild hair. The boys chugged the rest of their Moxies and put them in the box Fitzgibbons kept for empty bottles. He heard Fitzgibbons telling the other man, "I've been searching for a rare recording of 'Loves Old Sweet Song' by Edna Thornton."

"Back in my basement I have Richard Crooks singing that and Mother Machree," Barton said as Fitzgibbons began to thumb through the records.

"I have that one . . ."

They left the two old men to those conversations that only collectors of rarities would understand.

Chapter 6

River Adventures

Charlie, Foxy and another kid named Keith Aghy from the lower Highlands started hanging around the river. Keith wasn't big, but he was kind of a wise guy, which could be a dangerous combination. He was tough and wiry though, and had little fear of anyone. The big kids partied at the river on Friday nights, so if you went there on Saturday mornings, you could find leftover unopened beers they had lost in the dark or forgotten about in their drunkenness. Foxy said they could save it all up for a month and then have a party. They stashed it amid the wrecks of old cars and World War II jeeps and halftracks that rusted away in the lot on the river behind Alexander's Market. Charlie told Foxy that he was going to sit down and drink six beers at one time, just to find out what it was all about.

At one point, a path opened to a small clearing where a rope swing hung from a tree that grew out of the riverbank. On a sunny Saturday, they found Boo Boo Botelho, Timmy

Shaden and Stevie Spellisy in cut-off shorts, swinging out to land on a discarded washing machine that protruded from the river. They were diving off the washing machine into the deeper channel of the river.

"Come on in!" they shouted.

"That water's dirty!" Foxy said.

Boo Boo waved that answer away, saying, "Ya take a showa when ya get home."

"The fuckin' germs get into your mouth and everything," Foxy said. "You can't wash that off."

"Ah, yerra pussy."

"Ah, fuck you."

"That river is gross," Keith said.

"Ya mother's gross!" Boo Boo said.

"Hey, hey!" Charlie intervened, "No mothers! That's over the line!"

"All right, all right. Sorry."

They left the swimmers and moved along the riverbank, looking for flat stones to skim over the water. "Wish we had enough dough to get a frappe at Burbeck's," Keith said.

They came to a gravelly lot where a car was parked amid islands of brush and scrub trees. There was a pile of granite blocks that must have been left there by the city, and the boys started to climb on it. Charlie noticed that a man in the car appeared to be watching them. After a few minutes, he got out of the car and approached them, carrying a rolled-up magazine in his hand. He struck Charlie as a salesman, dressed neatly in light chinos and a plaid shirt. His black hair was combed back and gleamed with Brylcream or something; his long jaw was darkened with a five-o'clock shadow.

"Hey boys," he said.

"Hi," they said.

"I was just admiring these girls." He opened up the magazine to reveal a centerfold of a naked woman holding her ample breasts like an offering. "How would you like to take a bus tour around that?" he asked.

The gesture and the stupid question immediately put Charlie on alert. An adult showing them pictures of naked women? Something was not right with this guy. He waited, tense with anticipation of a confrontation.

The other boys looked at each other, puzzled or embarrassed. "Yeah, I guess," Keith mumbled.

"I got a date with a really hot babe tonight," the man said. "The only problem is, I'm gonna be over-excited. That's why I got a job for you guys, or one of you, if you want it."

"You got a lawn we can mow or something?" Foxy asked.

Charlie gave Foxy an incredulous look. He stood and said, "Let's go."

The man ignored him. "You see, I'm gonna be so excited, I'm gonna come too fast. So I gotta jerk off before I go on this date, but I'd rather get someone to do it for me. It would be worth twenty bucks to me."

Keith actually blushed and burst out laughing.

"No, we don't wanna give you a hand job," Charlie said. "Screw."

"Calm down. It's just a simple . . ."

"Screw! We're not interested!" Charlie shouted.

The man, suddenly indignant, hissed, "Fuck you!" He stalked back to his car, casting fierce backward glances. When he had closed the car door, Charlie picked up a rock and hurled it with a pitcher's accuracy. "Pervert!" It landed with a thud, and bounced off the hood. Foxy and Keith followed suit. Charlie thought the man might get out and chase them, but the car roared off under a rain of rocks, the tires flinging gravel and a cloud of dust.

As they walked back toward the tracks, Charlie said, "If either of you guys had done that. Even you, Foxy, I would never forgive you."

"Me? What do you mean *even me*? You think I'm gonna give some greasy perv a hand job?"

"You got any lawns we can mow?" Keith inquired in naïve tones, an index finger at the corner of his mouth. Charlie laughed in spite of himself.

"Shut up!" Foxy said, embarrassed, "I wasn't sure what the hell he was driving at!" The three of them laughed then, but beneath the laughter, Charlie felt a deep revulsion that there were men out there who would prey on young boys, and maybe find someone who had not grown up in the Acre and had enough street smarts to tell them to fuck off and to stone their cars. But you met all kinds of people along the river and in the world.

There was a clearing not far from the railroad tracks they had always heard called, "Bare-Ass Beach," but they had never seen anyone skinny-dipping there. Sometimes kids called it the "Hobo Camp," and they did find a hobo there one day with an opened can of beans, sitting on a bench seat that had been pulled out of some car. They watched the man, holding the opened lid with a rag, set the can over the glowing embers of a camp fire. Foxy and Keith wanted to take off, but Charlie said, "I never met a hobo," and they approached cautiously. They could see that he was a strong, well-built man. He certainly wasn't afraid of three boys, and he greeted them in a friendly way. "Are you a hobo?" Keith asked, getting right to the point.

He stirred the can with the spoon out of a Swiss Army knife and said, "I 'spose I am."

"So, you ride the rails?" Charlie asked.

"Yeah."

"How did you end up becoming a hobo?"

He looked up and squinted in the sun. "I'm livin' on the lam. A wanted man."

"What are you wanted for?"

"I killed a man."

Foxy gave Charlie the bug eyes and a nod toward 'outa here,' but Charlie went on. "Why'd you kill him?"

The air itself reminded the boys that they were breathing the atmosphere of a world that stretched far away from and beyond the mill city and was not ruled by its mayor or councilors. It was air laden with the swampy smell of the river, the blue smoke of the hobo's fire, the dead carp that littered the sandy shore and the creosote of the railroad ties.

It was a world where fugitives and hoboes and the world's lost souls rode the rails and passed like ghosts under starlit skies, across vast plains and along the banks of legendary rivers named by vanished tribes. The lonely rider of rattling boxcars told them his story. He had been a bridge builder, hanging from towering spans to weld metal. He'd had a nice home and a wife and took home a hundred fifty dollars a week. One night he got into an argument with a guy in a bar. They fought and he knocked the other guy down and his head struck the brass railing men at the bar put their feet on. And he died.

The hobo continued to stir the can of beans. "When I heard they were coming to arrest me, I left a note for my wife sayin' I was sorry and I loved her. I still do. I hopped a Hi-Line out of Missoula to Seattle, and I been on the run ever since. It's a lonesome life, boys, but hoboin' is better'n jail." He blew on a spoonful of beans.

"Couldn't you say it was self-defense?"

"This guy's family had connections in Montana. I was pretty sure I was goin' to jail. I was in jail when I was a little older than you boys for stealin' a car. I ain't goin' back. Not if I can help it."

They wished him good luck and left the lonely hobo, so far from Montana, eating his beans by the river.

They had gathered up quite a stash of beer, a half-bottle of vodka and some rum that they mixed together. That was called "rocket fuel." Foxy invited some kids he knew from

Porky's Bridge. Sherman Kelly, Paul Copley, Phil Comtois, Nick Andrianakos and some girls Charlie only knew as Irene, Denise, Donna and a couple of their friends he didn't know at all.

Somehow Charlie didn't believe that alcohol would affect him. It was as if everyone else in the world were operating under some illusion. He would be who he was, no matter what he drank—never one of the sloppy reeling drunks that his mother brought home. They carried the box full of booze down to the stone stairway behind the Gate House set above the swirling waters of the canal.

Charlie enjoyed the liberating feeling of being an adult, of doing something that only adults were allowed to do. He played drinking games and chugged beers while the other sang what sounded like a cheerful beer-garden song:

> *Here's to brother Charlie, brother Charlie, brother Charlie*
> *Here's to brother Charlie who's with us tonight.*
> *He eats it, he beats it, he even mistreats it,*
> *So here's to brother Charlie who's with us tonight.*
> *So drink chugalug, drink chugalug, drink chugalug,*
> *drink chugalug . . .*

Irene was leaning against him, smoking a cigarette, and he told her, "Those are bad for you," which she seemed to find funny. Things were getting boisterous. Charlie saw the moon through the leafy branches and felt as if he could float up through the branches and touch it. Irene tossed her cigarette in the canal and kissed his neck. He thought she was pretty, but the smell of her leather jacket, combined with her perfume, was making him slightly sick. He tried to forget that and focus on the girl, her blond hair and soft cheek.

He was roused from this dream by shouts, and looking toward the group, saw that Sherman Kelly had pushed Foxy to the ground, and had turned on Keith Aghy, who was telling him to lay off Foxy. Sherman was a couple of years older than the rest of the boys, tall and lanky. He liked fights, and he did not fight clean. Keith was backing up with his fists raised, knowing he was about to get his ass kicked.

Charlie stepped in. He remembered taking a couple of wild swings, and then Sherman had him by the hair and was bouncing his head off his knee. Charlie saw stars and fell. Sherman was on top of him. "You comin' after me, Tumulty? Apologize!"

Charlie looked up and said, "You're still an asshole."

He remembered nothing else until later. He heard distant voices; he was crashing along through the wooded lot beside the canal, and knelt to vomit.

The next morning, Grace asked if he had been in a car accident. He mumbled something, drank a big glass of water and went back to bed. He found his way to Fitzgibbons' shop that afternoon, an oasis of peace and calm, soothing to his throbbing brain.

"So. Alcohol one, Charlie, zero." The old man laughed, and said, "Any dumbass can soak his brain in booze all night, Charlie."

"I'm done with booze," Charlie said. "Done."

"Everyone says that. I've only known one guy who went on a bender and said, 'I'm done,' and he was. He never drank again."

"Now you know two," Charlie said. "I'll never be drunk again. You're at the mercy of whatever happens. The next time I see Sherman Kelly, I won't be drinking." He touched his badly bruised face gingerly.

"Well, we'll see. He did a number on you, all right."

"Drinking sucks. Now I see now why my parents are such . . . fools."

It was a warm night in June. Charlie was on the mound at Callery Park. The people from the neighborhood, the park kids, some parents—they were all leaning on the fence watching the game. Seated in folding chairs outside the fence, they chatted with each other or cheered their side. The Bartlett School was winning by a couple of runs late in the game against the Butler School. Charlie had two outs in the inning, and one strike on a kid named Griffin from Gorham Street.

"Come on, Griff! You babe! Knock it out!" Griffin's teammates crooned from the dugout, while Charlie's teammates cried, "Let's go, Charlie! Show him watchoo got!" The Butler coach, who was jumping around like he was in the World Series, was yelling, "Keep your eye on the ball, Griff!" which Charlie thought was hardly profound advice. And whenever one of his batters whiffed at his fastball, the coach yelled, "Now you're ready! Now you're ready, slugger!" And Charlie remembered Hornsby—confidence—and said to himself, "Yeah, now you're ready to whiff again, slugger."

When he glanced over to check the guy on first base, his body went tense, and the game receded for a moment. He saw a pile of silver ladders on a black rack moving past the parked cars on Parker Street, and between the cars, he caught a glimpse of his father's battered pickup. He dug at the mound with his cleats and watched him turn onto Wilder Street and prayed that the truck would keep moving on toward the Highland Tap or wherever else he might be welcome. He hoped his father didn't know that his son was pitching. But he watched the truck pull over near the swings. He knew.

"Let's go, sonny boy!" the umpire called.

Jack Tumulty had gotten out of the truck and was walking unsteadily toward the field. Charlie had to get this guy out and end the inning before his father came up to the fence. Ted Williams said great ball players blocked out every distraction. He tried to block out the advancing figure of his father. He took a deep breath and, staring at the catcher's mitt, threw a burning fastball. The Griffin kid swung late, and he heard it thud into the padded leather. The ump flicked a hand formed into a pistol to his right and said,

"Steeee-rikah!" F.J., the catcher, nodded his head as if to say, "Yeah, like that, Charlie. Like that."

"Thas' my boy!"

No, please.

"Thas' a pitcher right there!" the old man shouted. "He got the heat, you becherass! Let's go, Charlie! Show that whiffer whatcha got!"

Heads inclined in whispered conversations. Parents seated in beach chairs along the first base line craned their necks to get a look and shook their heads at the sad disgrace to his son.

"Fan that bum, Charlie!"

No one likes being called a bum. Griffin set his bat on the ground and leaned on it, gazing at the loudmouth beyond third base. The ump cast a warning glance in Jack Tumulty's direction and raised a hand, but said nothing, hoping the drunkard would get the message and that he would not have to stop the game and go talk to him and embarrass the Bartlett School pitcher. But the old man never got the message. He never ever got the message. The batter adjusted his helmet, took a practice swing, and stepped back into the box. *One more strike,* Charlie thought. He wound up and threw one hard and low. Too low—it bounced in the dirt and up, but F.J. blocked it with his chest, and it fell in front of him, where he fumbled for it, tearing off his catcher's mask. The runner at first had taken off. Charlie ducked as F.J. whipped the ball straight over his head to second.

"Safe!" the umpire called as Maloney swung the gloved ball into the sliding Yankee.

"He was out! Put on your glasses for Chrissakes, Mr. Magoo!" the old man shouted, cackling to himself. Charlie glanced over and saw him lighting a cigarette, swaying like a boxer who had just caught a hard left to the jaw.

The umpire held up a hand and trotted toward the fence. He tried to talk quietly to the old man, but everyone could hear Jack Tumulty saying, "Fuck you! This ain't a prayer service, it's a goddamn ball game! No, *you're* an embarrassment to the boy! To the whole fuckin' game! Thas' my boy out there, an' I can root for him if I wanoo ya fuckin' useless dope!"

One of the Butler players in the dugout said loudly, "What an asshole!" and their coach told him to shut up. The umpire turned toward Coach Burgess. His face was red, and Charlie heard him use the word "police."

Shame like he had never known fell on him. It burned him. He felt every movement of his body awkward, forced, unnatural. It was as if he were standing on the mound naked, and the eyes of all Lowell were on him. He heard his father howling as he wound up; "Fan that whiffer Charlie baby!" He hit the batter square on the shoulder as he tried to leap back out of the box. The ump must have asked him if he was okay because he nodded, dropped the bat, and trotted to first, holding his arm, but never looking at the pitcher. Charlie understood that to mean that he knew it wasn't intentional.

Coach Burgess spoke briefly with the ump and jogged out to the mound. "Are you okay, kid? Can you get one more out?"

"Yeah, yeah," he said reflexively. He had learned in his neighborhood, from the older boys, that you never admit you're not okay unless you need hospitalization. But he heard his father arguing with another parent. "Fuck you! And fuck the cops! There's no law against rooting for my boy out there! It's still a free country!"

Charlie called out. "Wait! No, I'm not okay, coach." He wanted to stay out there, but he just couldn't, because he was afraid he was going to start to cry on the mound, and how would he ever live that down? He handed the ball to the coach.

"It's not your fault, Charlie," Coach Burgess said. He made the long walk back to the dugout hearing his father shout "One bad pitch and you pull the kid? What the hellsa matta with you?"

Squiggles was warming up. No one in the dugout said anything to Charlie because no one knew what to say. He grabbed his glove, ran out the gate and jumped on his bike. The old man was yelling something, but he couldn't hear, didn't want to hear what as he pedaled away hard, crying. A while later, he pulled his bike into the brush by the Webber Street Bridge and ran along the narrow trail until the swamp pond opened up before him. He hurled his baseball glove as far as he could into the dark water of Black Brook. He knew that every time he stood on the pitcher's mound, he would hear his father's shit-faced bellowing, and the others would hear it, too. Baseball, for him, was over.

Chapter 7

Charlie's grandparents on both sides had come from Ireland. He remembered his father's parents, Sean and Delia. Before he died, his grandfather had given him a silver Celtic cross. It hung too low, and Charlie put it in his drawer until he was older. Delia was from Wicklow, a place called the Vale of Avoca. Charlie recalled a little ditty she recited to him:

O Vale of Avoca, Tom Moore called thee sweet
But if Tom had to walk twenty miles in bare feet
And sleep without a blanket or sheet,
He wouldn't give a damn where the bright waters meet.

Charlie's mother's name had been Hurley, but he didn't remember her parents. Grace Hurley had met his father at Fenway Park in 1942, not at a baseball game, but at a football game between Holy Cross and Boston College before his father had shipped off to the war in Europe.

His mother told him how she and his father and another couple had gone into the Cocoanut Grove, but it was too crowded, and his father wanted to go to the USO Buddies' Club because Buck Jones, the cowboy actor, was supposed to be there. Buck never showed up though, because he died in the fire at the Cocoanut Grove that night, along with five hundred others. "I shoulda taken that disaster on the night I met him as a warning, a whaddaya call it, a bad omen, but I started to write to him overseas. The guy who came back was not the guy who left, Charlie."

He liked school because it was a place where he could forget his mother's bad omens and hard luck and the alcohol that was the bane of the lives of both his parents. His teacher, Miss Walker, was what they called "an old Yankee." Being a Yankee meant Miss Walker was just plain American. Charlie supposed that way back her people came from England, but they fought in the Civil War, and one of them had his name on a plaque at the Pollard Library from 1880. He was on the city council that erected the great granite castle of the library. Charlie went there sometimes on Saturdays and locked his bike outside to the street sign. They had shelves full of books about Indians.

"Do you know what percentage of Congress has voted for the war in Vietnam?" Miss Walker asked. She was a gray-haired woman, but she wasn't frail. She moved about her students the way a queen might walk before her subjects. Her command was not to be questioned, and her word on any subject was final. As she passed Charlie's desk, she saw that he was cleaning his fingernail with a paper clip. She slapped his hand lightly and continued walking up the aisle. He put the paper clip in his pocket. She wore dresses with floral prints and reading glasses that hung on a cord around her neck. She put them on when she read, but not when she stood at the blackboard to write. She spoke the most perfect English Charlie had ever heard. She pronounced blue as "blyew." She never said, "Uhm,' or "Ah," or "Ya know." And she pronounced all of her r's, even in the word *February*.

"Would any of you care to tell me what percentage of the Congress of the United States has voted for war in Vietnam?" she asked the class. "Hmmm?"

Vera Quinlan's hand rose tentatively above her pig-tailed head.

"Eighty percent, Miss Walker?" she ventured.

"No, not eighty. Oh, no. Anyone else? Robert, get your hand away from your face."

Richie Shea raised his hand, but it was obvious from his voice that he was guessing. "Seventy percent, Miss Walker?"

She shook her gray head. "No. Not seventy." She let a long silence settle over the class to deepen the mystery. Her gaze traveled from the windows to the door, from the front row all the way back to the cloakroom, the expanse of her domain. "Shall I tell you then?" she asked, her arms folded beneath her hanging glasses. Charlie didn't know anyone else who used the word "shall."

"Zero percent!" she declared. "Zero! So, we have to ask ourselves, why are we fighting a war when Congress has never declared war? If it's not a war, then why are American boys dying in Vietnam? Almost six thousand this year! What is my nephew doing fighting in a war that Congress has not declared? If we are to fight a war halfway across the world, then let President Johnson ask the Congress to declare war the way Franklin Roosevelt asked Congress to declare war on Japan!"

To Charlie, Vietnam was the background music that you couldn't turn off. It was on the TV every night. It was in the overheard discussions of adults, and of the older boys at the park who talked about how to get out of the draft. They said that some guys put on a dress when they reported to be inducted and acted like girls or pretended to be crazy. They said one guy got a tattoo on his arm that said, "Fuck the Army," so they wouldn't take him. Some said we had to stop the communists there because they wanted to take over the world. Miss Walker's nephew was in the 1st Marine Division. She said it was a civil war and we had no business there, and Charlie knew she was pretty smart.

Miss Walker brought them down to the school library and asked them to find a book they wanted to read for a report. She was killing time because the year was almost over; Charlie knew they would never have time to do a report. She had to approve the book first, because they were in seventh grade, and the lazy kids would pick a third-grade book if she let them. Charlie had already started one he'd found there called *Captains Courageous*. You couldn't go wrong with a title like that. Miss Walker said it was an excellent choice, and he took the book to the back of the library where he saw Ed Peyton reading *The Light in the Forest* on his recommendation. He didn't disturb him, but found a table on his own.

There were a few words he didn't know, in *Captains Courageous*, like "frieze overcoat" and "sou'wester," but he liked the story. It was about Gloucester fishermen and a rich, spoiled boy they rescued at sea and how he learned to be a man aboard the fishing boat called *We're Here*. It was peaceful there in the library with the June sun streaming in the window and touching with golden light the shelved rows of books. He had entered the world of Kipling's story and could feel the wind at his back as the *We're Here* tore across the sea, straining her spars on the way to the northern fishing grounds; he saw the rugged crew swept with salt sea spray and heard their shouts above the roar of the gale.

"Charles." He heard Miss Walker's voice and was in the library once more, wondering what he had done to draw her attention. "Yes, Miss Walker?"

"I didn't get to see your mother on Parent Night."

"No, she works, and . . . am I in trouble or something?"

She smiled, which surprised Charlie because she didn't smile much in class. She took a seat opposite him at the table. "No, you're not in trouble—on the contrary. The composition you wrote in class last week, about being a secret agent. It was very good, Charles. Quite imaginative."

"Well, I like that show *Secret Agent Man*."

"Yes. You seem to enjoy reading. I mean more than the other boys. If I don't keep an eye on them, they won't read at all, most of them. But you find a place apart. If I were not here, you'd keep reading."

"I like words."

"What I wanted to tell your mother, I'll tell you. Because it's something uncommon, Charles, and valuable." As if she were imparting some great secret that would be the key to unlocking a door to a room full of riches, she said, "You have a literary mind."

"I do?"

"Yes," she nodded, her eyes large and serious. "I hope you keep developing it. I hope you can go to college. Maybe someday you'll write your own book."

"My own book. Geez, I don't know."

"Oh, yes. I think you could. Someday. School is almost over. Keep reading over the summer, Charles. Keep writing and thinking."

"I will. Thank you, Miss Walker."

Charlie thought he'd head down to Black Brook after school and take a raft out on the water and listen to the transistor radio. As he left the schoolyard and was cutting across the Common, he saw Bobby DeCola, Stevie Smith and Butchie Sales by the monkey bars. He was in 7A, and they were in 7B. They were laughing at something. Charlie was afraid it was at him, but he ignored them and kept walking as if he

The Pride of the Acre

didn't notice them. "Thass my boy!" DeCola shouted. "Oh my! Whatta pitcher he is! He's my pride and joy! I love to get drunk as a skunk and root for him!" The others were laughing hard.

"Faahhk you umpire!" another screeched.

Charlie dropped his book bag on the ground and walked over to DeCola. He didn't want to fight them all, but Kev Souza was a pretty tough kid, and he had told Charlie that when you're in a situation like that you gotta pick out the leader, and if you cut him down to size the others will back off. He'd seen Souza do it, too. Souza had this steely look. Charlie tried to imitate the Souza look, hard and a little crazy, as he faced DeCola. "You're cruisin' for a bruisin', DeCola." That was what he'd heard Souza tell Bobby Dexter, and it seemed to work because Dexter backed down.

The three of them hopped off the monkey bars, and while he tried to stare down DeCola, Smith and Butchie moved in at his elbows. He wished one of his friends would show up, even Squiggles, but he didn't see any of them.

"This is between me and Bobby," he said to the others. But he knew it wasn't. Souza said to knock out the tough guy; the others will fall in line, and if you stand there too long you look scared. Charlie had dropped his bag. He had walked over here. Now he had to do something about it. *Captains Courageous!* he told himself.

"Apologize," he said.

They laughed. "Or what, Tumulty? What are you going to do about it?"

"You're not as tough as you think, Bobby."

Butchie stepped behind him, and he glanced backward to keep an eye on him. He wanted to move so that his back was against the fence of the tennis court, but as soon as he turned his head to watch Butchie, DeCola nailed him in the mouth. He covered up the way Souza had taught him and looked for an opening. He saw it and took a good swing that would have knocked the stupid grin off Bobby DeCola's face, but Smith shoved him from one side, and he lost his balance and got nailed again, good. He knew he had to cover up until they got tired of hitting him, which eventually they did.

He didn't go to Black Brook. His mother was still at work when he got home. He cleaned himself up, and when she came home around 5:30, tried to act casual, but his eye was already swollen, his face bruised, and his lip cut. She put a bag with some groceries on the table. Charlie noticed more streaks of gray in his mother's hair. She looked tired. He read the little name tag on her waitress outfit: Grace. He had seen the photos in her scrapbook, as she must have been in the days when she went tobogganing with her friends at Mount Pleasant, or when she met his father at that football game, young, full of laughter and hope. He stared at the stained plaster where she had thrown the coffee pot at his father. Grace looked at his bruised face, and away as if it insulted her. "Can't you win a fight for a change?"

"Oh, I will," he said. "Ma, why did you tell him I was playing baseball at the park?"

She pulled a pack of cigarettes from the bag she had plopped on the table. "I wanted him to know we were doing just fine without him." He could see the hate for his father in her eyes. It was a cold fire, colder and harder than anything the tough guys could muster. There are some people that just don't care, Charlie thought. Like the song says, if you're lookin' for trouble you come to the right place. If you were lookin' for trouble, Grace Tumulty was ready for you. Most people are not willing to take it all the way, but she would take it all the way when she was pissed, and she was pissed at his father. The problem was that she would be willing to destroy everyone around her to get back at one person she hated. Vengeance was a religion with her.

She tapped the filtered end of the cigarette against the table. "Piece of shit," she said. "Oh, well. This world is a rotten place, and I'm sorry I brought you into it. You better get tough, Charlie. I'll tell you one thing. If you want respect, you don't ask for it. You demand it. You don't have a father and you don't have a big brother. If your mother gets involved, well, you'd never live that down. No one fucks with me, but I can't fight your battles. It's up to you."

He thought that for once she was giving him good advice. In that way, she was acting like a mother. She could be a good mother. "Ma," he said, "why do you have to drink so much? Can't you straighten out and we can try to pay our bills and get organized? I can help."

The hard expression that more and more, seemed never to change, didn't change now. "Listen, Charlie. I don't like myself—I don't like who I am and what my life is. Sober Grace works and worries and regrets. Drinkin' Grace is somebody else for a while, and she don't care about anything. It all just seems like a joke, and maybe that's what it really is." She lit the cigarette and leaned back, blowing smoke toward the ceiling. "A big fuckin' joke."

"But the joke is on you, Ma. We could be happy. Happier. We could . . ."

"Charlie, if I didn't drink, I'd probably kill myself—or someone else."

There was nothing more to say because the direction of the conversation frightened him.

Their phone had been turned off once again for non-payment, but Charlie pulled the thick phone book out of the drawer. He found Edward Tumulty on Wiggins Street and wrote the number on his hand.

He walked down to the phone booth at School and Broadway and dialed the number. A voice he didn't recognize answered.

"Is Eddie there? Tell him it's Charlie."

"Hang on."

Uncle Eddie came to the phone, "What's up, Charlie?"

"Are you busy?"

"Nah, just a little card game."

"Remember you said for me to call you if I ever needed you?

"Yeah, sure."

"Well, I need you. There are these kids at school, there are three of them, and they gave me a beating. I want to fight them, but one at a time."

Charlie heard indistinct voices and laughter. "One minute, boys," Eddie called. "Did you start the fight, Charlie?"

"No, I swear, Eddie. They made fun of me because my drunken old man showed up at my baseball game and made a fool out of me."

"Ah, I'm sorry, kid," he said, and Charlie could hear in his voice that he was.

"After school, if you could be at the North Common, like you're just passing through, and just make sure if you see a fight that it's one-on-one, that's all."

"You know, I'd rather not get involved in kids fighting, Charlie."

"They think I'm gonna walk home some other way tomorrow, but I'm going to walk the same way, whether you're there or not."

"All right, where on the North Common?"

"By the swings."

"I'll be there. I'll keep it one-on-one, but other than that, you're on your own, lad."

As Charlie crossed the common the next day, he saw them— in the same spot, sitting on the monkey bars. They spotted Charlie, and DeCola nudged Butchie and let out a howl: "Thas mah boy! Mah wunnaful boy! Heesh better 'n Sandy Koufax!" Charlie glared at him, but didn't see Eddie, so he kept walking. Then he let his book bag drop and froze. Eddie was walking across the basketball court.

The three stooges had jumped off the bars, but now looked not at Charlie, but at the man moving toward them. "Are these the guys?" Eddie asked as he came up.

"Yeah," he said, quietly. "These are the guys."

"Listen, you little cowards. There'll be no three on one today. You're tough when you're all together, aren't you? Who started it, Charlie?"

"DeCola started it," he said, "the chubby one in the middle."

"Well, here he is, Mr. DeCola. I'm just here to keep it fair. I won't lift a finger, but neither will you other two boys."

This startling change of affairs took DeCola by surprise, and he looked just a little nervous as Butchie and Stevie stepped away. He started to say something that sounded conciliatory, but raised his fists as Charlie charged. Focusing all the shame and hatred and humiliation into a continuous rain of body blows, Charlie beat him backward. Soon, very soon, DeCola's face was bloody, and Charlie hit him with a shot that sent him reeling back into the chains of the swings where he tumbled over a swing seat and flipped backward into the dust where he lay sobbing. Charlie moved toward him, but Eddie stretched an arm out to block him. "He's down. He's all done. Let's keep it fair."

"They didn't keep it fair," Charlie said.

"No, they didn't." He looked toward the other two boys. "Next?" he asked. "Let's go, he's just getting warmed up."

He was getting warmed up, the glorious warmth of revenge and the joy of vindication. "Come on!" he said. "One down, let the next one come on! You think you're so tough!"

Butchie and Stevie assumed the air of innocent bystanders. "Who's tough?" Butchie asked.

"I am!" Charlie roared into his face as Butchie stepped backward.

"What you did was a disgrace, boys," Eddie said. "In the future, fight fair. That's what a man does." He cast a look of disdain in DeCola's direction and said, "Take him home. Let's go, Charlie."

Stevie Smith mumbled, "Sorry we insulted your father. It was just a joke."

Charlie turned on him, still furious. "I don't give a shit about my father! You insulted me!"

"Okay, sorry," he said.

"Let's go, Charlie. I'll give you a ride," Eddie said. "These guys won't mess with Charlie Tumulty again."

Charlie felt that day changed him, but whether it was for the better or the worse he sometimes wondered. Uncle Eddie was right about one thing: those guys never messed with him again. They never even looked at him.

Chapter 8

Fall, 1966

Charlie had moved on to Lowell High School. The first day, in Lucy Larcom Park, he saw Sherman Kelly smoking a cigarette by the canal. He handed his notebook to Foxy and walked over to him. "Remember me?" Charlie asked and nailed him with a right. Kelly went down. He staggered to his feet, and seeing something in Charlie that he had not seen before, and the fact that he had grown, said, "All right, we're even." He hurried away, rubbing his jaw.

Charlie convinced Foxy McRae to go out for wrestling with him, but he quit after a week because the coach told him to get a haircut. He still spent a lot of his free time with Foxy, often at Black Brook. Neither of them knew who made the rafts that floated among the bracken or lay half-pulled onto the muddy shore. There were five of them. A couple were one-man rafts—what looked like sections of telephone pole with a few boards nailed across them. If Charlie and Foxy stood together on either of those, the raft would slowly sink into the swampy water. Two others were bigger, and could hold Charlie and Foxy, and the biggest could probably have floated three guys. The pond wasn't real deep; you could push the rafts around most parts with a pole. In the beginning, Charlie had always thought some bigger kids would come crashing through the woods and say, "Hey, get the hell off our rafts!" But no one ever did, and after a while, the rafts were theirs, and they hid them in a little cove that was hard to get to unless you didn't mind getting dirty, climbing over dead trees, and getting your sneakers wet.

They'd bring some rocks on the raft so that when they spotted a rat they could peg them at it, but the rats slithered into the water at the first splash around them. They dreamed of BB guns so they could plug those rats in their fat asses. Sometimes, Foxy brought his transistor radio, and put it on RKO to listen to "Sloop John B," "Secret Agent Man," and "See You in September." Their favorite was the Standells' new song. It always seemed fitting, out on the rafts, as they sang along: *Well I love that dirty water.*

No one ever seemed to come down there, except Squiggles because he lived nearby, but he didn't have a lot to say to Charlie these days; he hung out with Bobby Spinney. They were baseball teammates, and mainly interested in that or in fishing for hornpout up by the Middlesex Bridge. Charlie didn't have a fishing rod or much desire to pull fish you couldn't eat out of the dirty water.

Charlie and Foxy liked to go out on the two-man raft, poling across the flooded basin. Sometimes, Foxy would roll a joint and puff on it, though Charlie told him he should keep his wits about him, just in case those other kids ever did show up and try to claim the rafts.

"You shouldn't smoke so much hooch, Foxy. It's gonna make you dumber than you already are."

"You got that all wrong, Charlie. It expands your mind."

"Yeah, I'm sure. Just don't start bringing your pothead friends down here to party. The next thing you know everyone will be here and pretty soon Tiny Muldoon will be crashing through the woods and throwing people in the paddy wagon."

"He almost arrested me one night," Foxy said.

"What for?"

"I walked down to Pizza by Charles to get a cheese steak sub, right?"

"That's a long walk for you."

"I had nothin' else to do, and I like their subs." He took a toke off the joint and raised a finger, suppressing a cough and exhaled.

"That shit stinks," Charlie said. "So, what happened?"

"I was just walking home with my sub, minding my own business, and I turned and spit over my shoulder into the street. The chances that a cruiser would be going by at that instant were a million to one! The chances that my loogie would land on the windshield of the cruiser were a million to one! The chances that the cruiser would be driven by the toughest cop on the force, Tiny Muldoon, were a million to one!"

Charlie was laughing so hard that the raft bounced on the water and sent ripples out in widening circles toward the shore. "That could only happen to you. And he didn't arrest you?"

"Tiny, who sure ain't tiny, pulled over and got out, and he was pissed. I said, 'Officer Muldoon, I'm so sorry. Look, I have my sub from Charlie Pizza here. I just want to go home and eat. I could see if I was with my friends, and I was trying to be funny or something, but I'm all alone. Why would I do that?' I pulled the napkins out of the bag and went over and wiped it off and apologized. Boy, did I apologize. He asked my name, and I said, 'David McRae,' and he says, 'It's not that I don't believe you, David, because I do. It's just that anyone who has luck as bad as yours—I think we're going to meet again.' And then, guess what? He gave me a lift home in the cruiser. He's really a good guy. Told me to stay out of trouble."

Charlie nodded. "Well, they say he's tough, but fair." Foxy put out the joint and dropped what was left into a plastic vial he pulled from his pocket. "Yeah. He's all right. But I will never spit without looking where I'm spitting again." He looked around and said, "It's really pretty here, Charlie. Like a painting by some great painter like Louis DaVinci."

"*Louis* Da Vinci? You're too much, Foxy."

"What?"

Later, in jail, Charlie would often lie on his bunk and recall the carefree laughter, the smell of the swampy water, the flash of sun in leaves, the hum of cicadas as he and his oldest pal glided over the dark water, watching turtles scatter as their raft drew near, plunging into the murky shallows from the half-sunken logs where they sunned themselves.

The boys poled the raft to its hidden spot among the small brush islands of a swampy inlet and jumped to the shore. "You wanna go to see Fitzgibbons or go to the Boys Club?"

"We gotta go to the Boys Club, Charlie. There's a professional boxer coming in from the East End Gym to put on a demonstration."

"Oh yeah. Cool."

The boxer, who looked Italian or Portuguese to Charlie, took off his oversized robe. He wore high-top laced shoes, gold shorts and a white singlet bearing the logo of the East End Gym. He looked bored and said nothing to the boys who surrounded him.

Coach Canney, a tall man with thinning gray hair, who coached or had coached all the major sports, was the Athletic Director at the Boys Club. He had the booming voice of a guy who had spoken to teams of boys for thirty years. He called the twenty or so spectators standing on the basketball court to order. "Some of you may have heard of Manny Fragoso. He started as a featherweight in the Silver Mittens and has moved up through lightweight, to welterweight, which means he's near the weight of most of you guys. He's won more than fifty amateur bouts and a Golden Gloves title. He has agreed to come over here, for free, to give you knuckleheads a little demonstration of the science of boxing, and I say 'science' because it doesn't matter how tough you are, you have to learn the science. As you can see, he is dressed as he would for a regulation bout just so you can kind of feel what it's like to be in the ring with a real boxer. Is there anyone who would like to be the guinea pig and get in and spar with Manny?"

Murmurs rose around Charlie and the whole group of spectators shrunk back.

"He won't hurt you," Mr. Canney said. "Come on, who's got some guts here?"

"I'll spar with him," Charlie said.

"You're crazy," Foxy whispered.

Coach Canney helped Charlie push his hands into boxing gloves and laced them up. He secured the blue headgear and buckled the strap under his chin. Fragoso wasn't wearing headgear. The coach had marked off a square with tape. "The ring. Stay in the ring, Charlie. The rest of you take a seat in the bleachers, there." The boys climbed onto the bleachers while Charlie watched Fragoso. He looked like he was just getting ready to mow the lawn or something, while Charlie's blood was full of adrenalin, his heart beating in his throat. "You have two minutes. I don't have a bell, so I'll just say, 'Ding!'"

Fragoso walked out and stood, rather idly, Charlie thought, in the center of the improvised ring. Charlie raised his fists and moved toward him. He didn't expect to win a sparring match, but he hoped to make a good impression. When he felt he was close enough, he threw a jab and then quickly two more, but the boxer slid to his left and Charlie felt two light taps on the right side of his headgear. He refocused and was about to throw another jab when the boxer feigned a movement to his right and tapped him two more times with his left. "You got two hands, kid," the boxer said. "Throw combinations. Make it automatic."

Charlie lunged at him, throwing a jab and a roundhouse right. Fragoso, looking almost bored, bobbed and moved and tapped him again, on his ribs and then twice on the headgear. Charlie swung, but the boxer was somewhere else. "Don't drop that left, kid," Fragoso said. "Keep moving. You don't want to stand toe-to-toe with a guy like me."

Charlie was already sweating under the headgear and he knew the two minutes would be up soon. He charged, throwing everything he had with both hands. The boxer easily parried his blows, knocking his gloves aside as he moved smoothly within the improvised ring, and Charlie felt the taps on his headgear once again.

"Ding!" the coach cried. "Good effort, Charlie."

"Nice job, kid," the boxer said, off-handedly.

Charlie realized how easily this guy could have knocked him senseless without ever taking a punch. He had toyed with him. The coach was right. It was not just about being tough. It was a science.

"Thanks, Manny," he said, and he got a nod and a wink from the boxer.

"Next!" the coach shouted. Seeing that Charlie had not been pulverized, a few other kids tried their prowess.

Charlie studied the cool Manny Fragoso, the way he moved, stutter-stepped, leaning in, weaving, ducking low and then drawing back, bouncing on strong legs. At times, he made the boys miss without even moving his legs, merely bowing and moving his head between raised gloves or twisting his torso. Occasionally he dropped both hands, drawing his opponent in with what looked like a clear shot, only to slide rapidly away like a matador from a bull so that the blows of the frustrated youths sailed past him. No one touched him, while he tapped their headgear or their sides with light combinations at will.

Charlie Tumulty was at the East End Gym two weeks later, carrying the gear he bought with money he had saved working for Fitzgibbons. Baseball was over. Wrestling had lost its glamor for him. He would be a boxer, and he began his training with all the intensity that youth brings to a newfound passion.

Charlie felt, at the East End Gym, as he had felt at Black Brook. It was a place where he forgot about the rest of the world, about his drunken parents, about the strange men who frequented his apartment. He was intimidated at first by the other young guys he saw slamming fists into heavy bags, jumping rope or sparring while a trainer yelled out instructions. The sounds of punches landing on leather bags or into padded mitts, the shouts that resounded through the high-ceilinged gym, the smell of sweat and leather. It was all new and strangely exhilarating.

There was a retired boxer named Mike Dineen who trained fighters and worked as a cornerman with some. Coffee in hand, the older man talked to him, and Charlie could see right away that he was a solid man. "Mike," he asked, "what kind of guys am I going to meet here?"

"The best," he said, without hesitation. "Don't get me wrong. They're dangerous in the ring, but outside the ring they're gentlemen. That's what we teach here. See that kid working the speed bag? Edwin Pimentel. He takes his mother to church every Sunday. The Black kid hitting the punching mitts with Arthur? That's Ray Ramon. Academic scholarship to Merrimack College. That kid in the corner? Johnny Rivera. He sits there and does his homework every day before he trains. Arthur won't let any troublemakers in here, and they don't last anyway. They don't have the self-discipline. You come in here, you work your ass off and you show respect to everyone else. That's how it is."

Charlie watched the speed bag flying before the rhythmic punches of DosSantos and the rapid combinations that Ramon unleashed into the mitts that gym owner Ribeiro held before him. "I'm gonna make a fool of myself, Mike. These guys are really good."

"You're gonna stink, Charlie. Everyone stinks at first. Just like if you were playing piano. You're a wrestler, right? So, you know something about balance. That's a good start. Just work hard. No one will laugh. You'll get good if you stick with it. Whether you get very good, time will tell. It's a tough game. You'll see."

Mike put his coffee down and said, "Let me lace up those gloves, Charlie, and I'll show you some of the basics you can work on with the heavy bag and some of the common mistakes."

And so it began. In front of the heavy bag, the cagey old fighter raised his fists, and showed him, at first slowly and then more rapidly, basic combinations. He showed him how to stand, on the balls of the feet, how to throw a straight jab, turning the hips to transfer the weight into the punch. He showed him how to move his feet, left foot first when moving to the left, right foot first moving to the right. "Never cross one leg behind the other, Charlie. You get hit in that position, you will go down."

Charlie took up his stance in front of the bag.

"Imagine the bag is your opponent. Stand back here, get your range, feint with a right, throw your left. Imagine how your opponent reacts. Move in when you throw punches," Mike said. Charlie listened and tried to follow the trainer's advice. "Toe in line with the heel of your front foot and hit the bag with some jabs and crosses. Be a moving target, see?" Once again, he demonstrated the movements and the combinations.

Now Charlie jabbed and punched while the trainer critiqued his movements. "Keep the chin down, Charlie. Just the chin—don't lean forward. Don't drop that non-punching hand, or the other guy is gonna drop you. Are you holding your breath when you throw punches? Breathe, Charlie. Exhale as you throw the punch but keep breathing."

After a while, Mike nodded and said, "That's better, but don't push the bag, Charlie, hit the bag. And when you throw that left, don't bring it back to your chest, always bring it right back to your cheek." He went to a side locker and came back with a timer. "Three-minute rounds. One minute rest. Five rounds. That's fifteen minutes of punching, five minutes of rest. Hit the bag and move away." He raised his fists and demonstrated again. "If your last punch is a left, move to your left. If your last punch is a right, move to your right. Keep moving and keep your balance. Don't rest for more than two or three seconds between punches. There's no resting in the ring until you hear the bell. I'll be back."

Twenty minutes later, his arms felt as though they were full of hot cement. He stopped and began to walk toward the boxing event posters and the photos of current or former champions that hung over the painted brick walls. Beau Jaynes, Dave Ramalho, Larry Carney, Paul Frechette, Billy Ryan, Al Mello, Manny Freitas, Bobby Christakos, Dicky Eklund. Mike came up and said, "A lot of tough fighters from Lowell, Charlie. Some of them are still alive, mostly the ones in the color photos. Some of them won a lot of fights, big fights. Some of them, no telling how far they might have gone. But they took wrong turns. If you want to be a champ, you got to stay away from the party life. And you gotta eat right. You don't put cheap gas in a Ferrari. And get your sleep." He pointed to another photo, an old black-and-white photo of a boxer named Phinney Boyle, wearing short dark trunks and peering between his gloves in a classic fighter's pose. "Poor Phinney," he said.

"What happened to him?"

"His son Arthur was killed at Pearl Harbor. Dead before we even knew we were at war." He shook his head and sighed, then said, "Would you like to be on that wall, someday, Charlie?"

"Yeah, I would. I think more than anything else."

"That's the right answer," the old man said. "I'm not saying you will be. I'm not saying you can be. But if that's not your answer, you never will be, that's for sure."

Charlie's alarm sounded every morning at 4:30. He did sit-ups, push-ups and ran before school. He ran on weekend mornings before he met Fitzgibbons to clear out a house or to work the flea market. He trained with a single-mindedness that even his mother remarked on, though lately it had seemed to Charlie that she would hardly notice if he disappeared. Some of the money he made he spent on good food, trusting Mike's words that a great athlete needed the proper fuel. No donuts. No French fries. No chips.

Charlie spent months at the heavy bag learning to "slip," and getting in position to throw a hard lead hook, transferring his weight from his left foot with a turn of the hip. He began to spar with more experienced boxers like Ray Ramon and work with some other trainers. They exposed his weaknesses without nailing him as badly as they might have, and he worked to correct those weaknesses. Mike was usually nearby, giving advice. "Combinations start from the legs, from the feet. Jab, body blow, head jab, slip with jab. Feint. Move. Don't be predictable. Be a puzzle. A dangerous puzzle."

In time, he developed an understanding of the mystery of the rhythm and mobility that separate a mere puncher from a boxer, the imperatives of lateral movement, head movement, feints, of keeping your opponent guessing when you're coming and of not being where you were when he counter-attacks. He learned how to survive on the ropes when necessary.

Charlie was impatient for fights. He and another boxer from the gym went to Lawrence a few times on Saturdays to fight for money, impromptu bouts in some makeshift gym where spectators made bets and drank beer, but in general there was some kind of a referee who tried to be fair and rules were followed. Mike got wind of it, though, and made Charlie promise not to go back. "You're going to be a legitimate boxer, Charlie. Cut the shit." After nearly five months in the gym, Mike told him, "The doctor will be here Monday afternoon. He'll give you your medical and your first bout is next Saturday. An Inter-Club match. You'll wear headgear. Three rounds. There'll be a ref, judges, and people in the stands."

"You think I'm ready, Mike?"

"For amateur bouts? Between you and me, Charlie, the guy who's in the best shape usually wins. Most of 'em can't fight when they're tired, and some of 'em are sucking wind by the end of the first round. If you can spar for six rounds you can fight for three rounds. You're ready, and there's no substitute for experience." Charlie began to run in the evening, too, after his workout at the gym, building his endurance so that when he got in the ring for his first bout, he was moving fast and throwing leather from bell to bell each round. Mike had little to say to him between rounds, but after the ref had raised his arm, he said, "You're undefeated. Don't think that will last long if you don't work harder."

He worked harder. He won, and he kept winning, eight of his next ten bouts. Mike said he'd arranged for him to go to the Somerville Boxing Club to train with a guy he knew named Bovino. "I'll drive you down, three days a week, how's that? They got the best fighters in New England comin' out of Somerville now. Bovino can polish your technique, your combinations—advanced skills. You got the heart—he's got the method."

On one of his early morning runs, Charlie saw a familiar figure walking a small dog near Lowell State College. "Miss Walker!" he called.

She turned and gave him a broad smile, such as she had rarely shown as the undisputed ruler of her 8th grade class. "Charles Tumulty! Staying in shape, I see."

"I've gotten into boxing, Miss Walker."

"It's a barbaric sport," she said. "And you can call me Liz, now."

"No, I couldn't do that."

"As you like. Are you still reading?"

"I am, and I have to thank you for being such a good teacher."

"Thank you. You had me in my last year. I'm retired now, but I took my responsibility seriously, and I was gratified to have such a receptive student as yourself."

"It's good to see you. How are you?"

The dog sat at her feet and looked about, blinking. Miss Walker shook her head. "Oh, I'm so angry, Charles, with what's going on. You heard about the poor Callery boy from Parker Street? Only thirty-four days in Viet Nam, and he came home in a coffin."

"Yeah. Awful. I heard they renamed Highland Park . . ."

"Yes, it's Callery Park, a well-meant tribute, but it's poor consolation. Oh, I hope it ends soon, Charles."

"And your nephew? Is he all right?"

"Yes, thank God he has returned, but my sister says it's quite a readjustment for him. I don't understand why we're involved in an internecine war on the other side of the world."

"It is a mess."

"It certainly is. Now, Charles, you take care of yourself. Don't stay too long in that boxing business. Do you ever write?"

"Not really, but I write notes sometimes. Maybe someday."

"I hope so. Well, it's lovely to see you. I think of you as one of my best students."

"And I'll always remember you as my best teacher," he said.

"That means a great deal to me. Be good, Charles."

He never would have presumed to embrace the great Miss Walker, but to his surprise, she embraced him. "God bless you," she said, and to the dog, "Let's go, Bertie."

He watched her walk away, thinking that he might never see her again, and what a difference a few good people could make in the life of a young man.

Chapter 9

1969

Charlie was seventeen years old and a senior at Lowell High School. In addition to the local bouts, he'd won both the 1968 Youth Open and the Eastern Regionals and taken second in the John Lynburn Memorial Tournament. "Well," Fitzgibbons said, from the heart of his smoky sanctuary, "since you've become such a practitioner of the sweet science, I have a book you have to read." He snubbed out the cigarette, got up, and moved through the familiar labyrinth of the shop to the sagging bookshelf at the back. He ran his finger over a few titles, picked out a book, and drew it from its place. He opened it and read, or declaimed:

> *Anger be now your song, immortal one,*
> *Akhilleus' anger, doomed and ruinous,*
> *that caused the Akhaians loss on bitter loss*
> *and crowded brave souls into the undergloom,*
> *leaving so many dead men—carrion*
> *for dogs and birds; and the will of Zeus was done.*

He snapped the book shut and held it up. "That's the book to read and internalize if you want to be a warrior."

"What's it about?" Charlie asked.

"They never had you read *The Iliad* in school?"

He shook his head.

"Just amazing that you can get a high-school diploma these days without ever reading *The Iliad*." He gave Charlie a sort of thumbnail sketch of the background to the story of the two sides in the battle at Troy, of ruthless Achilles, and Hector the hero. "Here," he said and found another book, Edith Hamilton's *Mythology*. "If you get confused, read that, but don't get too hung up on names. Just read the book. You'll learn about the courage you need for victory and the grace you need in defeat. You know, Charlie," he said as they made their way back to the front, "I've had friends—close friends—good friends who are dead now these twenty years or more, and already the memories I have of them begin to fade. I read Homer at your age, and I swear that after all these years, the images I have in my mind of Achilles, of Hector, of Odysseus, of the goddess Athena—they are more substantial, more vivid in my mind than the images of my old friends."

Charlie ran his thumb across the edge of the pages. "It's pretty thick," he said.

"You're pretty thick!"

Charlie laughed. Fitzgibbons raised his fists and gave him a playful punch. "Come on, Charlie! If you don't read, *you don't know.*" He dismissed the young man's literary lethargy with a wave of his hand, pulled a pack of Camel non-filters from his shirt pocket and shook one loose. "When I was your age"

"Here we go . . ."

"Damn right! First of all, I would have kicked your ass!"

"Sure."

"Then, I'd go home and read half a Charles Dickens novel in one night! Too thick!" He lit the cigarette and shook his head. "How am I going to make an educated gentleman out of a bum like you?"

"Maybe if I just spend enough time with you, some of your . . . what's the word . . ."

"Erudition?"

"What's that mean?"

"Learning."

"Yeah, some of your erudition will rub off on me. I'll absorb it, like they say in biology . . . through *osmosis*. There's some erudition for you."

Fitzgibbons picked a loose strand of tobacco off the tip of his tongue and nodded thoughtfully. "Well, you may have something there, Charlie. You're really using your noodle now. Yes, I do *exude* erudition, and who knows, maybe you'll soak some of it up. In the meantime, read the first three books of *The Iliad*. I don't even know who I'd be without Homer. As Gladstone said, '*The Iliad* teaches you how to die.' Can teach you how to live, too."

Charlie got Foxy to run with him out to the Dracut State Forest. They jogged along wooded paths and by ponds where beavers thumped the water with broad flat tails to warn them away from their flooded lodges. "I'll whip you into shape," Charlie told him.

"You think I could be a boxer, Charlie?"

"Nah, you like to party too much. To be a contender, you need what Mike calls 'singleness of purpose.'"

"Well, I'll try to get in shape, anyway."

He made Charlie laugh. He didn't do well in school, but it wasn't because he was dumb. He just wasn't interested in a lot of it. He didn't have goals. The drinking age was 18, and Foxy had taken to hanging out at some of the local bars. He just flowed along like a guy in a canoe on a river without a paddle. He would never look out for rapids ahead. But the way he spoke was original and Charlie appreciated it. Once Foxy told him that in McCullogh's Bar, "Even the women are bullies."

Fitzgibbons wondered about Foxy. "You think he's good company for you, Charlie? I think he may pull you down."

"Ah, he's all right," Charlie would say.

One Saturday, Charlie stopped by Foxy's apartment, a one-room studio on East Merrimack Street. "Come in," he heard, in answer to his knock.

He found Foxy sitting there at the kitchen table with a book.

"So, you do read books?"

He showed the cover. "You gave it to me. It's a hell of a book, Charlie."

"*The Count of Monte Cristo*. Yeah, it's great. I didn't think you'd actually read it."

"The story really makes me wonder, Charlie. Could I survive in prison? Could I take it, or would I just go crazy?"

"You'd want to survive for someone you love or to get even with someone you hate. Edmond Dantès had both."

"Mercedes and Mondego."

"Right." Charlie scanned the room. Bed, neatly made. Foxy kept it surprisingly organized for a guy who liked to smoke weed. His eyes rested on a print of Jesus and then on a little statue of the Virgin beside a lamp on his night table. "You're still into the religious stuff, Foxy?"

"My mother gave 'em to me when I moved out. They remind me of her. She said, 'Take those, David, you need somebody up there on your side.'"

"That's probably true."

There was a little silence, and Charlie could see that Foxy was recalling something. "I was an altar boy, you know," he said.

"Yeah, I remember you told me that."

"But I missed my assigned Mass a couple of times and, you can't do that, so . . ."

"Oh, well. Seems like you took something away."

"Yeah. If I was imprisoned like the Count of Monte Cristo, I'd probably need religion to get through."

"And some weed."

"Don't think I'd like to be high in jail, Charlie. But I think in case I ever get in trouble or get busted, you know, you can be in the wrong place and end up in jail, and like Tiny Muldoon said, with my luck, that could happen to me.

I gotta be prepared. I need to get my mind tough just in case. So sometimes I just sit here and look at the walls."
Charlie laughed. "You practice for jail?"
"Yeah, Charlie. I do. I practice for jail. Just in case."

Later, Charlie remembered those remarks, and how ironic it was that he, and not Foxy, who should have been practicing for jail. Foxy was the wild one—the party guy. Charlie thought he could stand back and observe the foibles and craziness of the people around him because he was above it all. He had never forgotten Miss Walker's comment that he had a literary mind. He was merely collecting experience and gathering notes for the book he might write someday, like Jack London in the Klondike, or Hemingway in Spain.

He was thinking about quitting working at Eddie's Bar because Foxy said that he knew where they could make better money faster. He knew this guy named Beak Malvert.

It was just before graduation, and Charlie ambled into the old junk store. Fitzgibbons was writing up a slip for a grizzled workingman in farmer's overalls. "Charlie, will you help this gentleman get those tools out to his station wagon there?"

"That's all right, Fitz. If I can't pick them up, I won't be able to use them, will I?" the man said. Fitzgibbons handed him some change and his receipt, which he stuffed in his pocket.

"You're still a bull, Wally," Fitzgibbons said. The man chuckled and shrugged and said, "You gotta keep movin'."

He picked up the large wooden crate overflowing with a jumble of tools. The old dealer called out a thank you, and Charlie opened the door for the departing customer.

As soon as the door had closed, Fitzgibbons launched into what he called his "tutelage" of the younger man. "You know, Charlie, William Butler Yeats has eclipsed Thomas Moore as the greatest Irish poet, and rightly so, but Moore was damned good. I was just reading his poems in the old John Boyle O'Reilly *Poetry and Song of Ireland*. Now listen to this. He picked up a massive tome that had been lying open on his desk and read:

> *At the mid hour of night, when stars are weeping, I fly*
> *To the lone vale we loved, when life shone warm in thine eye;*
> *And I think oft, if spirits can steal from the regions of air,*
> *To revisit past scenes of delight, thou wilt come to me there,*
> *And tell me our love is remember'd, even in the sky."*

"That's really good," Charlie said.

"Take the book with you when you leave. Got time for a game of chess?" Fitzgibbons asked. He had already begun to set up the board.

"Sure. Did you see the fight last night?" Charlie asked the old man. "Ali had no trouble with Wepner."

"Ali got knocked down in the ninth, didn't he?"

"One lucky punch in the ribs. But Wepner was completely outclassed. Cuts over both eyes, broken nose. Knocked out for the first time in his career."

"You study Ali?"

"Of course, you try to learn, but you can't imitate him, dancing and throwing that jab. He has a reach of 78 inches. That's eight inches over mine."

"Come on, Charlie. No one has a reach of over six feet."

"A boxer's reach isn't measured shoulder to fist. It's really wingspan, arms spread, from the tip of one middle finger to the other," Charlie explained. "Guy with a reach like that can camp out in a zone where he can hit you, but you can't hit him. Beat you to the punch every time. You have to find a way into the middle zone, the war zone, where either fighter can get hit."

Fitzgibbons looked at him and said, "Well, I learned something new, there, Charlie. Jesus, you're growing like a weed. Where have you been lately?"

"Working out. And this guy Foxy knows is going to get me a job on the railroad, cleaning trains, gassing up the engines. It's part-time, but I may be able to go full-time when I graduate."

The board was set on Fitzgibbon's desk, and he pulled up a chair for Charlie. He lit a cigarette. "What guy that Foxy knows?"

"Beak Malvert. He's . . ."

"I know who he is. How does Foxy know him?"

"Foxy used to work part-time at Anderson Little. Malvert would come in and buy clothes. He knew the manager, Ray something. Ray introduced Foxy to Malvert and one thing led to another. Malvert got Foxy to peddle those football cards where you bet on the point spreads. Foxy was picking up the football cards every Monday night at the Stadium Plaza. Someone tipped off the cops and they showed up at Lowell High. They searched his locker and found one card used as a bookmark. Foxy clammed up, and Malvert got him a lawyer from Brookline. He was suspended, but was let back in school when he got off."

"So, this is the guy you count on? What about college?"

"I don't have the money."

"Apply for financial aid. Ask your guidance counselor to help. Maybe there's a grant." He nodded toward the chessboard. "Open the game."

Charlie moved out a pawn. "I don't need a diploma to educate myself. It's a waste of time. I read."

The old man shook his head. He moved a pawn, and his chair creaked loudly as he leaned back in it. "Charlie, let's say you're going to fight a guy. Now, you know you can beat him. And you say, 'I'm not going to waste my time fighting this guy because I already know I can beat him. I don't need to prove it.' People don't say, 'Yeah, you're right Charlie.' They say, 'Charlie didn't want to fight him because he couldn't beat him.'" He paused, letting the words sink in. "And people will say Charlie didn't go to college because he couldn't do it."

"I don't care what people say," he said, bringing out his knight.

"Oh, well. Then you're a new kind of person." He raised his hands as if to surrender on that score, but added, "Look, plenty of bright people didn't go to college, including myself. Okay, you don't have to go to college. But Beak Malvert!" He shook his head. "Charlie, I think over the last few years, I've helped to raise you, in a way?"

"You have."

"I mean, I talked to you. I tried to educate you. I gave you books. I taught you chess. Introduced you to interesting people on the flea market circuit. What can I say? I'm proud of you."

"Thanks, really. I've learned a lot."

"Let me tell you something. Beak Malvert is no fucking good, Charlie."

The young man was taken aback because he rarely heard Fitzgibbons swear at all. "I'm not marrying the guy. He's just helping me to get a job."

"Why? Because he has a kind heart? He doesn't have a heart at all, Charlie, or a conscience. Listen to me. He's going to want a favor back. Of that, I'm sure. Those guys like boxers because maybe he's going to ask you to collect a debt—use you to intimidate other guys, protect poker games. Maybe he'll even tell you to throw a fight like Marlon Brando in *On the Waterfront*, maybe carry some drugs for him, tag along on a heist. I don't know what it will be, but it will be illegal, and it will be dangerous. He's a bum, a criminal. You're a bright kid. You were warned. I'll say no more."

Charlie thought about this while they played in silence. He had been reading *The Iliad*, and he associated Fitzgibbons with "the man of winning words," Nestor, the trusted advisor to the Achaeans. He recalled Agamemnon's words to Nestor, "Old man, everything you say is fit and proper." The chess game was close until Charlie made a careless move and lost his queen.

The next day, Charlie told Foxy to thank Malvert, but that he was going to work in Eddie's Piano Bar. "You're crazy, man!" Foxy said. Charlie tried to explain what Fitzgibbons had said, but his friend said, "It's a job with benefits, man!

"Yeah, I'm out," Charlie said. "And maybe you should think twice." Anyway, the job at the bar was convenient because, for cheap money, Eddie rented him a studio apartment upstairs from the bar. His mother didn't notice he was gone for a week. Emmet Byrne, a local plumber with a used car business on the side, sold him a Ford Falcon for 600 bucks, canary yellow with a black top. Eddie said it was a peach.

Chapter 10

Charlie Tumulty's record was catching the attention of those who followed the boxing game. Then, in 1973, three years out of high school, he made it to the final of the Golden Gloves, where he TKO'd his opponent in the third and final three-minute round. His photo was in *The Lowell Sun* with Mike smiling proudly beside him. The headline ran: "*Charlie Tumulty: 'The Pride of the Acre,' Wins Golden Gloves Middleweight Title.*" He never let up on his opponents or on himself. He was thinking about applying to college, maybe getting a degree in psychology so he could figure out his parents. Eddie's Bar was busier than ever with the lowered drinking age. Training, working, and reading. These three formed the round of his life for a while, and he was happy.

December 11th, the first snowfall of the year, a dusting over Lowell in the morning. By 9:00 am, the gray dullness overhead had cleared. The steeples of the churches and the towering smokestacks of the old city rose boldly into a cobalt sky. It was the kind of air that made you feel alive, Charlie thought, as he unlocked the bar and was greeted by the eternal smell of the barroom: stale beer and tobacco with a hint of disappointed hopes. He went behind the bar and turned on WBCN. Marvin Gaye, "Mercy, Mercy, Me." He sang along with it as he cleaned the Fryolator. After that, he filled a bucket with Pine-Sol and went to mop the bathrooms.

Trish, a sad-looking prostitute, with blond hair and dark roots, came in early, ordered a sombrero, and lit a Marlboro Lite. "This city sucks," she said.

Charlie pushed an ashtray toward her. "It's what you make of it, Trish."

Her smile was edged with scorn. She dragged on her cigarette. Then she shook her head and blew a disdainful smoke cloud. "Well, I can't make shit of it."

There was a phone booth in the back of the bar. She went to make a call. A minute later she emerged and headed to the ladies' room. "Off to work," she said. "I gotta put my diaphragm in."

"You don't need to tell me that," Charlie called after her.

She emerged a few minutes later, gulped the last of her drink, left a dollar fifty on the bar and headed out.

"Take it easy, Trish. Enjoy the day. It's beautiful out there."

"Oh yeah, fuckin' *goh-giss*. See ya, Charlie."

The radio was playing "Riders on the Storm," and the lyrics seemed a fitting commentary on her departing figure.

If I ran this bar, he thought, *I'd clean it up. Sorry, Trish. No more hookers, no more druggies. They give the place a bad name. Eddie is too kind-hearted.*

Eddie arrived as the lunch crowd gathered: city workers, some college kids, and a few regulars. It was a simple menu: hot dogs boiled in beer, burgers, fries, steak bombs. Sophie Stiles came in, too. She was a young woman from Mt. Vernon Street off Pawtucket Street. She worked at the Club Diner in the morning and helped with tending bar and cooking at Eddie's later on. Eddie called her "a sweet kid," and she was. She and Charlie had a casual sexual relationship. They liked each other, but for some reason, they remained friends who were sometimes lovers more than lovers who were friends.

One of the regulars was George Lee, a veteran and a retired railroad worker who usually started drinking at lunch and occasionally felt pugnacious. Today, it seemed he had started at breakfast. A Salvation Army Santa Claus came in and took a seat at the bar. George gave him the stink eye for a minute and then lunged at him, and soon the two of them were rolling around on the floor trading blows. Charlie vaulted over the bar, and he and Eddie separated the men and hauled them to their feet.

"What the hell, George?" Eddie shouted.

"This asshole attacked me for no reason!" Santa said, lunging at George. Charlie pulled him back.

Eddie poked George in the chest. "What's wrong with you, whacking Santy Claus?"

"He ain't even really Sanna Claus!" George retorted. "He's a phony! Look, his fuckin' beard and hair an' everything came right off!"

"Of course, I'm a phony!" Santa shouted. "You dumbass! There is no Santa Claus!"

Charlie heard Sophie burst into laughter behind him.

"Well . . ." George was considering the implications.

"Everybody sit down. You all right, Santa?"

"Yeah, I'm fine. Fuckin' dope!"

"Well, you got in some good shots, Santa," Charlie said, as he guided the less-than-jolly old elf back to his seat and handed him his hat and beard. Eddie was giving George a lecture and pointing at the door, no doubt making it clear that another escapade like that would result in permanent expulsion. "Alright, alright," George said, and he mumbled, "I'm sorry, okay?"

"Louder!" Eddie said. "Say, *I'm sorry, Santa Claus!*"

"Awright, awright. I'm sorry Sanna!"

"Ah, fuck you," Santa said, but his mood brightened somewhat when Charlie set a mug of beer in front of him and said, "On the house."

He looked over his shoulder at his penitent attacker. "What's your name?" he wanted to know.

"George Lee," the other man said.

"Hmph!" he replied, lifting his beer. "There are more Lees in federal prison than there are peaches in Georgia!"

It was at this moment of unbridled idiocy that Laila Grant walked into Eddie's Piano Bar. She held a gloved hand to her face, which was bleeding profusely, whether from her nose or mouth, Charlie could not tell.

"Oh my God!" Sophie cried, and the bar went quiet. Charlie told her to call an ambulance and helped the woman to a chair while Eddie went to get a towel. He suspected immediately that she had been beaten, but she waved away questions. She insisted that she was all right, but Charlie had seen broken noses before, and he was sure hers was broken.

"What's your name?" he asked.

"Laila," she whispered.

"What happened, Laila? Did some son of a . . . did someone hit you?"

Her head bowed, and her dark hair shook. "I'll be all right."

"The medics will be here soon. You're safe here."

Eddie handed her a damp towel and a glass of water. She pulled off her blood-soaked gloves, and Charlie was nearly ashamed of himself for noticing that her hands were beautiful and that the only ring on her finger was a small birthstone, emerald, what was that March, or May? He stood and said, in a low voice, to Eddie, "If I find the guy who did this to this poor woman, I am going to kick his ass."

"Let the cops handle it, Charlie. Don't get yourself arrested."

"But will the cops handle it?" He was getting angry, and Eddie put his hand on his shoulder and told him to calm down.

"We don't know what happened," he said

They heard the ambulance arriving. The Med Techs came in, and he stepped away as they attended her.

Charlie walked outside and saw, beyond the ambulance, a cruiser parked across the street. Two cops were talking to a man in a long coat over a white shirt. He was clean-shaven, and his dark hair was neatly parted and combed. He reminded him of Al Pacino in *The Godfather*. His hands were raised, palm outwards, in a gesture of innocence. In one of them, he held a cigarette; in the other, a pair of sunglasses. Apparently, he had removed them so the cops could see the sincerity in his eyes. Eddie came out and said, "That's Frank Sago. Stay outa this, Charlie. He's got bad friends."

The Med Techs came out with Laila. She glanced across the street and quickly looked away. As she passed Charlie, he saw her eyes on him, above the towel that still hid half her face. "Thank you. I'm sorry." He heard her voice clearly even through the towel.

"No. I'm sorry," he said. She was bundled into the back of the ambulance. One of the men jumped in and took a seat beside her. The door closed and away they went, lights spinning, no siren. Across the street, one cop was already walking away. The other was folding up his notebook. He heard Frank Sago say, "Thank you, officer," before turning and walking back toward the stairs.

Charlie crossed the street. "Aren't you gonna arrest the son of a bitch?"

"What business is it of yours?" Sago called, poking the air with his cigarette.

"I wasn't talking to you, fuckface."

"Hey! Calm down!" the cop said. "We'll get a statement from the woman after she's fixed up. That's all we can do."

Frank Sago was now standing with one hand on the railing of his front stairs. He glared at Charlie like he was shit on his shoe.

"All you can do. That's what I thought," Charlie said, as the cop stuffed his notebook in his pocket and watched him, sensing correctly that Charlie was a second away from charging up the walkway.

"Go back to the bar," Sago called.

As he took a step forward, he felt a strong grip on his arm and Eddie said, "Come on, Charlie. Sophie is all alone."

He hurled a final "Asshole!" in Sago's direction, and he and Eddie returned to the bar together. Dan Webster had come in and was playing "Christmastime in the City" on the piano. George Lee and Santa Claus, among others, were singing along loudly, but the spirit of the season had drained from Charlie's soul, the peace and good cheer now dissolved in a cauldron of anger.

Three days later, Charlie saw her walking down Market Street. Though she was wearing sunglasses, he recognized her because an inverted T of white tape had been placed over the broken nose. He crossed the street. "Good morning, Laila."

She stopped. A faint smile seemed to cause her pain. Her hand rose to the cross of tape. "I'm sorry I caused you so much trouble," she said.

"Not at all." He felt somewhat awkward. The only thing he knew about her was that she'd been beaten by a creep. "Glad to see you're better."

"I'm a mess." She lowered her sunglasses to show two black eyes.

He shook his head. "Did the cops talk to you?"

"Yes," she said as she raised the sunglasses.

"Did they arrest the guy . . . Frank?"

She paused. Her head turned slightly, apparently surprised that he knew the name, and perhaps a bit embarrassed. "No. I didn't want to press charges. I have a restraining order. I want nothing to do with him."

A bus rumbled by. One of its windows clacked down and someone shouted, "Hey Chaahlie! Haza goin'?" He wasn't sure who it was, but he waved.

"Anyway, thanks, Charlie."

"Can I buy you a coffee?"

"Thanks. I really need to . . ." She pointed vaguely up the street.

"I understand. You can always find me at my uncle's bar if you need me. Charlie Tumulty. And I hope your boyfriend stays far away."

She sighed. "My husband."

"Oh." He caught himself before he said, *That's too bad.* "I noticed you weren't wearing a ring."

"Yeah. No, I threw it away, actually, and I won't ever wear it again. I'm Laila Grant. But, legally, for now, I'm still Laila Sago." She shrugged and laughed lightly. "A mess all around. But thanks for your help. You guys were so kind."

"Look for me at my uncle's bar if you need me."

She thrust her hands into her coat pockets and nodded. "Yes, you said that."

"Right. Sorry. I feel—I don't know how to put it, but after seeing what that bastard did, I feel like your well-being is . . . well, let's just say I take a great interest in your well-being."

Her brows knit and she said, "Someone told me you were a boxer. You don't talk like a boxer."

"I like to read. And I've had some good teachers." He was tempted to tell her of the boxing matches at the funeral of Patroclus in *The Iliad*, or of Hemingway's boxing matches, or the even tougher Jack London, but he thought that might be overdoing it.

She nodded appreciatively. "That's good to hear. Anyway, I don't know why you should worry about me, Charlie, but thanks so much. Merry Christmas!"

"Merry Christmas, Laila."

He was left wondering the same question. Why should he worry? Why should he care? He supposed she was good-looking, but so far it was hard to tell. He really didn't know her. Yet there was something that did make him care about her. There was a certain electricity in the air when he spoke with her. It was clear that Laila possessed an inner strength, a determination to set her course and endure whatever might befall as a result. That kind of power, when it arose in a woman of no great physical stature, suggested a force that few men possessed. She hadn't cried or screamed after the attack, nor did she seem afraid. She knew that she needed help, yes, and she accepted it gratefully, but with as little drama as possible. He hoped to see her again, soon. The smoldering anger against Frank Sago that had begun when he had seen the bloody Laila had not been doused in the few intervening days. Coward bastard.

That afternoon at the Somerville Boxing Club, Mike watched as Charlie went to work on the heavy bag. He chuckled and said to himself, "Jesus, Charlie, what did that bag ever do to you?"

Two days before Christmas. Charlie could never pass Prince's Bookstore on Merrimack Street without stopping in to browse. He had finished *The Iliad*, and then reread it. Fitzgibbons was right. An entire world lived between the covers of that book. After that, of course, he read *The Odyssey*. Now he wanted to read a book he had picked from a pile at a flea market, *Ancient Irish Tales*, published in 1936, translated from what they called Old Irish, an older form of the Gaelic or Irish language.

He turned idly as he heard the door open. The woman who had come in wore a black beret over dark hair which was pushed back on one side behind an ear from which hung a shining spiral of silver. Her gray coat was open, revealing several necklaces of white and light blue pearls that hung at various lengths over a white blouse, some to the waist of her black skirt. His eye traversed her length, down to the black tights and winter boots. She was exotic and yet somehow familiar. He stepped behind a book rack and continued to peek over the book he held open in front of him. Her jawline, from earring to chin, was well-defined, and her skin was smooth and flawless; it was not until she turned toward him that he realized he was watching Laila Grant.

"Hi, Charlie," she said, breaking into a smile. He would never forget that smile. It was imprinted in his mind as the earliest evidence that she saw something in him that pleased her.

"Laila. I didn't recognize you." As he drew near, he inhaled the delicate scent of something like vanilla extract and a flower he could not name.

"I'm not surprised."

"Without the bandages and black eyes, you are a sight for sore eyes."

"You're not so bad yourself."

They talked about books. *Jane Eyre* by Charlotte Brontë was her favorite. He had not read it, but she was surprised that he had read *Wuthering Heights* by Charlotte's sister, Emily. She bought *Napoleon and Paris* by Maurice Guerrini for her father. "He loves history," she said. He bought *The Fellowship of the Ring*.

"Can we get that coffee?" Charlie asked.

She paused and turned away from the cashier, a middle-aged woman who seemed to be interested in their discussion.

She drew him on a few steps and said, "You seem like a real nice guy, Charlie, but I have to be so careful. I don't want to bring anyone else into my mess, and I need time to organize my life."

"I'd be surprised if you felt any other way after what you've been through. I don't want to make you feel uncomfortable at all. I'd like to get to know you a little better because I like you, but unlike that jerk, I respect you, too."

Her eyes, a light hazel, looked into his. She bit her lower lip, considering. "Are you really a boxer? Do boxers read *Wuthering Heights*?"

He chuckled. "Not as a rule. Books have always been a good escape for me. And I've spent a lot of time around books and book collectors in a side job. I've also had good teachers and a sort of mentor who has taken it as his job to develop my . . . erudition. Boxing is something else. It's just a way of proving something to myself."

"What are you trying to prove, Charlie?"

"That I'm as good as anyone else, I guess. And that I'm a winner, even if I come from a family of losers." He shrugged. "Winning at boxing is something you can never do if you're a drunk or have no self-discipline. Winning proves I'm *not them*."

She seemed to understand him. He saw the softening of her eyes and a slight tilt of her head. "Let's get a coffee," she said. The cashier called a "Merry Christmas!" as they left the store. They passed along the garlanded streets toward Brigham's.

The following day at the bar, Sophie asked, "You really like her, eh?" Her back was to the window, so that the light around her head formed a kind of halo, and he couldn't see her eyes.

"Yes. I do," he said. "Too bad it's so complicated."

"Things will work themselves out," she said, ever calm and reassuring. The fact that she had been his lover seemed not to cast the slightest shadow over the conversation.

"You don't mind?"

"You have to follow your heart. I still think of you as a close friend. That's how I'll always think of you." Her voice, as the poet had written, was 'sweet and low,' and Charlie felt for a minute as though he loved both Laila and Sophie.

"I don't deserve either of you. You're so good, Sophie."

"Focus on your next fight. It's a big one, right?

"*The* big one. For a shot at the Olympics. If I can win this, I'll say my career was a success no matter what happens."

The day before Christmas, he picked Laila up at her father's house in Belvidere, the most exclusive neighborhood in the old Mill City, very different from the Acre. She always referred to the family home as "my father's house." She had told him that her mother died when she was a child—cancer.

Laila called that she would be down in a minute, and her father ushered him into a parlor where a Christmas tree shed its light over a fireplace whose mantel displayed the holiday cards they had received. Bookcases stretched out on either side of the hearth. "So, you're Charlie Tumulty," he said, extending a hand. "Joe Grant."

"Hi, Joe."

He was a rugged-looking man, slim, in his sixties, a crown of white hair still thick. He had avoided the paunch of the aging male. "Care for a scotch?"

"I don't drink while I'm in training, but I'll make an exception to have a scotch with you."

"Good man."

He opened a liquor cabinet, took out a bottle of Laphroaig and a couple of squat crystal glasses and poured a good double shot into each. "Ten years in the wood," he said, as he handed one to Charlie, who thanked the older man as he scanned the book titles. "A lot of military history here." He sipped the scotch and learned once again that good scotch was wasted on him.

"I read history," Joe said.

"You don't read fiction?"

"Nah. Never saw the point. I did read *Animal Farm* at the beach one day. I have to say that was very funny. I got a kick out of that. But in general, I prefer history. Laila tells me you're a reader?"

"Yes, I like history, but I'd say I read more fiction."

The older man nodded and Charlie picked up a book that lay on the coffee table. *The Price of Glory*. "Are you a veteran?"

"I was drafted. Served in the 88th, the Blue Devils. Yeah, June 4th, 1944, in Italy, we liberated the Eternal City, then chased the Germans north." His eyes took on that faraway stare he'd seen in other veterans. "Voltera, Villamanga, the Gothic Line—a miserable, cold, muddy front. Thousands lost, and the brass thought the price was cheap considering the resistance we faced." He shook these memories off with a shrug and said, "Well, that's war. As Sherman said, it's hell."

He sipped his whiskey and sniffed and said, in a lower voice, "Charlie, before she comes down, let me say, you seem like a solid guy. I never liked the other guy. Never liked him. She's been through a lot. Just be, you know, be good to her. I'd tell you I'd flatten you if you weren't good to her, but those days are gone. I did try threats with Sago. Laila doesn't know that, but he laughed, and in the end, what am I going to do? I could shoot him, and sometimes I'd like to, but I don't think Laila wants to visit me in jail."

Charlie put the book down and said, "Joe, let me reassure you. I know you don't know me, but I will be nothing but a gentleman with Laila. I don't believe in trying to control women, or anyone for that matter. And I'd cut off my arm before I'd ever strike a woman. I've fallen for her pretty bad, to be honest, but where it goes is totally up to her."

He nodded gravely and put a hand on Charlie's shoulder. "It does me good to hear that. She said you didn't talk like a boxer."

"If I can make it to the Olympics, I'll retire and focus on the business."

"The bar?"

"Yeah, and I have a few other ideas. Maybe a restaurant at some point."

"Very good. One thing is a mystery to me, Charlie."

"What's that?"

"You don't seem to like that scotch."

"Sorry, Joe. Honestly, I just never developed a taste for it."

"Don't worry, Charlie. I'm not the least bit disappointed."

Laila came down the stairs saying, "Sorry, I was looking for my warm clothes for a hike."

"Well," Charlie said, "the end result is worth the wait."

They bid the watchful father goodbye.

He drove her out through North Chelmsford on the winding rural road that led to the Groton woods. They passed small colonial graveyards where tilted headstones bore the names of the early settlers who cleared the fields and bound the low rolling hills with meandering stone walls. They saw blanketed horses standing under bare trees and the red barns and rusting tractors of New England. She found a station on the radio that was playing choral Christmas music.

"That's beautiful," Charlie said.

"Isn't it?"

They listened in silence. The music seemed somehow to fulfill what was suggested in the charged stillness of the pallid sky.

> *The heavenly Babe you there shall find*
> *To human view displayed*
> *All meanly wrapped in swathing bands*
> *And in a manger laid*

Thus spake the seraph, and forthwith
Appeared a shining throng
Of angels praising God, who thus
Addressed their joyful song

'All glory be to God on high
And on the earth be peace
Goodwill henceforth from heaven to men
Begin and never cease.'

"That kind of music makes you believe in God," she said.
"I wasn't brought up in the church, were you?"
"Oh yes. I had to memorize the books of the Bible. Genesis, Exodus, Leviticus, Numbers, Deuteronomy.... You get the point. There are sixty-six."
"That's impressive. And are you a believer now?"
"Sometimes I think there must be a God. Other times, I just don't know."
"I wonder about it, too. Sometimes." He pointed. "There's Lawrence Academy, a private school for rich kids, and the old town church." They crossed Main Street and continued for a while until he pulled off the road into a small lot. It was a gray day, full of a sort of hushed expectancy that had something to do with the silence of the surrounding woods and maybe something to do with Christmas. A light snow shower seemed to presage a storm, but Don Kent had forecast nothing major.

"Can I leave my bag in the car?"

"I think so. We'll put it in the trunk if you'll feel better. It's pretty safe out here."

They passed through an old gate and followed a path that led to a monument. Stone hounds sat beside a curved granite wall on which a plaque was inscribed with the words:

IN MEMORY OF THE GROTON HUNT
MASTERS HORSES HOUNDS FOXES FOR
THE JOYOUS SPORT THEY GAVE

They walked on into the Sabine Woods until they came to a river and followed a path carpeted with rust-colored pine needles. They stopped by a glacial boulder that sat beside the stream.

"What river is this?" Laila asked.

"The Nashoba? No, I think it's the Nashua River. Flows into the Merrimack at Nashua."

Charlie turned and saw that her face was flushed with the chill December air. She wore a blue knit hat over hair as dark as a raven's wing. But it was her eyes that struck him. "You have the most beautiful eyes. In a certain light, they're brown gold, and at other times they seem to have a greenish tint."

She struck a pose, fluttered her eyes at him and laughed.

"God. If I were a painter . . ." he said. "Are you cold?"

"No, it's so lovely here." She leaned against the great boulder, looked up into the branches of the pitch pines, and took a deep breath. He wanted to tell her he loved her right then, but it was too soon. Snow still fell lightly and powdered the icy edges of the moving plain of the river.

"I know it's a bad time to ask, and if you don't want to talk about it, I understand, but how did such a bright, and classy and beautiful woman—how did you end up with that guy and living in those apartments near Eddie's Bar? It doesn't make sense. You should have been in a really nice house, and if I were your husband, I'd work my ass off to see that you were. What happened?"

She shook her head and sighed, looking off into the shadows of the wood.

"I'm sorry," he said.

"I was wondering when you'd ask. I mean, not that I think I'm so smart and classy, but that he is so awful. Can I give you the CliffsNotes version?"

"Sure. That'll do."

"When I met—that person, I was working at a bank in Boston, and I was taking classes in Finance at B.U. He was someone who was invited to a Fourth-of-July cookout sponsored by the bank and the Chamber of Commerce. He was invited not so much because he had a sizeable account, but because he had donated to community charities like the Pine Street Inn. Frank Sago, a pillar of the community—a philanthropist."

"Where did he make his money?"

"Waste management, supposedly. And he was charming. Asked me to the opera, can you believe it? The Boston Opera House—we saw *Turandot*. He came across as a gentleman.

It happened fast. I was taken in. A brief courtship and I married him. The first morning—we were living in a condo in the North End, and I had a coffee, and I left the cup in the sink. Out of the blue, he grabbed me by the throat and told me, 'Don't ever leave a fucking dirty cup in the sink again.'"

"What?"

"I realized with a shock that I had not really known him. That I had made a terrible mistake."

"I get angry just hearing that."

"The real Frank was unleashed. I remember at the library looking up the words, 'psychopath' and 'sociopath,' and trying to decide which he was. The definitions were similar in some ways, but the sociopath was impulsive whereas the psychopath could be charming and manipulative until he got what he wanted. That's Frank, all the way. Anyway, everything went down the drain, and not just our marriage. Turns out that he was not reporting a significant amount of his earnings. He was cashing checks without depositing them, requesting payments in increments that he cashed at different bank branches on different days. He owed $600,000 to the IRS and had to do six months in jail. Obviously, we lost the condo and moved to Lowell where he has connections. Bad connections as it turns out. This guy they call Beak Malvert is his uncle. That's why I want you to be careful, Charlie. You just said you get angry at Frank. I understand, but for me, stay away from him. I'm getting a divorce and under the circumstances, a felony conviction, adultery and spousal abuse, it won't be difficult. My lawyer is trying to pursue a no-fault divorce if Frank will agree. He says it's easier."

"Will he agree?"

"At this point, even he has to know it's over. I was just waiting to get a job closer to Lowell and save enough money to get out. I was too embarrassed at my stupidity to ask my father for money. I don't know why Frank wanted me—just to torture me? I guess people like that enjoy controlling someone who lives in fear. Things got wildly bitter. In the car on the way home that day, the day he beat me up, I threw my wedding ring out the car window. He pulled over, but he couldn't find it. I think he was angrier because he could have pawned the diamond than because of anything it meant."

"That's enough," Charlie said. "I get the picture. I'm sorry I asked you about this on, or near, Christmas Eve."

She reached out and rubbed his arm, smiling sadly. "I want you to understand."

"Can I tell you something?" he asked.

She nodded. "Of course."

"I know what a lot of people think about boxers, and I was worried about what your father might think. I tried to reassure him while you were upstairs. But I want you to know. You have to know. Boxing, for me, is about self-discipline and respect. Respect for the rules, for 'the game' as they say. I fight other men, and I respect them, too. The men are in my weight class and are trained to defend themselves and to fight. It's violent, no doubt, but I'm not a violent man. Outside the ring, it's peace on earth and goodwill to men. Most men. Only in that ring, where the rules are set, and the fighters are evenly matched. What I'm trying to say is that I would never, *never* be violent toward any woman, or to any man unless I was defending myself or someone else. I consider that a cowardly and a terrible thing to do and there is no excuse, ever, for that kind of behavior. You could hit me with a baseball bat . . ."

Laila laughed. "You needn't fear that . . ."

"If I were married, just for example, and I found out my wife was cheating on me, I don't think I'd be angry as much as sad. But never would it occur to me to hit her. Never."

"I believe you, Charlie."

"I just had to say it. You know the worst fight I ever fought?"

"Tell me."

"Well, there was a Dominican in Brockton who caught me with a wicked left that I never saw coming. By the time I got up, the ref was holding his arm up. Dominicans are tough. But that wasn't the worst. The worst was a fight in Fitchburg. This kid, a Filipino, they're generally good fighters too, but this kid wasn't. Coco Avelino. By the second round, I had got to him pretty good, but he kept coming. I was hitting him at will, and he kept coming. He didn't belong in the ring. By the fourth round, he was a mess, and still he came. Coco was game, and I realized the only way he'd stop would be if I knocked him out, but

I didn't see why I had to do that. I kept looking at the ref and saying, 'What the hell are you waiting for? Come on, stop the fight!' His legs were unsteady. When you get hit like that, you feel like you're on wooden stilts. But he was just charging in to get hit more, round after round. But the ref wouldn't stop the fight, and his corner wouldn't throw in the towel, as if they thought somehow, he was going to throw a lucky punch and floor me, but he was out of gas. I kept dancing away from him. The crowd was booing, and he kept coming at me and I kept nailing him and trying to back away. Finally, a cut over his eye was bleeding so bad he was blinded, and the fight was stopped. When you see boxers hug after a fight—that's why. I had so much respect for this kid, but at the same time, I felt awful that they let him go at it for six rounds. I didn't enjoy that at all. The victory didn't feel like a victory."

He was watching the snow falling between the green boughs of lofty pines, but he felt her watching him for a moment after he had finished speaking. "How long will you do it, Charlie?"

"Not much longer, Laila. I want to get to the Olympics and fight with that American flag on my shirt. After that, I'll retire, and years from now, people will say, 'See that old man? *He was an Olympian.*' That's the dream."

"And what will you do after boxing?"

"I'm learning from Eddie how to run a business. I like honest work. And I do pay my taxes."

"Thank God for that!"

"I have another dream, but I'm not ready to share that one, yet."

She moved close to him, and he embraced her with a tenderness of feeling that he knew was love. "There's no one here," she said. "It's so peaceful. So beautiful. Why don't you want to share your dream with me, Charlie?"

"It's just . . . I don't want to move too fast. I know things take time, and . . ."

"Anyone would say I was a fool to rush into anything after my experience with *him*. I would have said so myself, but I can't help what I feel. I could wait another ten years, and I would never meet another man like Charlie. So tell me your dream."

"It's a simple one. To marry you."

"Are you sure that's what you want, Charlie?"

"Yes, and if you marry me, you'll never find I've become someone else after the wedding."

"No, I think you are who you are."

"I guess I've just proposed. Not in the most romantic way, but, I love you a lot, Laila. Will you marry me? I know we have to wait until things are settled."

"Yes. As soon as I can. You know I had a dream, a sleeping dream, that you and I were raising our child. I woke up with a heart so full."

The snow was falling more thickly now, though they were the large flakes that never last as long. He held her in his arms, inhaling her fragrance and watching the crystals land and melt into the blue knit and thinking that he had never felt so happy as he did at this moment. "This is our place, then," he said. "This is where we decided." And in the shelter of the great rock, they kissed while the dark, icebound stream moved toward the Merrimack and the sea.

"Oh, I wish the divorce was through and I was free of him. I know what a man needs, Charlie. But I feel like I have to wait for us to be really together."

"Laila, you do whatever seems right to you. All obstacles are nothing now."

They walked on in the gray gloaming of a sacred stillness, the branches arching above them like the timbers of a great cathedral. Finally, they made their way back to the car. Charlie turned over the ignition, cranked up the heat and said, "I have something for you—a small Christmas gift."

"Oh Charlie, I have nothing."

"I don't need anything." He reached into the back seat and pulled a wrapped present from under a jacket that had lain over it. "It's just something I thought you would enjoy."

She tore the wrapping paper and found a book bound in green leather. On the cover, an elegant golden letter B was encircled with a wreath of gilded roses. She turned the book to see the title on the binding. *The Tenant of Wildfell Hall*, by Anne Brontë. "It's the Murray Edition," he explained, "published in 1920. Fitzgibbons located a beautiful 1854 edition where she wrote under the name of Acton Bell, but the price was way out of my league."

"Charlie, that is such a thoughtful gift. I've been thinking I'd like to read something else by one of the Brontë sisters."

"Glad you like it. I think you'll find you have a lot in common with Helen, the main character."

"In what way?"

"She married a charmer who turned out to be a master bastard."

"I can relate to that. She was as blind as I was! It's a perfect gift, Charlie." She slid the book into her bag and pressed her arms against her coat, smiling but shivering. *She threw away a diamond,* Charlie thought, *and cherishes a book.* The Falcon took a few minutes to warm up. She leaned toward him and kissed his cheek, and he hugged her warmly. "I don't think I've ever been so happy as I am right now," he said.

"We're going to be happy, Charlie."

Chapter 11

1974

January. The Worcester Armory. Regional Olympic Qualifying Events. Charlie was standing in the red corner of the ring, gloved hands resting on the ropes. He had ceased hearing the sounds in the arena except as an incomprehensible roil of noise that was in some way like the roar of a waterfall; the shouts, the conversations, the referee talking to the judges—it was all combined into one sheet of sound like a wave breaking on the surface when you dive below it. The noise was irrelevant in the calm stillness beneath. He was aware, too, of the smell of popcorn and of the cigarette smoke that curled under the lights. And then the true sounds broke through to him. He heard the opponent's cornerman giving instructions, and then the voice of Mike Dineen rose out of and above all the other sounds as he smeared Vaseline over his face.

"This is your shot, Charlie. Win this fight, and you'll be eligible to compete for a spot in the Olympics. How do you feel?"

"I feel good."

"Unbeatable?"

He nodded and slipped in his mouthguard.

"Like I said, I haven't seen this kid before, bein' a blow-in from the Old Sod. He's got the reach on you. You're gonna have to get inside. Otherwise, he'll kill you with jabs. Don't give him too much room."

The announcer, with his perfectly coifed white hair, and wearing a black tux and red bowtie, stepped to the center of the ring. "Ladies and gentlemen! Tonight, the Worcester Armory, in conjunction with the AIBA and Boxing New England, is proud to bring you our third bout of the evening with four rounds of qualifying boxing in the light heavyweight division. In the blue corner, wearing green trunks, hailing from Dublin, Ireland, with a record of 21-2, Worcester's own Sean Keenan!" There was a burst of applause and shouts, and someone blew a horn. "And in the red corner, wearing black trunks, from the Mill City of Lowell, with a record of 19-2-1, the Pride of the Acre, Irish Charlie Tumulty." Scattered applause drowned in loud boos.

The ref, a Black man with a Duke Ellington mustache, called the fighters out to the center of the ring and recited the instructions. He knuckle-rapped their crotches to make sure they were wearing cups and said, "Let's have a clean fight, gentlemen." Charlie assumed the cold and passive mask he had copied long ago from Kev Souza. Keenan looked him up and down with unconcealed scorn, and as soon as the ref had finished, muttered, "Irish Charlie! You're not Irish, boy."

Charlie gave him a thin smile but said nothing. Mike always told him, "Don't waste your time talking and don't listen to it, either. You want to scare your opponent? Show up lean and fit and strong and let him see you got plenty of gas in the tank."

They walked back to their corners and the bell rang. Charlie bounded out and met Keenan in the center of the ring. He threw a double left jab, but Keenan parried and stepped forward with a flashing jab that hit Charlie as he was moving back. It was a jarring punch, and he realized that if he had been advancing that jab might have knocked him down. Mike was right about his reach, he thought, and Charlie looked for a way to move in, but in the meantime, he was backpedaling, using the ropes, bobbing and weaving, trying to stay out of range of the jab until he could see an opening, hoping the other man would get careless. When Keenan got him in the corner, Charlie grappled with him until the ref separated them; then he moved, using the ring, concentrating on trying to slip that jab and get inside. The kid was tough. And smart.

When the bell sounded, Charlie dropped his gloves and turned toward his corner but felt a jab to the back of his head. He turned with raised fists, but the ref had come between them and was telling the Irishman, "Don't do that again. You hear me?" He nodded and walked to his corner.

The following rounds were equally tough. His mouth was dry and his hands were sweating in the ten-ounce gloves. He had managed to duck some crosses and land hard body blows and one overhand headshot, but he saw the grim and undaunted face of Keenan between his raised gloves, stalking him, driving him back and throwing that long jab and quick combinations that required all of Charlie's skill in using the ropes, slipping and weaving. Still, a cut under his eye had begun to bleed.

Before the last round, Mike sprayed water in his mouth and placed an icy face cloth over his head. "Lean back," he said. He took a bottle of adrenaline from his bag, poured it over a thick swab and pressed it against the cut. "You tell me you want to be a champion, and I don't believe you, Charlie! Right here. This is where you show who you are. You're behind on the cards. You can give up, or you can get inside and throw some leather. You get nothing for surviving the fight. You're here to win the fight. And I haven't seen Charlie Tumulty yet tonight. The Charlie with lightning in his blood! This guy has got the lead and he thinks he's going to cruise through the last round. You've got in some good shots amidships. Follow them up! Jump into the lion's den, Charlie! Don't wait for the perfect opening. There is no perfect opening. The guy's ready to be knocked out! He's ready! Get inside and come up to the head! Bang him for God's sake!"

The final round. Charlie's head felt somehow clearer, no longer singing as it had been in the middle of the previous round. His body, though, was more tired. The Irishman moved toward him, but instead of backing up, Charlie stepped forward and threw a couple of jabs and a cross. He ducked a jab and came up with a left hook. He felt it connect, but Keenan shook his head and grinned to try to show him that it had not hurt much. "Irish Charlie!" he said. "That's a good one, all right." But Charlie saw the welt on his face and told himself that he could do it again.

Once more, though, he gave way to Keenan's combinations. *There is no perfect opening. Into the lion's den. This is where you show who you are. The Charlie with lightning in his blood.* The words ran in his mind, driving out every other thought and forming a single determined purpose.

Charlie stopped backpedaling and slipped to the outside of a jab. Bending his core and his lead leg, he threw a hard right to Keenan's ribs that made him bend slightly forward as he absorbed the shot. Instinctively, he threw out a defensive jab. Charlie slipped to his right to avoid the punch and went into a crouch. The opportunity was there for Floyd Patterson's "gazelle punch," and he saw it immediatley. With all the energy left in his tiring legs, he sprang from the ring floor, lunging at his opponent and landing a hard left hook that he felt land solidly on Keenan's chin. As he landed, Charlie threw a second left, and Keenan went down. He heard a loud collective groan from the crowd, and Mike Dineen cheering wildly.

Charlie retreated to his corner so the count could begin, but the referee paused over the fallen fighter. Dineen began shouting at the ref, "What the hell are you waiting for?" The referee pointed to him and shouted back, "Quiet over there in the red corner!" He began the count, pausing between each number as the crowd roared for their homeboy to get up. Nearing the eight-count, the fighter rolled onto his knees and pushed himself up, rising on wobbly legs. "The Olympics, Charlie," Dineen whispered.

The ref held Keenan's gloves and spoke to him. The fighter nodded and the ref stepped aside, and Charlie, knowing this was his shot, flew across the ring and drove the dazed fighter into the corner where he covered up and absorbed the blows. He seemed to wilt and was beginning to sink under a rain of punches when the bell rang, and Charlie threw his arms up in victory while the crowd booed. He didn't care; he had killed the lion, and everything he'd gone through since he first watched the Portuguese fighter at the Boys Club had been the price he paid to stand here at this moment, the price he had paid tonight with his sore ribs and blood oozing through the Vaseline under his eye. He was glad he'd paid it.

Charlie stood at the center of the ring with the other fighter, the ref between them, holding their wrists. The bell sounded and the tuxedoed announcer ducked between the ropes and was handed a microphone. "Ladies and gentlemen, here at the Worcester Armory we go to the scorecards." The crowd suddenly went quiet as the MC's voice reverberated through the arena. Scott McKenzie scores the bout 115-113, Tumulty. Bobby Jean scores the bout 115-113, Keenan.

And Ray LaChance scores it 115-113, to the winner by split decision . . . Worcester's own Sean Keenan!"

The building erupted as the ref raised the Irishman's arm. Mike Dineen erupted, too; at first, Charlie could not hear him. He could not hear anything but the words, "Worcester's own Sean Keenan!" resounding through his head, as they would resound for years to come. Then he was aware of Dineen leaning over the ropes toward the judges, shouting, "Do you know what you just did to this kid you dirty bastards? You just stole the fight from him, you bums!"

Then, Security was in the ring, expressionless men in suits pushing the old man backward while he continued to shout, "You got no balls! Rotten bastards!"

The booing intensified, and Keenan's trainer pointed at Mike Dineen and shouted, "Control that guy!"

Dineen and Charlie left the ring together making their way through a gauntlet of booing fans. A plastic cup of Coke struck Charlie in the chest and one of the security men waded into the crowd to eject the offender, but the fighter was numb to all of it save the four words that had announced the victor.

Dineen was nearly in tears for the fighter he had trained from nothing to have earned nothing for a champion's performance. Walking back to the dressing room, pulling the tape from his swollen hands, Charlie felt as he had when he pedaled away from the baseball game. Boxing was over for him.

St. Patrick's Day morning, two months after the Worcester fight. The phone was ringing as Charlie was opening the bar. He pocketed the keys and went behind the bar to pick it up. "Eddie's Bar."

"Is this Charlie Tumulty?" a voice inquired.

"Yeah. What do you want?"

"You're a fuckin' loser, Tumulty. When the stakes get high, the Pride of the Acre shits his boxing trunks." Charlie heard delighted laughter.

He let the man on the other end of the line enjoy himself for a few more seconds. Then he said, "I only know of one boxer who never lost a fight: the Brockton Blockbuster, Rocky Marciano, forty-nine wins, zero losses, zero draws. It's a little harder to beat a man who's a trained fighter in the ring than it is to beat your wife in the kitchen. But any time you'd like to give it a try, you just let me know, Frank."

"There are different kinds of tough, Tumulty."

"Come on over and show me your kind."

"When you see my kind, you'll wish you didn't."

"Oh, right. The kind of tough guy who sends some thug to do his dirty work. Maybe with a gun? Just know that I have a gun, too, and I have friends who have guns. Anything happens to me, they'll show you their kind of tough, and they don't give a shit who your uncle is."

The silence that followed told Charlie that he was getting under the other man's skin. "Was it worth it, Frank? Do you feel better after making your cowardly, giggling little phone call and your big scary threats?"

"Fuck you, Tumulty!"

"And that's the best the cultured opera-lover can come back with?" Charlie hung up and went to mop the bathrooms.

If there was one thing boxing had taught him, it was self-control. He didn't want to say anything that would direct Frank's attention to the fact that he had lost something far more valuable than a boxing match, and that Charlie had won it: Laila's love. He didn't really have friends with guns who would go after Frank Sago, though Eddie might try. Still, he was pretty sure that Frank was the kind of bully he had dealt with on the North Common long ago. When they see the victim will not be bullied, they fade. One thing he knew; there was no sense telling Laila about the call. She was certainly tough enough to hear about it, but it would do no good.

The anger he might normally have felt at this fool was light in the balance against the ever-present bitterness that he knew was the result of the loss to Keenan. It had left him with a feeling of emptiness, or what Fitzgibbons had referred to as "a hole in the aura." If he had been knocked out or beaten squarely on effective punches thrown, he could have accepted the defeat. But to have the fight stolen was something that would always rankle. It was not the way to end a career, but the goal that had motivated him was out of reach now, and you need a goal. Charlie ran the sopping mop over the tiled floor. He had Laila's love, after all, he thought. Bouts and decisions and Olympic dreams be damned.

A while later, Eddie came in with coffees and a bag of donuts. The younger man, coming out of the back with a case of Budweiser, saw the goods on the bar and said, "I haven't eaten a donut in years. Not good fuel for an athlete." He set the case down on the cooler lid and reached for the bag. "Doesn't matter now, I guess."

"So, you're done?" Eddie asked.

"Yeah. If I liked getting drunk, I'd even do that to put the cap on my career."

"Better drunk than punch drunk," Eddie said. "You stay in that game too long . . . not good to keep taking blows. Some guys are fine, but some of them . . . look at poor Tommy Ellis."

"Mike and the old boxers at the gym are fine."

"Still . . . I'm glad you're getting out, Charlie."

"Let me get a breath of fresh air, Eddie. I got the smell of bleach and pee pads in my throat."

Outside, he saw a homeless guy coming around the corner. They called him Red, though if his hair had ever been red, it was white now. "Morning, Charlie."

"Morning, Red."

Red, whose last name no one seemed to know, was not bundled against the chill of March. He wore a flannel shirt and tweed suit jacket. He talked to everyone in the city's center and he knew everyone, beggars and business people, criminals and cops, addicts and priests. Red was equally comfortable talking to Depot Annie, the raucous queen of the downtown streets, as he was to the Mayor. "Wish I had a smoke," he said.

"Claffey!" Charlie called to a skinny guy walking a dog along Market Street. "Come here, will ya?" In a lower voice, he said, "Hang on, Red."

Claffey crossed over and came up. "Hey, Charlie. Sorry the fight didn't go your way."

"Them's the breaks. Hey, you got a cigarette for Red?"

"Sure." Claffey reached inside his jacket and dug a pack out of his shirt pocket. He pinched out two cigarettes and handed them to the old man who stuck one in his mouth and the other behind his ear. Claffey struck a match and cupped it as he lit his cigarette and handed it to Red.

The wanderer of the streets blew on the ash and pushed it against the end of his cigarette, puffing it to life while Claffey's dog investigated his worn leather shoes.

The dog was short-haired with a golden-brown coat, save for a white mask, and paws. "Cute dog, Claffey," Charlie said. "Is he a pup?"

"She. She's about six months. Some kind of hound mix. I call her Sheba, like the queen." Having concluded her inspection of Red's shoes, the dog took the leash in her mouth and was tugging on it. "She doesn't like me to stop and talk," Claffey said.

"Looks about twenty-five pounds now. Will she get much bigger?"

"I'm not sure, 'cause the guy I got her from didn't know who the father was."

"Oh," Red interjected, "like me."

After a few seconds' pause, Charlie burst out laughing. Then he said, "Red, tell Claffey about the Commodore."

Claffey bent and told the dog, "Stop it!" and pulled the leash out of her mouth.

"What about the Commodore?" Red asked.

"You know, about dancing. You told me the other day . . ."

Red handed Claffey's cigarette back to him.

"Oh, yes." He cleared his throat as if he were about to give a speech. "Well, as a young man I was quite a dancer, you see? Quite a dancer. The Lindy Hop, which became the Jitterbug, the Big Apple, the Collegiate Shag and even a little Tap. And in those days, God be with them, as my poor mother used to say, I loved to dance at the Commodore. I'm tellin' you, you could dance all night at the Commodore Ballroom and never be tired. You know why, Mr. Claffey?"

"Because you were young?"

"Well, that too. But the reason you could dance all night there, was . . ." He paused for effect, took a drag off his cigarette and spoke through the smoke. "They had metal springs under the floor!"

"Interesting," Claffey said, nodding appreciatively, while Charlie wondered how a young dancer becomes an old drunk.

"It was real nice," Red said. "There were a couple of dead spots, but I knew where they were. Yes, sir. Louis Armstrong, Duke Ellington, Count Basie, Tommy Dorsey . . . they all played the Commodore. Then Pearl Harbor happened, and pretty soon I was dancing across the deck of the USS Cassin Young."

Charlie pulled four bucks out of his pocket and said, "Go over to the Cinnamon Tree and get a coffee and a donut, Red."

"Thanks," he said, shoving the cash into the pocket of his frayed tweed suit jacket.

"By the way," Charlie said, "have you heard who broke into the pizza parlor on Suffolk and Merrimack? They're getting a little close to the bar, here."

"Between you and me and the lamppost, it was that kid Paulie something from Dracut, hung out at the Worthen until Arthur threw him out. Trouble. Robbed Rowan's Drug Store, too. But I heard he's gone to Florida." He gave them a salute and added, "I like your dog, Claffey. Just shows you, you can have questionable parentage and still be handsome."

"And a good soul!" Claffey said.

Red waved a last time, crossed the street and set off along the canal, contentedly blowing fogs of smoke. Charlie called after him. "Red!"

He paused and turned. "Yeah?"

"By the way, what's your last name?"

"McNulty," he called back. "Red McNulty." And, as some Irish writer that Charlie recalled had written: *He set his face to the road before him.*

The gold dome of the Greek church was beginning to gleam as the sun rose higher. On the telephone wires above Market Street, a pair of mourning doves left off their dolorous cooing and took flight with deep-throated chattering. Claffey went on his way, too, with Sheba dancing beside him, and Charlie stood for a moment breathing the chill air and thinking, "I love this city."

Eddie came out with the A-frame to which was attached a hand-printed menu:

"*St. Patty's Day Special: Hash Omelet.*

Irish Lunch Special: Eddie Burger: Beef patty on a toasted bun with lettuce, tomato, cheddar cheese, caramelized onions in a Guinness Stout sauce with bag of chips and 12 oz beer. $5"

As he was about to go back in, a station wagon pulled up in front of the bar and a Hispanic man of about fifty got out. He looked up at the sign as if to make sure he was in the right place and then said to Charlie, "You know where is Charlie Tumalee?"

"I'm Charlie."

"My name is Orlando. Orlando Rivera. You know my son, Johnny? I have a picture." He reached into his pocket. "I know you are boxer also like Johnny. Maybe you know . . ."

He took the photo in which the man before him stood with an arm around his son. The two of them, smiling, holding fishing rods on the deck of a boat. "Sure, I know Johnny. Good kid. Sharp fighter."

"You know where is my son?" he pleaded. He was thin and wore the paint-stained clothes of the working man. He looked haggard and needed a shave.

"No, I'm sorry. I don't. So, he's missing?"

"Since Friday, he went out, and I don't see him. I'm very worried because he never do that."

"I'm sorry Mr. Rivera. I can't give you any information. I see him at the gym. Sometimes we talk a little, but he never mentioned going away."

The man nodded grimly; that was what he had expected to hear. "I fill out a report at the police station, but I don't hear anything . . ."

"Listen, do you have a phone number? If I hear anything, I will definitely let you know."

"Thank you, Charlie." He handed him a simple business card and said, "You call me if you hear anything. I'm worried because they say he get in a fight with a guy I don't know his name, and he work for the other guy Malvert, and he's like mafioso, criminal. They are all the time at the Star Lite. I'm afraid for Johnny. I went to talk to Malvert, but he says he don't know Johnny. He try to give me money, he says because I take time off work to look for Johnny. I say, 'I don't want your money *hijo de puta!*'"

"You should let the police handle it, Mr. Rivera."

"I don't care. If he killed Johnny, he can kill me, too."

"I will keep my ears open, Mr. Rivera. I'm really sorry. Let's hope he turns up."

The melancholy man in search of his lost son thanked Charlie and walked back to his car. A crow came on dark wings to alight on the telephone wire and croaked a stark "Caw!"

Charlie looked at the card: "Orlando's Painting. Good work. Good price," and a telephone number. The mention of Malvert had made him thankful to Fitzgibbons for steering him away from the job he'd been offered, but it also made him concerned for Johnny. Orlando Rivera was what a father should be, and it saddened him to see him suffer for his missing son. The lighthearted mood of the morning fled and now images of Johnny Rivera at the gym came to him. He told Eddie the story, and how a big crow had alighted just as the man left. "Felt like a bad omen," Charlie said.

"Almost every omen is a bad one," Eddie agreed.

The St. Patrick's Day crowd began to arrive well before lunch. As Charlie heard one customer say, "You can't drink all day if you don't start in the morning." Tom O'Carroll, a young, Dublin-born balladeer that Eddie had booked, showed up around noon and launched into song:

> *I'll tell me ma when I come home*
> *the boys won't leave the girls alone*
> *they pull me hair and stole my comb*
> *well that's alright till I come home*
> *She is handsome she is pretty*
> *she is the belle of Belfast city*

Many in the crowd hooted and a few attempted a poor imitation of an Irish dance, beer mug raised and usually spilling a few ounces. As the day progressed, gaggles of pub crawlers stumbled out, bound for the Old Worthen or the SAC Club, and fresh crowds came in, but eventually word got around that O'Carroll was the best Irish music that the downtown had to offer on this high holiday, and Charlie, Sophie and Eddie fed beers and shots continually to the moving throng. A couple of cops came in, and one of them held his walkie-talkie in front of the balladeer so that someone back at the station could hear "The Rocky Road to Dublin."

He smiled near midnight when he saw Laila waving and making her way through the crowd. Before he could go to her, trouble began. A heavy woman sitting on a bar stool suddenly went down —how or why, Charlie didn't know, but accusations were flying between the man who was with her and another guy. "Calm down!" Eddie roared, but a punch was thrown, and soon a Donnybrook engulfed the entire bar. The music stopped as O'Carroll tried to protect his guitar, which was his livelihood, from misdirected blows and reeling bodies. His amplified voice implored the crowd, "Please now, ladies and gentlemen! If you please now! Let's all . . ." A lanky scrapper with a scraggly beard tore the mike stand away from him to swing at a hefty adversary. The microphone hit the floor with a resonant thud. Charlie saw one of the cops on his walkie-talkie, no longer looking amused.

Charlie slid over the bar, and with his arm draped around her bowed figure, escorted Laila into the empty Men's room. "The cops will be here in a minute," he said. "Alcohol has made fools of us again. How are you, Babe?"

"I survived the trip from the door to the men's room," she laughed. "How are you?" She stroked his head, almost in a maternal way, but unlike anything his own mother had ever done. "Charlie, I do love you."

Her tenderness nearly overwhelmed him. So, this is what it feels like to have the love of a good woman. He wasn't sure he deserved it, but he would do his best to be worthy of it. "I feel so lucky that you do. I love you, Laila." He kissed her, feeling entirely hers.

The door swung open and O'Carroll joined them with his guitar cradled in his arms. "Happy St. Patrick's Day for fuck's sake! What a load of gobshites! The local constabulary is clearing the bar." They could hear Eddie shouting, "Everyone out! I'm locking up!"

They emerged, and Laila and the Irishman sat down at a table near the stage. Tom began to pick out a jig on the guitar. Charlie stepped outside, where he saw a pile of the brawlers handcuffed on the ground, still trying to elbow or kick each other, like a pile of the damned in Dante's *Inferno*. A cop was chasing another guy around a pickup truck. Charlie shook his head and said to the struggling pile, "Have a nice night in the hoosegow, dopes!"

Charlie joined the others and set beers on the table for Tom and a cranberry and vodka for Laila. He went back to the bar for a cranberry juice and soda for himself. Eddie locked the door, poured himself a beer and joined them. Tom raised his beer, and looking over his shoulder at the framed map of Ireland on the wall, said, "May our hearts be as full as our glasses." The others expressed their approval and drank, and Laila squeezed Charlie's arm.

Tom strummed some chords and began to sing a plaintive song of that island that Charlie's grandparents had left to begin a new life in this city.

My young love said to me, "My mother won't mind
And my father won't slight you for your lack of kine"
And she stepped away from me and this she did say:
It will not be long, love, till our wedding day."

Charlie thought of Ireland as a misty island of rebels, saints, and banshees, where men peddled bicycles under leaden skies to the local pub, where women in shawls gathered at wakes in whitewashed cottages to lament the passing of village folk, smoking pipes and speaking in the old language, or in an English so shaped by the old language that it would be barely comprehensible to him. That must be the Ireland his grandparents had left, but no doubt it was changing. Laila leaned her head against his shoulder and they listened.

She stepped away from me and she moved through the fair
And fondly I watched her move here and move there
And then she turned homeward with one star awake
As the swan in the evening moves over the lake.

The people were saying, no two e'er were wed
But one had a sorrow that never was said
And I smiled as she passed with her goods and her gear,
And that was the last that I saw of my dear.

I dreamed it last night that my true love came in
So softly she entered, her feet made no din
She came close beside me, and this she did say
It will not be long love, till our wedding day.

When the sound of the final chord of the guitar faded, silence reclaimed the space briefly, until Laila spoke up. "My God, what a sad song," she said.

Tom laughed and said, "It's Irish, love. It's Irish." He set the guitar back in its case and they finished their drinks and Eddie said, "Let's do it again next year without the brawl."

"Please God, we're all able," the Irishman said.

Grace was incredulous. "In a bookstore? You met her in a bookstore?"

"Yeah, what's wrong with that, Ma?" Charlie had not thought it necessary to get into the gory details of his actual first meeting with Laila.

"I didn't say there was sumthin' wrong with it. Just in my day people met at dances and socials or someone introduced you, that's all."

"Anyway, I'll bring her by to meet you. She wants to. All I'm asking is for you to be nice to her, and if you talk to *him*, please don't mention it. I don't need him to show up half in the bag and embarrass me."

"Of course I'll be nice to her. Whaddaya ya think, I'm a monster?"

"Just coffee, Ma. I'll bring a small cake or something from Olympos Bakery."

"You said she lives in Belvidere. Won't she think this place is a dump?"

"She's not like that, Ma."

"She ever been married?" she asked as got up to fish through her purse on the counter.

"She's in the process of getting a divorce."

She paused with a cigarette in one hand and a lighter in the other. "Jesus, she's married?"

"Technically. Not for much longer. Ma, you of all people should know that a woman can make a mistake."

A moment's pause, and then she burst out in a hoarse laugh which turned into a fit of coughing. When she had regained her voice, she said, "She certainly can, Charlie. She certainly can."

"Are you okay, Ma? That cough sounds bad."

"Ah, I cough my ass off when I get up in the morning. Then I have a smoke and I feel better."

He shook his head. "Anyway, she's a good person, Ma. You'll like her." He saw in the sunlight from the kitchen window that she had aged in the last few years more than he had realized. "You should quit smoking, Ma. They're no good for you."

She shrugged. "If it ain't one thing that gets ya, it's another."

"Sunday at 1:00 pm. Don't forget!"

Charlie was coming out of the Athenian Corner with a bag that held a quart of lentil soup and some Greek bread. Lunch of champions. As he put the bag in his car, he spotted Red ambling down Market Street. He hailed the old man and held up a finger. "Wait up, Red!" He had been hoping to run into the old wanderer and had bought a pack of cigarettes to give him. Though he often urged his mother to quit, he was pretty sure it was too late for Red, and smokes were one of the few things he lived for anyway. That and a pint of Old Grandad.

"Hey, Charlie," he said as the younger man approached.

"I picked you up a pack of cigarettes."

Red accepted the pack somewhat reluctantly and eyed it suspiciously.

"What's the matter?" Charlie asked.

"Winstons?"

"That's a popular brand, isn't it?"

"It is, yeah, it is. But if you ever get me another pack, Charlie, I prefer Old Gold."

Charlie chuckled and said, "I thought a smoke was a smoke. Didn't realize you were a connoisseur of tobacco."

"Old Gold."

"Okay. Hey, listen, Red. Strictly between you and me, you know anything about Johnny Rivera?"

The old man shoved the cigarettes in his pocket and peered around nervously. "I don't know nothin', Charlie."

"Young guy? Boxer? He disappeared."

"I don't know nothin'. All I can say is I wouldn't go around asking people about it. I don't want to see *you* disappear."

"Just between you and me, like I said. What have you heard?"

"What's done is done. I like to stay away from rumors that might, I say that might, involve dangerous people. You live longer that way."

"But . . ."

"Thanks, Charlie. Next time, Old Gold. That's all I got to say. Curiosity killed the cat, Charlie." He set off, a living ghost of the downtown, with all the secrets of alley and street, and much of what he knew or suspected buried deep.

Charlie wondered, as he drove with Laila to his mother's apartment, if he had made a terrible mistake. He foresaw a possible if not a probable scenario. They might arrive to find the place in disarray, last night's bottles crowding a kitchen table, a half-eaten pizza in an open box on the counter and Grace snoring in the darkness of a heavily curtained room. He had warned Laila that his mother was not one to remember appointments.

"Well," she said, "from what you say, she does manage to show up for her job on time when she has to work."

"That's true," he said. He didn't say, *she can remember things that matter to her.*

The two of them climbed the old stairs, Charlie amazed that they still held up. He had been less nervous when he met Laila's father, with whom he had connected immediately. He knocked on the door and stood there with the bakery box under one arm and the woman he loved holding on to his other. He decided that if there was no answer, he would not use his key to go in. He did not want to see, and he did not want Laila to see the scene a non-response would suggest.

He heard steps within, though, and his mother opened the door. Charlie was relieved to see that she looked presentable. She wore a black V-neck sweater over a white blouse, and black slacks. They could have been her work clothes, but they were clean and she looked good. The tidied kitchen was redolent with the smell of coffee.

Charlie introduced Laila, and to his surprise, his mother took her extended hand in both of hers. "I'm pleased to meet you. Charlie has got it bad for you."

Laila laughed and said, "I have it bad for Charlie."

"Well, you make a beautiful couple. He never brought no woman here before that he wanted me to meet."

Charlie cut the checkerboard cake and Grace poured coffee. The sun spilled slats of light through the angled blinds, onto the kitchen floor. They agreed that the Greeks were good bakers. Grace asked Laila about herself and listened.

Charlie almost spit out his coffee when his mother said, "I know your soon-to-be ex-husband, Laila. He used to come into the Pineview. He's a real asshole. We married a couple of bad ones, you and me, but you got a good one now."

Charlie saw the color rise in Laila's cheeks somewhat. "Yeah. Yes, on both counts."

Grace asked the young woman what she was studying. "Finance, huh? Geez, that's great Laila. I know I'd fail that class. What the hell. I failed everything," she said, laughing.

"Come on, Ma," Charlie said.

"But you know what is strange?" she continued. "I know people, good people, with money, big houses. They send their kids to the best schools and they try their best, and sometimes the fuckin' . . . excuse me, Laila. I'm a hard case. Sometimes the . . . the kid is no good anyway. Now me, I admit, an' I take the blame. I was a lousy mother. Charlie raised himself. I was either working or drinking and causing trouble. And this kid here, he turned out better than all of 'em. I'm proud of him, but I got no reason to be proud 'cause . . . I didn't really do a hell of a lot."

Charlie was shocked to see that her eyes had filled. Laila reached out and grasped her hand.

"That's all water under the bridge, Ma," Charlie said.

"I never read him no bedtime stories, but he read himself. His old room there you can see is full of books. Charlie, he ain't like other boys, Laila. He's not just letting, you know, letting the river carry him wherever it's going, usually over the falls. No, no. Charlie knows where he's goin' and he steers the boat. He didn't start drinkin' and doin' drugs like a lot of the other kids around here. Who taught him that? It wasn't me. God gave me a shit husband, honestly," Grace said. "Charlie knows that, but he gave me a good boy, Laila. Better than I deserve. So, when Charlie tells me he met a girl who's special, I know she is special. He won't just fall for a pretty face. Not him. He sees into things. He thinks, and he knows what's important. That's all I'm gonna say. An' you know what? Even I can see you're special, Hun."

"Oh, thank you, Mrs. Tumulty."

"Grace."

Laila asked her about growing up in Lowell, and she told them about the Irish immigrants in those days that would come to their place for what they called a 'kitchen racket,' with a couple of fiddlers and someone with a squeezebox. And then, as a young girl working in Woolworth's, when a charming young Jack Tumulty came in and sang to her, "I found my million-dollar baby in the five-and-ten-cent-store."

They were laughing at the idea, particularly Charlie, who had never known that side of his father. "That was all before the war," Grace said. "It was different then. Jack was different. So different."

"Where is Jack Tumulty now?" Laila asked.

"Wherever he is, just be thankful he's not here," she said.

And Laila saw Charlie nodding ruefully. He shrugged and said, "Sad but true."

Chapter 12

Jack's Story

The bar had been relatively busy all day, with Charlie flipping Eddie Burgers and Eddie and Sophie taking orders and pouring beers. As evening approached, Dan Webster, the pianist, arrived and Charlie unplugged the jukebox while Dan's soulful voice and the flowing chords of the American songbook filled the room. Eddie came in and told Charlie to relax—his shift was over. He took a seat at the bar and listened to the piano man sing "I Could Write a Book," which recalled to Charlie's mind Miss Walker's words of encouragement long ago. That was followed by "You Do Something to Me," which made him think of Laila, and "The Boulevard of Broken Dreams," which brought him back to the white canvas under the hot lights and the ring announcer's loud and false proclamation that he had lost the fight.

Various friends came and spoke with him and a part of him listened until he glimpsed, through the crowd, a familiar face. Jack Tumulty. His father saw him, too, and approached. The guy beside Charlie recognized him and gave up his seat at the bar. Jack thanked the guy and sat down. "I heard you got robbed, Charlie."

"You heard correctly."

Eddie, who was working behind the bar with Sophie, came over. "Hi, Jack. How are you?"

"I'm dandy. How's my boy here?"

"He's great," Eddie said.

"He's livin' upstairs? Best thing he could do—get away from his mother. Crazy bitch."

"Her life hasn't been easy, Jack," Charlie said. "Shit, she was married to *you*."

"He still defends her," Jack said to Eddie.

"Look, if that's why you came . . ." Charlie began.

"Come on, Jack. She's the man's mother after all," Eddie said.

"All right, all right. Whatever. She's the mother of the year. Let's have another beer, or whatever John L. Sullivan here is drinking, and two shots of Jamie."

"You want a shot of Jameson, Charlie?" Eddie asked.

"Sure. Why not?"

"Atta boy," Jack said. "I just wanted to come down and tell you, for what it's worth, I'm proud of you, Charlie. You acquitted yourself well, as they say, in the ring. I wasn't much of a father . . ."

"You got that right, Jack."

"Okay. I'm sorry."

"He's sorry. That's great. Makes up for growing up with a guy whose idea of being a father was to stop by every now and then and cause trouble. Or come to my baseball game drunk and embarrass the shit out of me in front of the whole Highlands. Crazy bastard."

Eddie brought the shots and beers and Charlie saw Sophie giving him a meaning glance though he wasn't sure what the meaning was. Probably to stay calm. They knocked back the shots. "You know, Charlie," Jack began, "you call me crazy. All right. I'm crazy. Of course, I'm fuckin' crazy. I was a kid your age and they threw me out of a fuckin' plane in Holland. The 82nd Airborne under General James Gavin. Well, first Ridgeway, then Gavin. 'All the Way,' that was our motto. All the fuckin' way."

He pulled open his jacket and lifted his shirt to show a long red scar. "I took some shrapnel in a place called Mook. A dirty place. Shit flying everywhere with the 88mm shells exploding—the impact would loosen your teeth. Before you know it, there are one hundred and fifty of the 82nd dead and eight hundred wounded, and we're pinned down."

He was leaning toward Charlie and speaking in a gravelly whisper. "I ended up in a ditch with another guy, Dominic Santino from Philly." Jack's mouth turned down and he shook his head. He stared at his beer, but Charlie knew he was seeing the shattered dead of Mook. "Dominic was bad, Charlie. I didn't know if I'd survive, but I sure as hell knew he wouldn't. His stomach was just torn open. Every time I hear the expression 'he spilled his guts,' I think of

Dominic. He kept moaning and begging me to kill him. I couldn't understand how he could stay alive with his stomach open like that. It would have been easy if I had my M1, but when the shell exploded, we both got knocked head over heels. I pulled him into the ditch, but we lost our rifles. I had a Camillus combat knife. Double-edged. The battle went on—we couldn't move, and the kid started having convulsions, just slowly bleeding out. It was horrible. He needed to be at peace, Charlie, so I did it. Quickly."

He took a long drink of his beer, and Charlie caught Sophie's attention and pointed two fingers at the shot glasses. "And you know, Charlie, when he was dead, he was at peace. And I envied him. Because I thought I'd be a long time dying alone in that ditch. I was weak and it felt like something was eating me from the inside. I passed out, and later I woke up on a stretcher and they had taken the metal out and sewn me up. And they gave me a Purple Heart and a new rifle."

The pianist was playing "God Bless the Child," and Sophie brought the bottle of Jameson and poured the shots. Jack thanked her and pushed a ten-dollar bill toward her, but she pushed it back. "The patch we wore on our shoulders, Charlie, the 82nd Airborne AA. The All Americans. And that's what Dominic was—just an All-American kid." He was quiet for a moment and finally said, "Like the song says, 'God bless the child.'"

Charlie said, "Well, I'm sorry you had to go through that."

"I don't tell you that for sympathy. I tell you that to kind of explain—that's why I'm crazy. Shit like that. I was just a kid. What did I know about weapons and killing people? And after all the crazy stuff I saw over there—I remember an RAF Lancaster bomber, a huge aircraft just falling out of the sky, and all of us running for our lives. Left a crater the size of this building. You'd never find the guys that were killed. So many things I never imagined. And I'm supposed to come back here and forget it all? I'm supposed to care about going to church and being a good citizen? It wasn't fair to you. All right, and it wasn't fair to your mother. But I didn't care, Charlie. I just could never give a shit."

"You didn't care about your own son?"

"I left all my caring in a ditch in Mook. You care about guys—good guys, Charlie, brothers, and then you watch 'em die, and it tears you apart. Then the replacements come in, and you don't let yourself care. In Sicily and Normandy and later at the Bulge. There are things you don't ever talk about. I mean not even in confession. People don't understand. They can't understand. Eddie has heard my stories, but I never told anyone else. And I didn't give a shit about anything anymore, so what I did, what I do, is, I drink and I let people down."

Charlie looked at his father for a moment and sighed. "Well, you didn't let Dominic down."

For the first time in his life, Charlie saw Jack struggling to keep his emotions in check. Then, in a whisper that sounded like a gasp, he said, "I pray to God I didn't. I was so young. There was nothing in our training and no one to ask."

He pushed a shot in front of his father, who swiped at his eyes with a bar napkin, and the two of them drank. Charlie shook his head, squinting, and said, "Whiskey really is awful stuff."

His father pulled a pack of cigarettes from his pocket and said, laughing, "What do you think, I've been enjoying myself all these years?" The Jack he knew was back.

How strange. It was the first time that Charlie could ever remember sitting at a bar with his father or sitting anywhere with Jack Tumulty and hearing any sort of explanation for the disaster he had been as a husband and a father. It didn't change anything, but it explained something. As James Joyce had once said, "It seems history is to blame." Bad luck for him and his mother. Very bad luck for Dominic and Jack Tumulty and all the others.

Toward midnight, the crowd was getting louder until Webster began playing the "easy and sad," song, "One for My Baby, and One More for the Road," and the drinkers grew quieter, and some began to sing along with the chorus. Jack spun his chair around, lit another of his endless chain of cigarettes and leaned back, one elbow on the bar. Everyone could relate to that forlorn feeling at the end of a romance, and Charlie thought of Laila and hoped that it would never come to such an end, but whether it did or did not, he hoped at least that she'd never have to endure the threats of Frank Sago again.

He was surprised to see a familiar figure moving toward him through the crowd, someone else he had never seen in Eddie's Bar. Mike Dineen didn't drink. He introduced him to his father. "What are you doing here?" Charlie asked.

"Looking for you. Get off the sauce, sonny. You're back in training."

"What?"

"I got a call late this afternoon. Two of the judges in that last fight were not certified to be judges in Massachusetts. That means the decision is invalid. That means you get another shot."

Charlie had not been aware of how badly he wanted another shot until he heard those words. He felt a sudden surge of energy and purpose coursing through him. "Same opponent?"

"Maybe. Maybe not. Luck of the draw. And this time we may have to go to New York."

It was a reprieve from failure, and he remembered the heroes of *The Iliad*: "Let me do some great thing that shall be told among men, hereafter."

His father raised his bottle and said, "Well, I'll drink to that. Not that I need a reason."

Charlie drained the rest of his beer, put the empty on the bar and said, "I'm done with that."

Mike nodded approvingly. "I'll see you at the gym, Charlie," he said and walked off. Charlie told Eddie and Sophie the news and went to the phone booth to call Laila.

When she answered, he apologized for having called her so late. "I had to tell you the news."

"I'm so happy for you Charlie. I know you were disappointed. Still, I wish you didn't have to fight."

"If I lose, it's over. If I make it to the Olympics, I'll retire an Olympian. That's it."

"Well, I have news, too. I was going to tell you when I saw you. I didn't want to call the bar."

"What is it?"

"It seems you can contest the no-fault divorce, and Frank threatened to do that, but my lawyer explained to him that while this way was cheap, contesting would be expensive, and the result would be the same. He was not happy, but he gave in. I'll be free of him soon. A month or so to settle it all."

"And we can be married. Jesus, I should have bought a lottery ticket today. This is the best day ever."

"Do you love me, Charlie?"

"So much, Laila."

"I dreamed again last night that I had your baby, a little girl. That we were raising her together."

"That's a beautiful dream."

"Oh, I could feel the love we all shared, Charlie."

"You're going to get me all teary-eyed, here," he said. He turned and saw his father approach Dan Webster and say something in his ear. The piano man nodded and struck up "Happy Days Are Here Again."

A week later, he found out he would be facing Sean Keenan again, and he was glad. He understood his opponent's strengths now, his style and what it would take to beat him. And the judges would not save Keenan this time. He worked on his core and on his legs. To beat a man who had the reach on him would be all about twisting his hips, ducking the elbow toward the opposite knee, slipping to the outside, staying low, becoming a smaller target, a constantly moving target, rolling under hooks and looking for the uppercut, the shoulder jutting of the feint and the quick lead with the other hand. There would be no discernable pattern to his movement, and when the chance came, his combinations would be lightning, and they would land like dead blow hammers. He would be the better boxer and the more devastating puncher.

Chapter 13

Foxy's Story

The new qualifying fight was scheduled for June. When he wasn't working, Charlie was at the East End Gym or at the boxing club in Somerville. He found time to take Laila to see *The French Connection* at the Route 3 Cinema, but he was so tired from his workout he fell asleep halfway through the movie, and she didn't wake him until the credits rolled. He drove her to the bookstore in Concord one day; another day they went to walk in the Carlisle woods, though the paths were wet with melting snow and April's showers. The final days of peace. Later, he was to consider how the wheels were already set in motion, how the unseen train was roaring along the tracks to where he stood between the rails, blind and unsuspecting.

He had closed the bar and was upstairs reading "The Death of Cúchulainn" in his *Ancient Irish Tales*. In it, the great hero Cúchulainn converses with his friend, the warrior Conall Cernach. "How quickly will you avenge me if I am killed?" Cúchulainn asks. Conall assures him it will be before the sun has set that day. "And how quickly will you avenge me?" Conall asks. "I will avenge you before your blood has cooled," Cúchulainn replies.

Sometimes he read books so quickly that he hated to finish them and leave the characters behind. It helped him to escape for a while from thoughts of the fight that otherwise might consume him. The ancient myths of his people, separated though they be by time and a sea, spoke to him and reaffirmed imaginatively the power of that virtue without which all other virtues were useless: courage.

His eyes were beginning to close, and he had decided to turn the light off when he heard a knocking on the door downstairs. He looked at the alarm clock on his night table—nearly midnight. The furtive knock sounded again. He threw the book on the night table, pulled on his jeans and went down the narrow stairs. He found Foxy out on the back porch. "Are you drunk?" Charlie asked.

"No, I ain't drunk. Listen, man." He closed his eyes, cupped his hands over his face and shook his head.

"What the hell are you into, Foxy?"

"I got a problem, Charlie. A big problem."

"Come on up."

Charlie's studio apartment was spartan. A bed and nightstand, a table, a stove, a small refrigerator and a chair. The bathroom was off the hallway at the top of the stairs. The blinds were drawn, but Foxy raised a slat and peeked out over the street, then let it fall and drew the curtains. Charlie sat on his bed and Foxy took the chair.

"All right, what's up?"

He scanned the room nervously. "You got a drink?"

"I'm in training. I got nothing. What's up?"

"You were right about Malvert. I shoulda listened to you. I shoulda listened to you, man."

"Tell me what happened."

Foxy drew the chair closer as if someone might be listening outside the door. "There's this guy, they call him Catfish. I don't even know his real name. He's a crazy bastard from down South." He paused and took a deep breath, rubbing his eyes with the palms of his hands. "Wait, lemme start at the beginning. Last Friday night, I was having a beer in the Star Lite, and Frank comes over to me."

"Frank Sago?"

"Yeah, Beak's nephew or something. Thinks he's a classy guy. He listens to opera and wears expensive suits. Has a little office in the back near Beak's where he takes action. I hear he also supplies some drug dealers around the Valley."

"I know who he is. And I've heard that."

"Anyway, Sago tells me Beak needs me to help Catfish with something. So, I say sure, and he hands me a set of keys. He tells me there's a Lincoln parked out in the alley—to bring my car over and get a couple of bags of lime out of the trunk and put them in my trunk."

"Lime? Shit, you know why they use lime."

"Of course, I know. For burying a body. But I couldn't get out of it. So, I put the bags of lime in my trunk. And I go back in. And Frank tells me this guy they call Catfish is gonna drive my car, 'cause I'm gonna have to be blindfolded! He says it protects me and everybody. I asked if this is something that could get me in trouble. He says, 'The only way you're gonna get in trouble is if you open your yap. Always remember, Foxy, like the Beak says, there are very few mutes in jail. And jail will be the least of your problems if you can't keep your mouth shut, but you know that. Just go with Catfish. Give him a hand with whatever he needs and come back here. It's nine o'clock now. You can be back here easy by midnight, and the Beak will talk to you then. He'll have somethin' for you.'"

"Dammit!" Charlie said. "Right then, Foxy, you should have said, 'He can have my job. I'll keep my mouth shut, but I'm out.'"

"Well, I didn't!" Foxy's shoulders slumped, and he heaved a hopeless sort of sigh and said, "Fuck!"

"Why didn't you?"

"I don't know! I'm sorry I didn't pull a *Profiles of Courage*!"

"*Profiles in Courage*." Charlie shook his head. "What happened?"

"I don't know how long we drove, but it was a long ride for me, Charlie. I kept thinking, I don't mind bein' Foxy the bag man, the rent collector, the errand boy, but Foxy the fuckin' body-disposer? And Catfish. Jesus Christ, he's a nasty fucker.

"The car stopped, an' I said, 'Can I pull off this blindfold off, Catfish?'

"He says 'Ah'll tell you when.' He pops the trunk an' comes around and opens my door. He pulls off the blindfold and I see that mangy beard and his long greasy blond hair under a John Deere baseball cap. He's got one of those twelve-inch flashlights that you could probably kill someone with. 'Y'awl get the *lahm*,' he says, like that, that's how he talks.

"So I get out. Christ, it was dark out there, wherever it was. We get the lime bags and I stumble after that lunatic with the spot of light bouncin' over the path in front of us, nothin' but woods. Five minutes on, he stops and shines the light around for a minute. 'Sheeit, ah walked raht by it,' he says. We backtrack a bit and then he stops again and moves the light around. He shines it on, like a forked birch tree; then he goes off the path and crashes through some thick woods with the branches whipping my face and the lime bags pressing down on my shoulder.

"Catfish stopped again. He flashes the light around until it's on the body of a guy, face down beside a hole and a pile of dirt. I dropped the bags. There was a shovel, a pick, and an axe for the roots lying on the ground. I felt like throwing up, Charlie. 'Fancy meeting you here,' Catfish says to the dead guy. He shines the light up under his chin so I could see him grinning at his joke, ugly bastard with the big gap in his teeth. It was like he was saying, in case you were wondering what a cold-hearted fuck I am, well, now you know.

"There wasn't a damned thing funny about it, but I thought it was smart to laugh along, and I said, 'What did you think, he was gonna leave, Catfish?' You know, *ha ha*.

"'Hell no,' he says, 'like we say back home, he jus' lyin' there like a no-legged dog.'

"He said his back was killin' him and told me to keep diggin', make it deeper, which I did. Took a while. Then he laid the flashlight so it shone across the body, and he pulled something out of his pocket. I heard a click, and a blade flashed out of his hand. I stepped backward, 'cause I thought he might kill me too, but he bent over and ripped open one of the bags of lime. He stood up and wiped his forehead on the sleeve of his jacket. 'Throw that shit awl over the bottom there, Ahm sweatin' like a hooker on nickel night,' he says. He's full of that kind of shit.

"I poured it all over the bottom of the hole. I was chokin' on that lime dust, a white cloud that came up out of the grave, and then Catfish grabbed the two arms of the body and said, 'Gimme a hand with the deceased.'

"I just said, 'Right,' and grabbed hold of his two ankles. One of his sneakers slid off.

"Catfish started to swing him. The dead guy's head hung down. 'One, two, three.' I let go and heard the body thump against the ground. 'Yer new home,' Catfish says. He picked up the light and shone it into the grave. The body had turned slightly, and Charlie, I felt like crying when I recognized. It was Johnny Rivera. His face was all blue and swollen and there was a hole in his ear, but it was him. He was one year ahead of me at St. Patrick's. He drove a forklift at Friend Lumber."

"Jesus. Poor Johnny," Charlie said. "Good kid."

"Then Catfish took off his cap and held it over his heart: 'Dearly beloved, we are gathered here this night to bid farewell to a fellow whose big fuckin' mouth got him killed. May it be a lesson to awl us honest Christians.' He was having fun, Charlie, the sick bastard, and threatenin' me at the same time. He kicked the sneaker into the grave and ripped into the other bag and covered Johnny. It was awful, Charlie. He looked like a ghost of Johnny all covered in white like that. Catfish threw the empty lime bags in the . . . in the grave, and then handed the shovel to me. I was filling in the hole, acting, you know, just like I was shoveling my car out in a snowstorm. But inside, I was sick. When I was done, Catfish gathered leaves and branches and spread them over the grave and we were outa there. There was a little pond or swamp nearby, and he tossed the shovels and shit into the water. I leaned over the water to scrub my hands. The lime was burning my neck, and that sight of Johnny Rivera was burning my mind."

"Did you see Sago or Beak when you got back to the Star Lite?"

"Yeah. That stupid tinsel disco ball was spinning over the phony parquet dance floor and three or four couples were slow dancing, 'Baby, I Love Your Way.' Can you believe people feel romantic in that hell hole? I just went to the bar. Sago spotted me and waved me toward the door to the back room, where a blonde and a few other broads and Artie, the club manager, and this punk Wayne Barnette who sells Sago's dope for him, they were sitting around a table snorting lines of coke. 'The Beak is in his office,' Sago said, and just then the boss stepped out of his office into the hallway, with the stupid cigar poking out of his mug, and he called me in.

"He sat down at his desk. There was nothing on it but an adding machine and a notebook and a coffee mug that said *The Sands, Las Vegas*. Jus' to let you know he's a high roller. There's no chairs in front of the desk, so I stood there like the flunky that I am. He looks me over while he rubs his nubbly chin, and loosens his ugly tie. He puffs the stinking cigar, still just looking at me, like checking for cracks in the concrete, and then leans back, and the chair creaks 'cause he's a heavy bastard, an' he says, 'Any problems?' I'm trying to act casual. 'None, Beak. Very simple job.'"

"'Good. Good,' he says.' He just keeps fuckin' staring at me. I could feel my heart beating, because when you're looking into the eyes of a man that really doesn't have a conscience, well, you know he could kill you and then go get dinner at Ho Jo's and think no more of it than you would of swatting a fly. He leans over and he spits in the ashcan, an' he says, 'Too bad about the kid.'

"'Yeah, well, he musta had it comin',' I said, like I got no conscience, either.

"'You got that right, Foxy. He could have hurt some friends of mine, bringing attention to a situation where it was not wanted. Reckless with his mouth. Dangerous. Shoulda known better. What are you gonna do, right? Lesser of two evils. Sorry to put a damper on your night, but I need someone I can trust for something like that and Scully and Lyle are still in Florida.' He opened a drawer, took out an envelope and slid it across the desk. I was wondering if the payment was recorded in his notebook. Hopefully not with my name. I kept tryin' to look, you know, almost bored, but all the time I was thinking: *Accomplice to murder.*

"That's OK, Beak,' I said. 'You don't owe me nothin'."

"The envelope sat there on the desk in front of me like those thirty pieces of silver in the Bible. Dirty money. Weed money is one thing. Cash for planting a guy you know—that's dirty money. The Beak nodded and he sucked on his cigar for a few seconds. The wheels are spinning behind those dead eyes. He's just like, calculating, *what does this guy mean he doesn't want the money?*

"'Take it,' he said, finally. It wasn't a suggestion, Charlie. 'And listen,' he says. 'Don't worry about a thing. Four people know what happened to the kid. There's me and Frank. That don't even count. Catfish did eight years hard time down at Parchman Farm and never ratted out his friends. And there's you. Nobody else. I know I can trust you, absolutely. Absa-fuckin-lutely. So, you can forget about it. It's what my old man used to call *a clean sneak.* Just make sure you bury it, deep, that's all.' He poked his cigar at me. 'No pillow talk with the sweetheart. No whimpering to some shrink about your fuckin' nightmares. You *never* mention it. To *anyone*. *Ever*. That's what *secret* means. I don't ever want to have to do anything about *you*. But if it came to that…'

"I'm just standing there nodding and shifting my weight from one leg to the other like a kid in front of the principal's desk. Then Beak, he relaxes again and smiles and he says, 'But what am I sayin'? I had you doped as a trustworthy guy from way back. Back when you used to collect the football cards and take 'em to the bookie for me, huh? Jesus, you were in high school. Remember that? An' when you got caught, my name was never breathed. Never fuckin' breathed.'

"'Course not,' I said.

"'Because you're a stand-up guy.'

"Even when the Beak smiles, you can't relax, Charlie. Finally, I said, 'It would be disloyal. And it don't take a genius to know that nobody in the business got nothing to gain and a lot to lose by flapping his jaws. Like we've all heard you say, Beak. 'There are no mutes in jail.'

"He laughed at that, and gave me some quote he said was from the Bible. What was it? Oh yeah, he said, '*Whoever guards his mouth preserves his life*.' Yeah, can you believe this guy quoting the Bible, Charlie? Back in the car, I opened the envelope. There were five crisp C notes inside. That must be the going rate for putting a guy in a hole."

Foxy shook his head and repeated, "Jesus Christ. I'm an accomplice to Johnny's murder."

Charlie had listened quietly. He closed his eyes for a minute, now, and kneaded his temples with his fingers. Then he opened his eyes, and said, "An accessory *after the fact*. I shouldn't have let you get mixed up with those guys. Poor Johnny. It's a damned shame. But why do you say you're in trouble now?"

"The kid's father, Charlie."

"I met him. Sad."

"Someone must have mentioned my name, that I knew Beak Malvert, and he came up to me. I didn't know who he was. And he put it to me—'You know my son Johnny Rivera?' He took me by surprise, and I think he could see I was freaked out. He saw something in my eyes. Now he keeps showing up, haunting me, asking me 'Where is Johnny? What happened to Johnny?'"

"I don't like it," Charlie said. "I don't like it one bit. First of all, I don't believe that Johnny had anything to do with Malvert or that he was a danger to his plans. That's bullshit. He crossed him somehow. Does Malvert know that Orlando Rivera has been talking to you?"

"I got a phone call from Sago two nights ago. He says, 'That Rivera guy been botherin' you?'"

"I was ready for that, Charlie. In case they saw him talkin' to me. 'Yeah,' I said, 'pain in the ass.'"

"'Whadja tell 'im?' he asks."

"'What'd I tell him? I said I'm sorry your kid disappeared, but I don't know a damned thing. He kept houndin' me and I finally told him to fuck off.'"

"'Well, he's been askin' all around. Even tried to buttonhole the boss, but he's got nothin', so the Beak wanted me to remind you – you know.'"

"'No mutes in jail.'"

"'Exactly.'"

"*Or with a bullet in the brain.* That's what I was thinking, Charlie."

"An' he says, 'Just remember, he's got nothin'. He's just fishin'.'"

"I said, 'I know that, Frank. Sergeant Shultz was my hero.'"

"'What?'" And he chuckled. "'Oh yeah, that guy on *Hogan's Heroes*. 'I know nothing! Nothing!'"

"'I didn't see anything. I don't know anyone. I just got here, and I'm leaving.' I had him laughing, Charlie."

"'You know, I do feel sorry for the poor guy,' he says. I could just picture Malvert, hand cupped over the extension phone, you know, hunched there beside his nephew, listening, calculating. 'Fuck him,' I said. 'He shouldn't have had a snitch for a son.'"

"He laughed and he sounded relieved. 'You're beautiful, Foxy.'"

"I laid it on, you know. 'Let him go cry to Dear Abbey. I don't know shit.'"

"'They don't call you Foxy for nothin',' he says. 'You're crazy, but you ain't dumb.'"

"Bet yer ass."

Foxy stood up, pushed the curtain aside, and peered through the blinds again. Charlie noticed that his friend's hands were trembling and imagined that the stress had been killing him. "So listen, you're covered," Charlie said. "You just have to stop talking to Rivera's father. Why do you say you're in big trouble?"

"I haven't been able to sleep. I went to St. Patrick's Church. I put the five hundred in the poor box. The red sanctuary light was shining on the altar. That's supposed to mean that God is present, Charlie. I remember that from when I was an altar boy. And I think I could kind of feel it. And I made a promise."

"Oh, shit, no. What kind of a promise?"

"I got out of work at the trains last night, and there was Orlando Rivera. 'My friend, *por favor*. Tell me. What happened to my son?' I had to pry myself loose and push him away. 'I don't know anything about it!' He looked right into me, and he knew. So, I told him to meet me at the Savoy in Davis Square."

"Oh, Jesus. Are you kidding me?"

"Listen, he doesn't want the police. He just wanted to know what happened, and if he's definitely dead. He knows a Spanish priest who will say a Mass for him. That's all. But you can't say a Mass for the Dead for a guy you don't know definitely if he's alive or dead. I mean he assumed Johnny was dead, but he didn't *know*."

Charlie's shook his head and looked up at the crack-veined ceiling. "Oh, Foxy. And you're telling me he knows Johnny is dead now?"

"Yeah. Now he knows."

"Oh, my God. Bad move, Foxy. Bad move. None of this will bring Johnny back, and it's gonna get you killed. Are you sure you were not followed here? I could get killed, too."

"I drove all around before I came here. No one was following me. Do you know any good cops, Charlie? Maybe someone could get me in the witness protection program."

"Shit," Charlie said. "That may be your only out now. Go to see Andy Robinson. He's a detective. You remember him from the Boys Club. Black guy. From the Acre. Solid."

"Yeah, yeah. Thanks."

"What a bane these guys are on the city. I don't really care when they kill each other, but Johnny Rivera? He was a good kid."

Foxy's blond head bowed into his hands, and he seemed to shrink into the stained army jacket he'd worn for so many years that it was finally beginning to fit him. Charlie imagined blood pouring from a wound in that head; he saw the blond hair matted with gore, streaming crimson. He stood and tried to banish those thoughts. "Foxy, you can stay here tonight, though if I were you, I'd go to the cops right now. If you stay here, go to the cops early in the morning."

"Will they put me in jail? I'd be no good in jail." He bit his lips and Charlie saw the fear in his eyes.

"You didn't do anything. You were just scared for your life. You're not a killer. Maybe they'll put him away, Foxy." Charlie suspected it would be difficult to put Beak Malvert away without a body, but Foxy's story was certainly compelling.

The two young men got up and walked toward the door. "Where are you going?" Charlie asked.

"Maybe I can explain it to Malvert. Orlando didn't want vengeance. He just wanted . . ."

Charlie lunged and grabbed him by the collar. He slapped his face and shook him. "Are you out of your fucking mind? Listen to me. You've already talked to Orlando. The cat is out of the bag. Go to the cops. You go try to reason with Malvert, and you can just wait for the bullet." He jabbed Foxy in the forehead with an index finger to make the impending bullet real.

"I know. I know." He kept nodding and crying. "I'm going to talk to Father Walsh, then I'll go to the cops. In the morning."

"You and your priests. The longer you wait . . ."

"I know." Charlie walked down with him and looked up and down the street. All was quiet.

"Where's your car?"

"Up by the Olympia."

The two men walked in silence toward the Greek restaurant. Foxy's Chevy was the only car in front of the place. They tensed when a young guy on a bicycle pedaled down Market Street toward them, but he glided to the other side of the street and slid up Broadway. Charlie hugged his friend and said, "Don't fuck with me now, Foxy. Go see Andy Robinson in the morning. He'll take care of you."

"I really got myself into a mess, Charlie," he said.

"It'll be okay. Just do the smart thing, now."

Charlie walked back and paused at the door; he saw the red tail lights of Foxy's car receding along Market Street. He remembered the print of Jesus and the small statue of the Virgin Mary in Foxy's studio apartment. "Watch over him now," he said quietly to the stars and whatever angels might hover there. He went inside.

Chapter 14

The Edward Wood House, (ca 1878), at 34 Wannalancit Street is a fine example of the Queen Anne style, popular in what, even in America, is often referred to as the Victorian period. It is an imposing home, many gabled and asymmetrical, with high angular expanses of slate roof segmented by copper-lined valleys. Two great chimneys rise through adjacent ridges. From an upstairs window, the view gives out to the west where the Pawtucket Canal flows darkly between 19th-century granite walls. The view from a window on the north side of the same room presents a sloped street that runs down to the Merrimack River just before the falls.

The house was vacant, undergoing renovations as the new owner modernized the interior. Orlando Rivera had arrived early, as the morning light glinted on the high windows. He was thinking that although he would never live in such a grand house, he would have been proud to tell Johnny that he had painted it, and as he had done many times each day since his son had disappeared, he whispered a prayer, "*Dios te salve, Juanito.*" Today he added another vow. "*One day Malvert will pay, te prometo.*"

He parked his truck at the end of the long driveway and carried the extension ladder around to the back of the house. He set the shoes against the foundation and walked it up, his hands moving from higher to lower rungs until it stood against the house; he pulled the base of the ladder out and hauled on a rope as the pulley system raised the extension to 32 feet. Two men, standing on a walkway on the far side of the Pawtucket Canal heard the rung locks clatter over the aluminum rungs as the ladder rose against the great house. One nodded to the other, and they began to walk over the Pawtucket Street Bridge and across the field toward the Edward Wood House.

They came up quietly and found the house painter perched near the top of the ladder, scraping the flaking paint around the windows of a dormer and priming the trim. He was singing a song in Spanish. One of the men set his feet against the outside base of the ladder. The other man stepped inside under the ladder and pushed. Orlando saw them and began to shout something, they didn't know what, nor did they much care. When he landed with a heavy thud, the paint bucket exploding in a white spray, and the ladder clanging beside him, one of the men stepped close and appraised the body. A long final gasp escaped the shattered figure and stillness settled over him, as if the man had been replaced by a broken statue.

"Chillin' like a villain," the taller man said.

"Damn right, Scully. When you're dead, you're deader than you'll ever be."

"That don't even make sense, Lyle. Shit, I got paint splattered all over my pants. Some fuckin' blood, too. Let's book." They walked unhurriedly down the hill where they blended with the shadows under the pines by the canal.

Mario Santiago from Emerald Flooring found Orlando a couple of hours later. He was surprised at what must have been the carelessness of the dead man, whom he had always known to be steady on a ladder.

Foxy McRae did not sleep well. Somewhere around the time the descending moon began to fade into a brightening sky, he slipped into uneasy dreams. He was standing on a stairway in an abandoned house. He heard water running in the darkened upstairs and stood there nervously asking "Hello? Hello?"

Something out of the darkness reached out and struck him with such force that he awoke to find Lyle and Scully standing by his bed. The first thing that he noticed with some alarm was that they were wearing gloves. Lyle wandered over to the portable TV and flicked it on while Scully slapped him a second time.

"What the hell, Scully?"

"Who else did you tell?" he asked.

"What? About what?"

"You know about what. Who else did you tell besides the Rican?"

"I didn't tell anyone anything. Not a word." He swallowed hard. "Listen, let me get up and get dressed." He began to rise, but Lyle, who had left *The Waltons* on the TV, shoved him back.

"Relax. You're fine," he said, and began looking around the room as Scully sat down on the bed beside Foxy.

"You got a girlfriend, right?" Scully asked. "So, you musta told your girlfriend."

"I don't have a girlfriend. Malvert told me not to tell anyone, so I didn't tell anyone. I'm not stupid!" he said without conviction. All three of them knew he was lying.

Lyle stepped up to the other side of the bed and the two men stared at him. An ambulance passed outside, siren wailing, heading no doubt to St. John's Hospital.

"Okay, who else did you *not tell*?"

"I told you . . ." Foxy had never felt so vulnerable nor in such danger. Here he was in his underwear lying in bed with two of Malvert's enforcers hovering. Killers. His heart drummed madly in his chest. He suspected that he would never leave this room alive.

"Didja tell yer pal, the boxer?"

"Malvert didn't tell me to tell him, so I didn't tell him. I haven't even seen him in ages. He's always at the boxing club or working I guess, I don't know. Why would I put myself or a friend in danger yakking about business?"

"Why?" Scully asked. "That's a very good question." He seemed to ponder it for a few seconds, looking up at the print of Jesus of the Sacred Heart. "*They know not what they do,* right?" He fixed the young man with a cold stare. "Foxy. Funny name for a stupid bastard. Foxes are supposed to be smart, ain't they, Lyle?"

"That's what I always heard," the other man said.

"But this fox? Giving foxes a bad name. Very fuckin' stupid." He poked the young man's chest with a stiff finger. "You were seen with the Rican in the Savoy. Did Malvert tell you to go socialize with Johnny Rivera's father?"

"I was just trying to comfort the guy," he protested weakly. "Okay, I felt bad for him. But . . ."

"You don't need to feel bad for him anymore, Foxy. He's with his boy. In heaven. Because of you."

He gave the merest glance and the slightest nod to Lyle, who pulled Foxy's pillow out from under him and slammed it over his face, leaning into it with his forearm. Scully jumped on his chest and held down his arms. The young man's body twisted and thrashed wildly for a short time. Then the struggling stopped. Lyle pressed the pillow down a while longer.

"Jesus, Scully. It woulda been much easier to fire a bullet into the pillow."

"Easier to do. Harder to explain." He drew from his pocket a small case and opened it. A hypodermic needle and a rubber band were nestled within. Scully wrapped the band below Foxy's bicep; he put the dead man's fingers on the barrel and the plunger of the syringe and pumped the contents into the corpse. He replaced the pillow under Foxy's head, and looking at the wild grimace, put an index finger at each end of his mouth and pushed it into a smile. "Cheer up, kid."

Lyle watched with distaste. He had always hated needles, not to mention playing with a dead man's face. He shivered and said, "Let's get the fuck out of here." The phone on the table began to ring.

Scully raised a calming hand. "Wait a minute," he whispered. He pulled a bag of dope and other drug paraphernalia from an inside pocket and left it on the night table. Then he parted the curtains, peered out, and signaled his partner. Lyle looked at *The Waltons* on the TV and then, glancing in the direction of the murdered Foxy, said, "Goodnight, John Boy."

They slipped out the door, leaving the phone ringing and the smiling body of David McRae on the bed with a syringe hanging from its arm under the sorrowful gaze of Jesus of the Sacred Heart.

Charlie heard on WHDH that a painter had been killed at a house on Wannalancit Street after falling from a ladder. He saw the gentle house painter in his mind's eye and recalled his tortured plea for his lost son. A man who cheated no one, who worked for every penny he owned. A man whose only hope lay beyond this world. Heaven, and his son waiting at the gates. Charlie's eyes filled with tears and his heart with rage. For a minute he thought of reaching for the gun that Eddie kept under the cash register. If they had killed that poor man, he felt as though he could kill them and never lose an hour of sleep. But that would put him in jail. There would be no future with Laila, and her divorce was coming any day.

Eddie sidled up and asked quietly, spatula in hand. "What's wrong?"

"Long story," Charlie said.

The phone rang, and Charlie picked it up and heard a voice he didn't recognize. "Is Charlie Tumulty there? David McRae's friend?"

"Speaking."

"My name is Father Walsh over at St. Pat . . ."

"I know." The tone of the priest's voice was scaring him. "What's wrong?"

"Charlie, David was supposed to see me early this morning. He never came. I've been calling him at his apartment. There's no answer. I'm worried because it's not at all like him to break an appointment without calling. I called 911 . . ."

Charlie let the phone fall and ran out the door without a word to Eddie; he kept on running along the canal and down Merrimack Street, over the Eastern Canal and up the hill to Foxy's apartment.

Cruisers and an ambulance. Charlie stopped cold. Then he ran. Subdued voices, flashing lights, crackling radios and running engines swirled in a surreal diorama in front of

Foxy's place. His instincts suggested the worst, but he tried to hold onto hope that Foxy was not . . .

"Dead? Did you say McRae is dead?"

"Sorry, Charlie," the cop said. "He's gone. Looks like a drug overdose. Father Walsh over at St. Pat's asked us to do a wellness check. TV was on, no answer, we went in. All you can do now is pray for the kid. Send a card to his mother."

"He didn't do hard drugs, ever," Charlie said.

The cop shrugged. "That's what it looks like."

The EMTs came out pushing a gurney on which a figure covered by a sheet was stretched. The empty shell that had contained a simple kid with a good heart. Charlie turned and headed back toward Merrimack Street, wiping his eyes on his sleeve, and hearing Foxy's voice reverberating in his mind: "I shoulda listened to you, man."

I should have made you listen, Foxy, he whispered. *Another kid who never hurt anyone is dead. But I'm not.*

Charlie Tumulty, in a dark watch cap and windbreaker, was standing at a pay phone at the top of John Street pretending to talk; he was watching the Star Lite Bar at closing time. It was almost one o'clock. The drunks, the sad construction workers who had gone in for a pop after work and kept swallowing away their pay, a few couples with no more romantic place to go, the hard core of the city's drinkers—they had all either straggled past him or headed the other way toward the Boott Mills. One guy, wearing a green baseball cap over long blond hair, passed him coming down from Merrimack Street and went into the bar.

After a while, Charlie hung up the phone and crossed the street. Softly, he pushed on the door, but it had already been locked. He walked around the corner and down the alley where a Lincoln Continental was parked by the back door, which meant that at some point Malvert would come out this way. He tried the back door; it opened a crack. He listened intently. Voices near the bar. He slipped into a dimly lit kitchen.

". . . good day's work."

"Boss, don't trust nobody else."

"You guys were away, and it was so simple. Knew the kid for years. Dumb bastard. I really thought he was smarter than that."

"Anyway, loose ends tied up. Ga'night, boss."

"Catfish, let 'em out and lock the door if you want another drink. I gotta put the cash in the safe."

The others were moving away toward the front. He heard footfalls. Someone mounting the stairs. Malvert taking the money up to the safe. He peeked through the space in a swinging door and saw the disheveled man in the green cap pouring a big whiskey. He was crooning, "After she left me, I ordered more whiskey . . ." He turned on a TV over the bar, got some old Western, and settled into a seat.

Now the reality of revenge presented a puzzle to Charlie, watching from the shadows. He had to do something, but what? There were knives here. But could he plunge a knife into a man? Even a worthless killer who thought that Johnny Rivera's dead body was an amusing prop in the stage play of his life as a dangerous outlaw? God knows he had it coming, but any attempt against him would alert the man upstairs, the deranged puppet master. He had certainly ordered Foxy's death. He remembered once again the sad young man who had felt the presence of God in the burning sanctuary lamp, and the godless bastards who killed him without a thought, leaving his mother to believe he died a junkie.

"How quickly will you avenge me?" Conall Cernach asked, and Cúchulainn answered, "Before your blood is cold, I will avenge you."

He stood indecisive for a few moments and then heard steps. Malvert was coming down. He heard the two men talking, and then the scrape of Catfish's chair as he pushed it away from the bar and got up. "Ah'll see you 'round, Boss, an' thankee for the whiskey."

Malvert walked him out the front and Charlie heard the click as the front door was locked again. The adrenalin was nearly making Charlie shake as he slipped out the back. He waited behind the dumpster. A few minutes later, Beak Malvert exited the Star Lite and locked the door. He was opening the car door when Charlie flew at him from the shadows, throwing him back against the wall.

Malvert shouted once, but Charlie slapped him hard and said, "Shut up! Here are your choices, cigar breath. We walk over to the police station and you confess to murder or I get justice for Foxy McRae and Johnny Rivera right here." Malvert tried to pull away, but Charlie held him fast.

"I know you, Tumulty. Just 'cause you're a boxer don't mean you gotta be fuckin' dumb. You drag me over to the cops—that's duress. A confession made under duress is no confession. Not to mention the cops on my payroll, you dumb shit. So, what are you gonna do, kill me? Are you a killer, tough guy?"

The clouds in the night sky sailed on. The naked moon cast a silver light over the alley, and Charlie hesitated. *I'm not a killer, I'm an avenger.* That was what he wanted to say, but he froze, not knowing what that really meant in action. He might have left the scene, but as he stood there, eye to eye with Malvert, the mobster spit in his face. He released his hold on the man and recoiled involuntarily, wiping his face on his coat sleeve.

Charlie saw Malvert reaching inside his jacket and lunged at the mobster as the gun barrel was coming up. He drove Malvert's arm aside and muscled him back against the brick wall. The gun went off and Charlie heard the bullet thud into the side of the Lincoln. He grappled with Malvert for the gun, each man covering it with his hands and trying to bend it toward the other. The gun fired a second time, and Malvert cried out, "Motherfucker!" and slumped to the ground. He groaned once or twice more and was quiet. Charlie was holding the gun.

Someone else was shouting, and thinking it was one of Malvert's men, Charlie aimed the gun at the figure silhouetted at the top of the alley. A voice was shouting at him, and through the ringing in his own head, he heard the words, "Police! Drop it, Charlie! Hands up! Now!"

He never understood why Officer Jake Hutton had not shot him dead right there, but he didn't. Charlie dropped the gun. Later that night, in a cell at the Lowell Police Station, he learned that William "Beak" Malvert was dead. He felt no remorse on that count, but tears welled in his eyes for the future he had dreamed of with Laila, which now, he was sure, had fallen into the region of broken hopes . . . *what might have been.*

Though he was a public defender, Kevin Cavanaugh seemed to Charlie to be a competent lawyer who took his cases seriously. They sat down in plastic chairs in a cheerless room at the Middlesex County Jail, which was at the top of the high-rise Middlesex County Superior Courthouse in East Cambridge, the "Slammer in the Sky," as it was known to inmates. Cavanaugh set his briefcase down on the laminated table and snapped it open. He was a balding middle-aged man in an ill-fitting gray suit who seemed to emanate airs of courtrooms and legal briefs; a true creature of the legal profession and the only friend that Charlie had in the system.

He pulled a folder from his briefcase and closed it. "So, how are you, Charlie?"

"I've been better. If I can't post bail I'm stuck here. I keep an eye out for any friends of Malvert's I might run into."

"Listen, in my experience, guys like Malvert don't inspire genuine love or admiration. He's the paymaster. Once he's dead and the pay stops, his boys don't really give a shit about who killed him or why. They wouldn't go out of their way to avenge him the way you did for your friend, David . . . " He opened a folder and began to peruse Charlie's sworn statement. "David . . ."

"David McRae. He didn't overdose. He was a pot smoker. He didn't shoot drugs."

"Oh, they know he was murdered, Charlie. I was going to explain that. When they drew blood from his other arm, there was no heroin in the blood at all. It pooled in the area where they injected it. It stayed there because the heart was not pumping it through the body. Which means they injected the dope after he was already dead. Anyway, no tracks on the kid. He OD'd his first time?"

"Will that help my defense?"

"Well, here's the thing. The story that David told you . . . we don't know who this guy Catfish is. Whoever he is, he's made himself scarce, and we don't have a real name. Nicknames are not really a legal form of identification. Second, David's story makes sense, but that's not enough. The fact is that we have a story from a guy who is dead told by a guy facing time. And we have no body of Johnny Rivera. That means no evidence. On the other hand, we have incontrovertible evidence . . . by which I mean . . ."

"I know what incontrovertible means."

"Sorry. We have incontrovertible evidence that you killed Malvert."

"Right. That puts me behind the eight ball."

"Now, I believe your story, I'll tell you that. However, even if it's true, you and I don't get to be the judge and jury, right? Everyone is entitled to their day in court, and you killed a guy. And the prosecutor will probably try to pin David's murder on some mysterious guy with no name except 'Catfish.' Frank Sago supposedly told David McRae to go with this Catfish, allegedly to bury Rivera, but Sago says the only Catfish he's ever heard of is Catfish Hunter, the pitcher. So where's our proof? We have none, Charlie. Again, just the word of a guy facing time quoting a dead witness." He loosened his tie and leaned forward, eyes narrowed. "Let me ask you this—did you intend to kill William Malvert?"

"I didn't care. He murdered my friend. Or had him murdered."

Cavanaugh pulled a packet from his pocket and unwrapped a piece of gum. "I'd offer you a piece, but it's that Nicorette shit. I'm trying to quit smoking. I'd almost kill for a smoke, but I promised the wife."

Charlie nodded. "Good idea."

"So, anyway, 'I didn't care' is not the best answer, Charlie. I'm not advising you to lie. I'm just saying. And you being a trained boxer, your hands are weapons and all that. I'm sure the prosecutor will raise that point. It may not be hard for him to convince the jury you went there to kill him."

"He had the gun."

"There's no evidence that the gun was his. It was unregistered, Charlie. The prosecution will say it was yours. You were holding it. And you were there, in the alley, waiting. Looks premeditated."

Charlie could hardly hide a feeling of jaded disillusion. "What is a *good* answer?"

"You were in a rage. You believed that this man had ordered a hit on your friend and you had evidence . . ."

"Incontrovertible evidence," Charlie added.

"Okay, well, that's in the eye of the beholder, but you had no doubt . . . let me see, you wanted to confront him, and maybe . . . I don't know. I don't want to put words in your mouth, but obviously things escalated."

"Words, words, words."

"Words can mean years if they're not used the right way, Charlie. We need to establish a frame of mind. Little planning aforethought, right? Spontaneous. The prosecution is going to say you didn't go there immediately, in a rage, that you went to the alley much later, and you waited there to ambush him. That's malice aforethought. We need to try to show that you were driven by . . ."

The lawyer went on with the suppositions and explanations of his trade. The words wound their way through a labyrinth of legal definitions, levels of crimes, motivations, jury considerations, mitigations . . .

Though his future hung in the balance, Charlie's mind wandered from legal argument to the image of Laila. He was more concerned with what words he could use to explain this to her rather than how he could explain it to a jury. He could hardly explain it to himself. All he knew was that Beak Malvert had it coming.

He interrupted the lawyer, "Mr. Cavanaugh . . ."

"Kevin."

"Kevin, all right, I'm not the judge and the jury as you said. But what do you do when a jury can't hear witnesses because they're silenced by a killer? Who will testify for the dead? Where do Johnny and his father and Foxy McRae get justice if not from me?"

Cavanaugh was quiet for a moment. Outside the room, they heard the institutional sounds, doors opening, jumbled voices on two-way radios, buzzers sounding and doors opening and closing. He tapped his pen against the yellow legal pad and said, "Look, I'm not saying I can't understand that. Maybe justice was served, but it is not the way we serve justice. Sometimes it just starts a whole chain of violence. That's why the law doesn't allow it, and so I'm pretty sure you're going have to pay a price for it."

"More than you know . . . how long will I stay in this place?"

"Pre-trial detention. Probably a few months. Maybe up to six months." The lawyer glanced at his watch, and citing another appointment, offered a few words of encouragement and took his leave. Charlie watched him bustle off to the world of the free, the world that had lately been his.

The food was not the sort of fuel that kept an athlete running on all cylinders. A bologna sandwich, a carton of milk, and a withered apple. Charlie forced it down half the sandwich, and gave the other to his cell mate, Otoniel, or Tony, a slim Hispanic guy who knew basic English but still called him 'Carlos.' He took the proffered half sandwich. "Gracias Carlos."

Charlie was sweating. There was no air conditioning "above the red," the stripe around the building's exterior that marked off the floors above the 17th story as the jail section. It had been built for 160 prisoners. It currently housed 380. Charlie was suffocating, physically and emotionally. Cavanaugh was right. The justice he had carried out would cost him, already was costing him, heavily.

He heard a C.O. open the locked door in the corridor and call out: "Wilbur Creighton and Charlie Tumulty, you have visitors. I will escort you to the visitation area." He let the two men out of their cells, and on the way explained the rules to Charlie. "You may embrace the visitor when you see them, or give them a quick kiss. Once you are seated, no physical contact is permitted. You cannot accept anything from the visitor, and any visitor who attempts to pass something to the prisoner will be crossed off the visitors' list."

He tried to prepare himself because he knew the visitor was Laila. A buzzer sounded and the door opened; he saw her seated at one of the tables, looking forlorn. She was wearing jeans and a purple, long sleeve blouse. A light raincoat hung over the chair beside her. She rose as he approached and they embraced. The fragrance of her hair and the closeness of her form overwhelmed him with a feeling of loss. They sat facing each other. She pushed away strands of her dark hair, damp with rain or tears.

"How could you do it, Charlie?" Laila's voice seemed to reach him from a great distance, from the world he had left behind. He felt disoriented, disconnected; sitting there in a new reality with his heart twisting in his chest for the old one. He could see the raindrops on the long window, and the sky, a gray woolen blanket. He could not take her hand.

He gripped one sweating fist in the other, and shook his head. "What can I say, Laila? Foxy was a gentle kid. He never hurt anyone. Malvert murdered him, or sent someone to murder him in cold blood. And he murdered that poor house painter and . . ."

"But you threw away our future. The divorce came through."

The words cut him. "I wish there was something I could say. I'm sorry."

"Was it worth it, Charlie? Your revenge?"

"I can't think of it that way. I'll go out of my mind, Laila. Nothing is worth being separated from you. I love you. But Malvert had poor Foxy murdered in his bed like he was nobody. Like he had no friends who would care."

"I understand, but I can't help being angry with you, Charlie. You didn't just do this to him or to them. You did it to me, to us. You should have thought of us."

"I don't blame you. I'm sorry. You're free. I'm not. You have to move on. I understand."

It was a tragic balm to his soul when she said, finally, "I can't. I told you I'd never find another Charlie." She seemed to take a new resolution and tried to put on a bolder face. He saw, in the light from the window, the golden flecks in her hazel eyes. She told him she had got a new job at Enterprise Bank, and would be saving money for the day of his release.

He thought of the old prison ships on which Irish rebels and criminals had been sent into Australian exile. He felt as though he were on board such a ship; the snow-white sails were unfurled, and he was bound for the far side of the world, while Laila stood on the shore wrapped in a dark cloak, watching the ship grow smaller. "You're so loyal, and I'm so sorry," he said.

Sudden shouts erupted at a nearby table. They had allowed a visitor to bring in an instamatic camera to take a photo of her inmate boyfriend or husband, but a C.O. saw him flash a gang sign as she snapped it. Two guards stepped up and told her to hand over the camera. She refused and quickly found herself restrained. 'You fuckin' communis' bitch!" she screamed at the woman who tore the camera from her grasp. Her inmate companion had been in the system long enough to know that he couldn't win. "You take care, baby. I see you later," he said, as they rushed the woman, shouting curses, out the exit. The C.O. did not have to urge the inmate toward the door that led back to his cell.

The resolute mask fell away. "My God, Charlie. It kills me to see you here."

"I'll survive. You know the old saying, 'What can't be cured, must be endured.'"

She shook her head and wiped her eyes with a Kleenex. "No, I never heard that."

"We'll both have a lot to endure."

"Oh, Charlie. I love you so much and it's just so sad."

"I can't let myself be weak, Laila. I just can't. Whatever happens . . ." The C.O. informed them that the visit would end in two minutes. His mind rejected the word that tried to edge its way into his consciousness: *hopeless.*

"I'll be better when I come again," she said. "I don't want to make you sadder." As he watched her turn at the door to look back and attempt a smile, he struggled to retain the mental toughness he had learned as a boy in the Acre.

Endure.

He realized he had not known the true meaning of the word 'hopeless' at the time of her visit. But two days later, when he learned over the radio in the Rec Room that Laila Grant had been shot and left for dead in the parking lot of Enterprise Bank in Lowell, he fell to his knees crying like a child and felt for the first time that hope, along with love, had abandoned him. For days he hardly ate and would not speak. Hardie Bangs did his best to keep him out of trouble because his fuse was short and burning with the red flame of hatred.

Eddie came to visit him and told him that Frank Sago was a prime suspect, but, as usual, there were no witnesses, and there was no murder weapon. He had been questioned and released. Knowing the identity of the killer is not the same as proving the identity of the killer. "Maybe he paid some kid to do it," Eddie said. "It's a horrible situation, Charlie."

"It was his way of getting back at me for killing Malvert and for having Laila's love," Charlie said. The cycle of violence the lawyer had mentioned had begun. Foxy's murder was unforgivable, but this was worse. "I should have been there, Eddie. My God, I got her killed."

His uncle, who seemed older and more world-weary since Charlie's arrest, sighed and said, "Poor Laila was bound for trouble the day she met that son of a bitch."

"One day I'm going to kill him, Eddie."

"Charlie, let the police handle it. Please."

That night on his cot, while his Tony snored, Charlie remembered a conversation with Foxy about *The Count of Monte Cristo*; his friend had wondered if he could survive in jail or if he would go crazy. He had told Foxy, "You survive for someone you love, or someone you hate." He had lost the one he loved, but the flame of hatred had been kindled and burned unceasingly beside her memory.

Charlie was friendly with one of the correctional officers in Cambridge. His name was John Crowe. He had been a boxer, so there was mutual respect. Crowe was firm but fair.

When Charlie asked him about the possibility of going to Laila's funeral with an escort, he shook his head. "Sorry, Charlie. I feel for you. I can have you fill out papers, but I'll tell you it's a waste of time. Immediate family. That's it. Girlfriend, even a fiancé, won't cut it."

"I have time to waste," he said. Crowe gave him the papers. He filled them out. His request was denied within a few hours.

"Can I send a letter to her father?" he asked.

"You can write it. If they approve it, and if her father wants to receive it, they'll send it. Do you know what you want to say?"

"That I'm sorry. And that Frank Sago will pay . . ."

"The ex-husband? No, no, Charlie. You can't say that. You mention Sago, they shit-can the letter. Immediately."

In the end, he wrote a simple note to her father:

Dear Joe,
I'm so sorry. Laila deserved life, a good life, which is what I hoped to give her. I will always love her. There's nothing else I can say. I'm sorry.
Charlie Tumulty

Charlie was sentenced to fourteen years for manslaughter, but Cavanaugh told him if he behaved he'd serve nine or ten at MCI Concord. During the day, they kept him busy with a job in the cafeteria, or, in the prison nomenclature, 'Culinary.' It was the nights that belonged to Laila as they had since his first one in the "Slammer in the Sky" while she was still alive. Charlie saw her so clearly in the darkness behind his eyes, standing by the river beneath the twilight pines of the Groton woods while the snow fell. He seemed to feel the calming grace of her presence, while around him, he heard the rattling of the guards' keys as they made their hourly count, the opening and closing of the cell block doors, inmate banter, and sometimes the sound of metal on the cement floor when an inmate in the block was grinding a shank. He had no love, no living love, to survive for, but he certainly had anger and hate. He longed for freedom, often. But more than that, he longed for vengeance. Come what may.

His father had told him how he had been forced by events or by history to become a killer. Charlie had never thought himself capable of killing either, but he knew if fate ever put Frank Sago in his path, one of them would die, and there would be an end to the cycle. *Anger be now your song.*

Chapter 15

1988

*There's little joy in life for me,
And little terror in the grave;
I've lived the parting hour to see
Of one I would have died to save.*

—Charlotte Brontë,
"On the Death of Anne Brontë"

Charlie's mother had sent him Christmas cards in jail, usually with cheery illustrations of Old Saint Nick with his red cheeks and fluffy beard waving a greeting from a skybound sleigh. Shit like that. A line or two written inside. *Charlie, Have a Merry Christmas. Love, Mom.* Oh yeah, Ma. We are a merry band here at MCI. Sometimes, probably if she were drunk when she wrote it, she'd add, *I miss you, Charlie. Sorry I was such a rotten mother.* And he would think, "I'm sorry, too."

As for his father, it seemed he had disappeared. There had been a high-stakes poker game somewhere in South Boston, a game run by a mobster named Neily Boland. Two guys had driven the bodyguards up the stairs at gunpoint and surprised the players, who were made to lie on the floor. Rumor had it the thieves collected ten thousand in cash. To add insult to injury, the robbers made the men strip down to their underwear, laughing hysterically when one of the men was found to be wearing women's underwear; the bandits threw the players' clothes out the window into an alley.

Apparently, one of the men on the floor recognized Jack Tumulty's voice and was dumb enough to say so, for which he got a kick in the head and was told to shut the fuck up. If Jack went back to his apartment at all, he did it fast, because the South Boston guys were no doubt there looking for him within a couple of hours. He was gone, or at least that's what the word was. Maybe they did catch up with him; maybe he was already dead. Finally bit off more than he could chew. The other robber would probably have liked to see him dead, too, because if those guys got him, they'd make him talk. Charlie imagined the conversation. "Who was the other guy, Tumulty?"

And wiseass Jack, "I don't know. He was wearing a mask."

That bravado doesn't last long when they put your head in a vise. Yeah, they'd make him talk before they killed him.

Once, about a year before his release date, his mother came to see him, wearing yellow plaid pants and a yellow shirt, her sunglasses perched atop the paisley scarf tied over her now bleached blonde head. Alongside her was a bald guy in a suit who carried a briefcase and smelled of expensive cologne—had to be a lawyer.

"Hi, Ma." She seemed impatient with his hug. Charlie felt a gnawing pity for her. What had made her so cold? The old Grace he remembered, not the warmer version who had been so kind to Laila. She had aged of course. Her makeup could not hide the fact that hard living had taken its toll.

"Charlie, this is Dave McLaughlin. He's a lawyer, and he has some papers for you to sign."

"What papers?"

"Your uncle, Eddie Tumulty . . ." the lawyer began. "I'm sorry to say he has passed away."

"Goddammit," Charlie said, half to himself.

"And good riddance," his mother snorted.

Charlie shook his head. "A guy who never said a bad word about you, Ma. A guy who was more of a parent to me than either of my real parents. You can't get along with anyone."

"Not with any holier than thou who wants to tell me how to live my life!"

"Oh no. You had it all figured out."

"Anyway, Charlie," McLaughlin continued. "As I was saying, I'm sorry, but he has passed on and has left instructions with me to inform you that he has left you the bar, the entire property. There's money set aside to pay the taxes until you are released, even to do some renovations, which I'd recommend, and then you can either sell it or run the business. Or if you like you can sell it as is."

"Sell it," Grace said.

"Was he sick? He just came to visit me a month ago. I thought . . ."

"It was his heart."

"When?"

"About a week ago."

"Why didn't you tell me, Ma?"

"What difference does it make? I didn't. Just sell the bar. What do you know about running a bar?"

"I know a lot of guys who run bars, and I know they're not all geniuses. Anyway, I know a lot."

He thought for a minute. The days were long here. Having a bar, thinking about it and planning for it, could keep his mind occupied. He recalled the interior. The long, polished bar. The rich mahogany of the baby grand piano gleaming at the back of the room. It always seemed out of place, like some classy lady sipping champagne from a fluted glass in a whiskey dive. And when the lid was raised, music resounded through the bar as Eddie himself or one of the other pianists who came in played "Oh! You Crazy Moon" or "Autumn in New York." Money is money, but the bar could be a living. "I'm going to keep it," he said.

His mother let out a cry of disgust. Charlie ignored her and continued. "Mr. McLaughlin . . ."

"Dave."

"Dave, there's a carpenter in Lowell by the name of Brian McNamara. He's honest and reliable. Bring him in and ask him what he would do to make the place, you know, better. I want more light, bigger windows. I trust his judgment. Check out the flooring. Let me know what he says and tell him what the budget is and just let him go to work."

"You're crazy, Charlie," his mother said. "You want to spend your life with drunks?"

"Why not? I grew up with one."

She pushed her chair back noisily, grabbed her bag and stalked off, as the Irish song had it, 'with no word of farewell.' He shook his head regretfully and called after her, "I'm sorry, Ma!" She kept walking.

The lawyer took his hand in a firm grip and said, "I'll be in touch. I was a fan of yours. You were robbed of that bout in Worcester, and everyone knows it."

"I was robbed of much more than that, Dave. By the way, did she mention anything about my father? Has she heard from him? Does she think he's dead?"

The lawyer shook his head. "She doesn't know, but frankly Charlie, she has no interest." Then he rose, too, but before he turned away, he said, "I know it didn't end well, Charlie, but you made us proud."

"It's too bad I could never make my mother or my father proud, or be proud of them, but that's life."

"Eddie was proud of you," he said. The lawyer left, and the guard who came to escort him back to his cell pretended not to notice that Charlie was wiping tears with his sleeve.

Plans for the bar did give him something to think about. He got a letter from Fitzgibbons expressing his condolences. The old antique dealer had never judged him. Once when he visited, Charlie said, "I guess I was a fool. I avenged a friend and got the woman I loved killed."

The old man shrugged, his face inscrutable, eyes large behind the lenses of his wire-rimmed glasses. "Fools rush in, as they say, Charlie, where angels fear to tread. But remember it wasn't for money or for any self-serving reason. You avenged an innocent friend, and you've paid a heavy price pretty much without complaint. I wish you had spoken to me first, but . . . the Star Lite is a Cambodian market now. That gang is gone, and we're better for it."

"Another gang will fill the vacuum and find some other front. Has anyone heard where Frank Sago went?"

"If they had, I wouldn't tell you, Charlie. Let God judge him and send him to hell."

"If only I could be sure that He would."

"Have faith, Charlie. You don't want to come back and die in this place."

Chapter 16

1989

Ten years behind the wire. And now he was free.

His first night as a free man in so long. He had picked up the keys to the new doors to Eddie's Piano Bar from Dave McLaughlin. Brian, the carpenter, had done good work. The floor had been refinished, the long bar shortened and formed into an L shape so there was more room for tables, and the front windows replaced with larger ones while a new window had been cut into the side.

One thing he had told Brian: "We need a light above the piano." He remembered how once he had told Uncle Eddie that the pianist he'd hired was playing in the dark at the back of the bar. Eddie had gone over and opened the door to the men's room so that a shaft of light fell over the player, and considered the problem solved, at least until someone used the men's room. Brian had set the piano up on a sort of small stage or deck with its own lighting, with room for other musicians, a trio at least. Above the bar, was a framed poster of Charlie with gloves raised. "Irish Charlie Tumulty: The Pride of the Acre." He smiled wistfully but took it down and brought it to the back room. He told himself he would replace it with a photo of Eddie.

The phone was not turned on yet, so he walked down to the corner and dialed a number he knew by heart. "Sophie?"

"Wait. Is this . . . ?"

"Charlie," he said before she might say any other name.

"That's what I thought! Are you calling from the prison or are you out?"

"I'm a free man."

"Then you need to get laid! Come on over—same place."

Charlie laughed for the first time since he had left the prison, and probably for a while before that. "I just hope it works," he said.

"I'll make it work."

"I'll be there soon."

"Bring condoms," she said.

He hung up and set off on foot for the CVS on Merrimack Street, and on to her house. He had no car yet. He was eager to see his old friend Sophie. The last time he had heard from her she was not married, and by her reaction, it was clear she still wasn't.

No one would say that Sophie was a knockout, but she had a fine figure, and she was one of those women, Charlie thought, who are so kind and good, that the more time you spend with them, the better-looking they become. She sure looked good to Charlie that night. She had put on some soft soulful music, Bill Withers singing "Lean on Me." She greeted him in a housecoat, and when the door closed, she let it fall. She was naked except for a red bandana around her neck. The girl he had once thought plain might as well have been Helen of Troy.

He picked her up in his arms and carried her to the bedroom, where, with her help, he undressed quickly. She had lit some candles. The warm glow of the light on her body made him ache for all the years of female company he had lost.

"Where is your Celtic cross?" she asked.

"Probably around the neck of some corrections officer. They said they lost it."

"You lost so much. Years."

They kissed, and Sophie, reaching down, whispered in his ear, "You're so ready." She opened the condom and put it on him. He raised her up and kissed her again. After so many years, he was nearly overcome by the power of it—the electricity of this touching. He ran his hands along her curves, as smooth as marble and as soft as down. More welcome and more warming than a longed-for hearth to a weary winter traveler. They lay on the bed and she was astride him, rocking gently. He thought he would never forget this image—her dark hair falling over his chest, the red bandana a splash of color above her white breasts.

Later, as they settled side by side, he said, "My God. I'm weak."

"Good thing you don't have to get in the ring."

"Those days are gone."

"I could never watch fights, but I know you got screwed by the judges."

"Turned out two of them weren't even certified to be judges in the state. If you recall, the decision was invalidated and I would have had another shot, if only . . . . Ah, well. *Sing no more this bitter tale, that wears my heart away.*"

"Shakespeare?"

"No. *The Odyssey.*"

"Of course. You want a beer?"

"That would be great."

Charlie watched her naked form move away, thinking he really didn't feel that tired anymore. She came back with a glass of wine and a long-neck bottle of Budweiser. "Did you want a glass?"

"It's in a glass."

"Right." She held out her glass and said, "To Eddie."

He clinked his beer against it. "We'll never forget him." They drank and Charlie said, "It was very good of you to send me those letters in jail and let me know what was going on in the Acre. Made me laugh a few times in a place where I didn't laugh much. You'd be amazed how many people forget you after a couple of years. Mike Dineen always wrote. He's retired now. Eddie visited regularly. And Fitzgibbons. He's still haunting his old House of Forgotten Dreams." He sipped his beer and repeated, "Forgotten dreams."

"I just couldn't face seeing you in there. But I thought about you every day, Charlie. We were always good friends."

"I understand." He chuckled. "I remember Johnny Gallagher said to me once, 'What's going on with you and Sophie Stiles?' I said, 'We're just good friends, and sometimes we sleep together.' He was taken aback by that and started ranting about how I was a 'friend fucker,' like that was some class of criminal."

When they had stopped laughing, Sophie said, "I'm afraid you're going to have to find another friend to sleep with, Charlie. My mother is in her eighties, and she needs help. I'm planning to move back up there to take care of her."

"Move back where?"

"Home. Jonesport, Maine. Up past Bar Harbor."

"I forgot. That's why you don't sound like a Lowellian."

"Exactly."

"Well, that sucks. I mean it sucks for me. You're my best friend, really. It's good for your mother. She was a good mother, I suppose?"

"Yeah. She really was. I love her." She shrugged, "She's my mother." *Yeah,* Charlie thought, *it's as simple as that.*

"Have you been back much?"

"I went back every summer during college, and usually at Christmas. There's this guy up there."

'A French-Canadian fur trapper?"

She laughed. "No, wise ass. Jeff Nichols. My mother says he told her he intends to marry me. And he's knocked out more people than you!"

"Really? Nasty left hook?"

"He's an anesthesiologist. At the regional medical center."

"Good job."

She took a sip of wine and then nudged him good-naturedly. "Can you believe some sucker wants to marry me?"

"Easily. I've often felt that I was in love with you."

"And then you came to your senses," she said.

"I kind of feel it right now. You don't think it would work?"

She took a deep breath and shook her head thoughtfully. "We'll never know, Charlie. Unless you want to move to Jonesport. And I heard you inherited the bar."

"Yeah. Eddie's Piano Bar is now Charlie's Piano Bar."

"So, you have a business in the city."

"Northern Maine. Jesus. It is quite a trek."

She shrugged, acknowledging the hard reality. "It is." She was about to continue, but she paused and bit her lip. Then she said, "Charlie, it's probably not something you want to talk about, but . . ."

"I got your card after it happened. Thank you, Sophie." He exhaled and passed a hand over his still short prison haircut. "It's been hard. Especially since no one has ever paid for her murder."

"I cried when I heard. For her and for you. I know you two had something special. It's so awful and so sad, but please don't do anything that . . ."

"I understand." He took her hand. "Believe me, Sophie, whatever I do will not be done lightly or accidentally. But it's something in my path that I'm going to have to deal with before I feel . . . really free."

"Even if you lose your freedom for it?"

"There's a battle going on inside me. I'm not sure yet which side will win, but you're right. The consequences will not be light, but they never are in questions of love and murder and vengeance."

She nodded, accepting that he had heard her, but that the actions he took would be the result of his own decisions, after weighing everything in the balance. "Just be careful," she said. "I know you won't be reckless." They were quiet for a moment, in which Charlie relished the concern of this dear friend, and even more, the silence. No raucous shouts or forlorn cries. No clang of metal doors. No C.O.'s pacing the hallway, whistling casually in the knowledge that when the shift is over they would rejoin the world.

"You downed that beer pretty fast," Sophie said. "Let me get you another one." She jumped out of the bed.

"That Jeff Nichols better treat you right!" he called after her.

"He's a nice guy! I bet he's not a 'friend fucker!'"

She was hard not to love, but it seemed, as usual, he thought, that luck, or fate, or the gods were against him. She came back and handed him the beer and raised her glass, "Another toast. To Charlie's Piano Bar." They drank, and Charlie said, "Shit, it's been so long. I'll be half-drunk on two beers." She arranged the pillows behind them, and they looked at each other with that deep regard that is so close to love. The candle had neared the wick's end and cast fitful shadows over the room. "Come here," he said, pulling her into his embrace, loving her and trying not to love her too much because it made things complicated, and maybe because in some corner of his heart, he felt it might be a betrayal to the lost Laila. The candle flame died, and Sophie held him tightly in the darkness.

He dreamed of Hardie Bangs. He spoke in the deep and resonant voice that suggested a lifetime of sad experience. "You was born under a bad sign, Charlie. I know you'll be back." He woke in the dark, disoriented, his heart pounding. A digital clock shone the hour in red, 3:10, but there was no such clock in his cell. *Where?* He turned and saw Sophie sleeping beside him as reality settled and his mind cleared of dreams and confusion. He needed to go to the bathroom. But there was no toilet in this room. He sat up, feeling an odd panic in the still of this strange night in a room with such high ceilings, such space, such quiet, with only the occasional hum of the refrigerator in the kitchen as it kicked on.

Sophie had awakened. "What's wrong, Charlie?"

"It's . . . I need to go to the bathroom."

"So just go."

"Right. Just get up and go."

"You break my heart, Charlie," she said, caressing his cheek. "You're not locked in a cell. You don't need anyone's permission. You're free. Just get up and walk out of the room. You know where the bathroom is."

He took a deep breath. "Yeah, of course. I don't know what came over me. It's just . . ."

"I understand."

"I have to pull myself together. It's my first night out. It's hard to explain. Like it's some other reality. Some other planet."

"Do you want me to walk with you?" she asked.

"Thanks," he said. "I'll be okay." He got up and walked out of the room, but as he passed through the kitchen, he imagined he saw Hardie Bangs in a darkened corner, idly shuffling a deck of cards. "I won't be back," he whispered to that phantom.

He heard Hardie's voice in his head: "If you find him, you'll be back."

Charlie could not deny it. Hatred is such a powerful force when a beloved ghost wanders unavenged under the weeping stars.

The grand opening of Charlie's Piano Bar was a subject of some conversation throughout the Acre and the downtown, particularly in the other bars of Market Street, the White Eagle, the Cosmo, and the SAC Club. The news echoed through every other joint from the Old Worthen up to Saba's below the Overpass, Fury's and the Three Copper Men, on to the Highland Tap and Captain John's in Cupples Square, over to the Whipple Café in Lower Belvidere and across the river to the Cameo Diner and the East End Social Club. In smokey bars where pool balls clicked and tumbled into net pockets, where men gathered after work for a couple of beers, their hammer holsters still on their belts, where women laughed at the men's insinuations and fearlessly cracked back; in short, in the bars and diners of Lowell, the word was out.

"That the boxer who shot the gangsta?" asks the grease-stained mechanic.

"Yeah, Charlie Tumulty. The gangsta murdered his pal so he went after him and shot him," says Diane. She holds a whiskey and ginger in one hand and makes a pistol with the other. She fires a couple of imaginary shots at her boyfriend with her index finger to illustrate the point. "Pow! Pow!"

"I heard one of 'em killed his girl while he was in jail. Shot her dead."

"Son of a bitch. They ever get him for that?"

"Nope. No weapon. Couldn't put any of 'em at the scene."

"You think Tumulty will go after 'em?"

"Be surprised if he didn't."

Charlie had asked Eddie to sell the Falcon once his prison sentence was handed down. Now he bought a '64 Pontiac Grand Prix with a rare four-speed transmission down at Jack's Used Cars. The idea of just getting into a car and driving, with permission from no one, to any destination, was daunting at first, and then exhilarating. One late afternoon, he drove out to the place he had dreamed of so often, the Groton woods where he had spent that unforgettable twilight with Laila. He found the rock by the river where they had embraced, climbed to the top, and rested there for some time, remembering. The shadows lengthened and the declining sun shed a golden light over the river and through the trees. Later, as darkness spread, Charlie saw a couple of coyotes trot along the trail, stopping to sniff the air, perhaps catching the scent of the man who sat atop the glacial boulder. The pair of shadows moved into the darkening woods. Before he left, he picked up a stone from the riverbank and put it in his pocket.

Though he had never been religious, he prayed for Laila's soul, and apologized over and over to her ghost, a presence he seemed to feel was near; he recalled Fitzgibbons once reciting the magical lines that he had memorized later from the book he'd given him:

At the mid hour of night, when stars are weeping, I fly
To the lone vale we loved, when life shone warm in thine eye;
And I think oft, if spirits can steal from the regions of air,
To revisit past scenes of delight, thou wilt come to me there,
And tell me our love is remember'd, even in the sky.

Charlie's celebrity as a boxer and as the deadly avenger of his old Acre friend drew a considerable crowd to the grand opening. Sophie came down to help out behind the bar, and

Charlie had hired Mike Dineen's nephew, Will, to help out as well. Charlie thought it better to try to socialize and do all the hail-fellow, well-met stuff.

Dan Webster was back at the piano, playing "Ain't Misbehavin'" from the newly illuminated stage. It was all a blur for the first couple of hours. Charlie was still not accustomed to normal socializing and the easy banter of the free. There were a lot of old friends from the Acre and friends of Eddie's who wanted to express their condolences.

Scanning the faces and wishing Eddie could be here to see it all, he saw one face that surprised him. The last time he had seen the man, he was peering over raised gloves and driving him back with hard jabs. Sean Keenan. The fact that the boxer was smiling, or that that face could wear a smile, surprised Charlie.

"What'll you have?" Charlie asked.

"Just a bottle of Bud and a few words," he said.

Charlie retrieved a beer from the cooler for Keenan, and they walked to the end of the bar. "I heard about the opening through the grapevine as they say. I just wanted to tell you that I know you won the fight and fair play to ye. I wasn't part of that whole farce. It was decided by others. I was still reeling, to tell you the truth."

"I appreciate your coming here. No boxer is going to overturn his own win."

"All the shite I was talkin' was just to get under yer skin, a' course."

"Of course. Part of the game."

"I was not lookin' forward to fighting you again, but the way things turned out . . . it was a damned shame, Charlie."

"How did you make out?"

"I lost the final trial fight to a kid from New York. Tell you the truth, I lost something in the fight with you. Deep down I felt like an imposter, and it drained somethin' in me, you know."

"That fight could have gone either way. It was going the wrong way for me. I needed some luck."

"And you had it. Luck and guts. That last gambit, the gazelle punch . . . Jaysus."

"It was a risky gambit. You get hit while you're in the air, you're going down hard."

"Like I said, luck and guts. Oh well, those days are over, and I don't mind."

"It's very decent of you to come, Sean."

He had been aware of a small dark woman standing close by, watching him intently. "Excuse me, Sean." He turned toward the woman. "Can I do something for you?"

"My name Griselda Rivera. The mother of Johnny. The wife of Orlando."

Without warning, she embraced him hard, burying her head against his chest. He felt the sting of tears in his eyes. She stepped back and slapped his arms like some brave and hearty companion. She gave him the thumbs-up sign and said, with narrow-eyed conviction, "Good Charlie. *Good* Charlie!"

He was speechless. Speech, however, was not necessary. All he could say was, "Thank you."

"*Dios le bendiga*," she said. "I light candles for you." He watched her departing figure, a woman suddenly alone in the world. Yes, he had killed a man and he had taken a bitter punishment for it. He wasn't sure if it was right or wrong or whether he might pay again on judgment day if there were such a thing. But, like his father in the ditch in that "dirty place" in the war, he had done what he felt he had to do at the time. It was not Malvert's ghost that haunted his dreams. And he was sure that Griselda, at least, slept better.

"You have a fan for life, there," Sean said. He cast sidelong glances as if checking for eavesdroppers, and turning back to Charlie, said, "I need to tell you something."

They leaned over opposite corners at the end of the bar and Charlie inclined his head as Keenen's voice grew quieter. "There's an Irish bar in Southie called Brooksie's. I sometimes stop in to see some of the old boxing crowd. You want to mind your business in there. It's a hard-boiled crowd, Charlie. But you hear things. This fella you did in . . ."

"Malvert."

"Right. His demise was welcome to certain gangsters. Neily Boland, whose name I never mentioned, by the way, was wanting to take over his bookie operations, slot machines. And Malvert's what's the word . . . his thugs, or . . . ?"

"Henchmen?" Charlie offered.

"That's the word. His henchmen, Lyle something and Scully Bolek, bein' good for nothin' but being henchmen, when Malvert died, they went to work for a rival of Neily's, more of a Rhode Island guy called Albani."

"Understood."

"There was a bookie who was connected to, and protected by, Neily Boland. Albani thought he'd been screwed by him, who knows. Albani tells this bookie, 'Pay me the money or I'll send a couple of guys for you.' The bookie says, 'Send a couple of guys you don't like. They're not coming back.' And the Rhode Island boss sends this pair of gobshites, Lyle and Scully, to fuckin' kidnap the bookie."

"Did they come back?"

"They did not. Walked right into Neily's trap. They're as dead as doornails."

"Glad to hear it." Charlie recalled the name of Neily Boland. It was Boland's high-stakes poker game that his father had robbed. Jack might also be as dead as a doornail.

"Albani decided to stick to Rhode Island," Keenan added.

Sophie came over with two more beers, and Charlie introduced her to Sean. She shook her head and said, "Boxers. You go in a ring and try to beat each other senseless and then you sit and drink together like old friends."

Sean nodded and said, "It is a strange thing when you think about it."

"The ring is another world," Charlie said.

"But she's right," Sean said. "When you think about it."

"An opponent is a problem to be solved, not an enemy to be hated."

"Ah, yerra philosopher, Charlie."

A patron called for Sophie, and as she turned, Charlie called after her. "How's the kid doing?"

"Will? Good. He's learning."

They listened for a moment to the tumbling chords of the piano and Charlie asked, "Do you ever hear anything about another henchman they call 'Catfish'? I don't know his real name. Or of Frank Sago?"

"Catfish? No, never heard that name. Frank Sago, well, I did ask around. I was curious on your account. The police couldn't put him at the scene of . . . I'm sorry what was her name?"

"Laila Grant."

"Right. Laila. Lovely name. Seems there was a lack of evidence. But I don't think Sago wanted to be around when other guys moved in after his uncle met his end. I'm hearin' Malvert was a rat."

"But do you know where Sago is?" Charlie asked, as casually as he could.

"If I did, I don't think I'd tell you, Charlie. You've suffered enough for that crowd, haven't ye?"

"That's what everyone tells me."

Grim, remembering it all: poor Foxy, Laila, as beautiful as the morning in Prince's Bookstore—the warm smile and deep heart, a gun discharging and Malvert falling and a silhouette in the entranceway to the alley shouting at him to drop the gun. Then the walls and the monotony and the hopelessness. The kid, younger than Charlie had been, who hanged himself in the next cell. And the guards complaining because they'd have to fill out 'a shitload of paperwork.' All of that experience was now a part of who he was. "The question, Sean," he said finally, "is whether Frank Sago has suffered enough."

"Ah, it sounds like you'll be heading back to jail, Charlie," he said. The warning of Hardie Bangs again.

"I know. Sometimes, I kind of hope I never find him."

"Anyway, the oul' henchmen are dead. Sure, I thought you'd like to know that."

"Yes. That's good. Probably the ones who carried out the hit on Foxy."

Charlie swigged his beer but nearly choked on it as he saw his mother apparently looking around for him. "I'll be damned," he said and waved at her.

She spotted him and wedged through the crowd like the veteran waitress that she was. "Ma, this is . . ."

"For God's sake, Charlie, get me a gin and tonic, will ya?" She turned then to Sean and said, "Hi, I'm Grace, this ex-con's mother."

"Well, right, so. Sean Keenan, a sort of old friend of Charlie's."

Charlie waved at Will. "A gin and tonic over here, Will, when you get a chance!"

"Well, Charlie, I told you to sell the place and I still think that was a good idea, but I have to say it looks nice. Real nice." She glanced up at the photo of Eddie over the bar and studied it for a few seconds. "You think I was too hard on him, Charlie?"

"You were definitely too hard on him. Were you serious about working here?"

"I been thinkin' I'd rather work for my Charlie than for some guy that . . . anyway, yeah, why don't you let me work here for a while?"

"You still have to be on time."

"Even when I'm hung over. One thing you can't say is that I ain't a good worker. An' I don't drink when I'm workin' either. You know that."

"Just kidding. You've always been a good worker. Sophie is moving and sure, I can use you."

"Jus' for a while." She picked up a neatly folded beer-stained paper menu and added, "I can cook, too. Anything on this menu."

"We call it 'the bill of fare,'" Charlie said, winking at Sean.

"Talk American for God's sake. I got a car now, too. No insurance, but I got a car!"

"You're driving with no insurance?"

She waved away his scruples. "I drive wicked careful, Charlie."

"Ma, that's why they call them 'accidents.'" He knew that reason was not an effective tool in a discussion with his mother.

She fished a pack of Parliaments out of her handbag and pinched one out of the pack. "Maybe I was too hard on Eddie," she admitted even as she eyed the portrait with distrust. Charlie knew that her prejudices, once formed, resisted all evidence. She held the unlit cigarette in one hand and a lighter in the other, thinking.

Will came with her drink which she accepted with a smile. She drank. And then, as if Charlie were not there, and as if Sean Keenan were an old confidant, she said, "I was a crappy mother, Sean."

"Oh boy, here we go," Charlie said.

She continued, "Sometimes I feel bad about it. But I do love him, and I am proud of him, even if he is a jailbird. I think he forgives me. Right, Charlie? You forgive old Gracie, don't you?" The lighter illuminated her face as she dragged the cigarette to life.

Old Gracie. Yes, she was old now. Fading into gray. Eyes, still defiant, sinking in a face now pale and lined, her voice deep and raspy with decades of smoking.

"Sure, Ma. You could have done better, but . . . nobody's perfect."

"Except Eddie. He was perfect, right?"

"Yeah. I guess he was."

"But you forgive me, Charlie, for being such a lousy mother?"

"Yeah. Yeah. I forgive you, Ma."

"As long as he forgives me, Sean." She blew a cloud of smoke toward the freshly painted tin ceiling and tapped the ash into a glass ashtray on the bar. "I'll make it up to him someday," she said.

Sure, Charlie thought. *Someday. Somewhere, over the rainbow.*

Down the bar, he overheard an old gaffer saying to Sophie, "I guess it's like marriage. You have to hope for the best."

"I know your wife, Jerry," Sophie said. "You got the best."

The old man smiled faintly and said, "You women stick together."

Charlie chuckled and said to no one in particular, "I love this city."

Chapter 17

Officer Jake Hutton was now Captain Hutton, and he sat across from Charlie in his office at the Lowell Police Station. The walls were adorned with photos: Hutton surrounded by members of local charities or golf buddies. Smiling broadly as the recipient of a commendation. At the beach with wife and family. He was the largest man in every photo. A gray crewcut and a military bearing.

"A couple of things I wanted to ask,' Charlie began. "First, have you heard anything about my father? Do you know if he's alive or dead?"

"He disappeared. Frankly, if he's alive, he'd better stay disappeared. That was a dumb move, Charlie. But we have no idea, honestly."

"He was never known for thinking things through." A two-way radio on Hutton's desk crackled, and he turned down the volume. Charlie nodded and asked, "So why didn't you shoot me?"

Hutton leaned back in his chair, his blue eyes keen below white brows. "I was stupid, that's why. You were pretty stupid that night, too, as I recall."

"I thought you were one of Malvert's men. I wouldn't have aimed a gun at a cop."

"Well, you had about one more second to drop it. I kind of knew you, and I knew Eddie. I didn't think you were a killer, but I wouldn't have risked it for more than a couple of seconds."

Charlie nodded. "Thanks."

"I had some crazy idea I could bring him in. He said he had cops on his payroll."

Hutton shook his head and laughed softly. "It was the opposite, Charlie. He was picked up on gaming charges for the second time. He was terrified at the thought of serious time. So he gave up information on the mob's horse race-fixing schemes on east coast race tracks, bribing jockeys. It was big. Suffolk Downs, Pocono Downs, Rockingham Park in Salem, New Hampshire, Lincoln Downs in Rhode Island, and the Atlantic City Race Track. Malvert ratted the scheme out to save his own skin, Charlie. Shortly after you went down, Fat Francis Ferrara, Neily Boland and others mobsters found out. After that, he would have had to go into witness protection fast. You did their work for them, Charlie."

"Oh, well. Water under the bridge. A cozy life under a new name is something he didn't deserve, anyway."

Hutton shrugged. "I don't miss him, but it was a high price you paid." He sighed and continued. "Anyway, how you doin'? I know you took over the bar."

"I'm all right. So can you tell me more about Laila Grant's murder?"

"She was your girl, right?"

"We were pretty serious. Planned to marry. I think it was my fault..."

"Listen, Charlie. We both *think* we know who did it. Thinking you know is not the same as proving it in court. Especially with no evidence. If you go try to find this person and beat him to death or throw him out a window, you will die in jail. And it won't bring Laila back." His eyes seemed suddenly to grow tired with experience.

"If you guys would do your job..."

He leaned forward. "We have to do our job within the law. And you need to respect that."

Charlie nodded resignedly. "I understand. You're right. I'm sorry. Can you tell me what happened? I mean, I know she was shot. Were there no witnesses? Nothing?"

"She had started a new job for the Enterprise Bank. Apparently, she stayed late to review some loan applications. Security guard let her out around 8:00. A minute later, he heard three shots in quick succession. He went out. She was down. He drew his weapon but saw no one. Laila died before the ambulance arrived. I suspect the shooter was parked up around Merrimack and took off up the alley by the old city hall."

"You brought Frank in. He had an alibi?"

"Not much of one. He and some other dirtbag were watching a hockey game at his house. We got a search warrant based on the restraining order. No gun. No clothes with residue. No witnesses. Nothing."

"What was the name of the guy who alibied him?"

"I'm not gonna tell you that, Charlie. The Laila Grant case is open. New evidence may come up. It happens. Someone may rat on Frank Sago, assuming he is the culprit, or we may get him for something else."

"Or he may never pay . . ."

"That's possible. But you need to stay out of this. You really need to stay out of it, for your own good. Dead or back in jail. Those are the consequences for you. You paid your debt. The past is the past. Move on, Charlie."

"Did she say anything before she died?"

"Unconscious when the guard arrived, then . . . she passed."

They shook hands and Charlie took his leave. When he was alone, Captain Hutton sat back down at his desk and said to himself: *I couldn't tell him that before she died, she said his name. I'm afraid this is going to be a problem.*

Grace parked her rusting Olds on Market Street. Walking toward the bar, she was surprised to see an ambulance pulling away. She tried to hurry but lost her breath and had to slow down. A cop was leaving as she arrived. "What's up, Officer? I work here."

"Guy had a heart attack at the bar. He died."

"Shit. Ya never know, right?"

"Ya never know," the cop confirmed.

But Grace knew. The letter from Doctor Bleckman at Lowell General ran in her head like background music she couldn't shut off. *Radiology confirmed and all that crap. Whatever. No one gets out alive. Maybe there's a place that's better than this. Getting hard to breathe right, but I can still work. For a while.*

Inside, a few early customers were milling about, rehashing the sad details. Willie, 'the red-haired boy,' as Grace called him in her mind, came over. "When is Charlie coming?" he wanted to know.

"He said he was getting some supplies at United. He'll be here later. Why?"

"Well, I was gonna tell him something."

"Out with it, Willie."

The young man stepped closer. "The dead guy. His name is . . . was, George. George Lee. He comes in every day. Charlie said he was a regular when Eddie ran it. And he came back and sat on that stool every day since the bar reopened. He drank a lot. Smoked a lot, too."

"So, he had it comin' is that what you're saying? Jesus, you look like you're scared. What's goin' on?"

"It's just that, he just fell off his stool. Boom. And he was dead . . ."

"A good death. So what?"

"There's this guy . . ."

Grace rolled her eyes. "Another guy . . ."

"His name is Barnette. Wayne Barnette. I heard him say he lives above Forza Pizza. Thinks he's a gangsta . . ."

"What about him? I'm getting old, Willie."

"Well, when George, when he . . ."

"Boom. Hit the floor . . ."

"Yeah, when he hit the floor, Barnette was sitting there, and he jumped up and I saw—he was leaning over him acting like he was checking on him, and he pulled his ring off his finger."

"He stole the dead guy's fuckin' ring?"

"Yeah. That's right."

"Did you tell him to put it back?"

"I didn't tell him anything. He's not that tough, but he's tougher than me, even if he's on drugs. But Grace, that ring should go to George's family, right?"

"Of course! Asshole."

"So, I was gonna tell Charlie. He'd be scared shitless of Charlie."

"Charlie don't need that shit. I'll go get the ring back."

She left Willie stammering his *buts* and *whatifs* and went back to her car. A minute later she was at Forza Pizza. There was a stairway on the side of the building and two mailboxes. She read W. Barnette on one. Latin music filtered through the graffiti-tagged door of the first-floor apartment. She headed up the stairs to the second floor but had to stop on the landing, wheezing for breath. Finally, she pushed herself on, thinking, *Grace, come on. You can take care of this crap for Charlie. Show him he can count on you for somethin'.*

She smelled weed and could hear someone moving inside. She took a minute to collect her breath; then she knocked on the door and said, "Barnette. Open up. It's Charlie Tumulty's mother." She could hear steps approaching the peephole.

"Whaddaya want?"

"Open the fuckin' door. Whaddaya think I'm gonna beat you up? I hardly made it up the goddamn stairs."

After a brief silence, he opened the door. Scraggly beard, unkempt hair, too thin, eyes like a hunted animal. Just about what Grace would have expected from a guy who would steal from a dead man. "You took George's ring. Give it back."

He swallowed. His eyes widened as his slow brain tried to conjure an alibi. All he came up with was, "What?"

"I come here to get the ring back to give to the guy's family 'cause if I don't get it, Charlie will come over here and . . . well, you don't want to see Charlie here."

His dull eyes flickered as he imagined the scene and a mournful expression came over him. He tugged his stained tee shirt downward like a child and said, "I don't got it. I traded it for some weed."

She saw that he was about to cry. "Asshole. Who did you give it to?"

"A guy hangs at the Highland Tap. They call him Skid. Skid the Kid."

"What did the ring look like?"

"It was gold. Heavy. US Army with a red stone."

"A dead veteran. You stole the ring off the corpse of a dead veteran? You really are a piece of work. I hope Charlie kicks your ass." As she turned to leave, Barnette said, "But wait! Tell Charlie I can help him, 'slong as he don't mention my name."

"How the hell can a loser scumbag thief help my son?" She felt a sudden pride, and beyond that, love, when she said the words *my son*.

"I can help him because everybody knows he's after Frank Sago."

She searched his eyes for an instant, then said, "And you don't like him, right?"

"He ripped me off for a half ounce of hash."

"So you want Charlie to settle your score. But you'll testify against him in a heartbeat."

"I ain't sayin' nothin to the cops."

"Sure."

"I'm sorry I took the guy's ring. Tell Charlie I'm really sorry."

"Where's Frank Sago?"

"There's a girl, she's a stripper at the Three Copper Men. She goes by the name of Destiny. I've known her a long time. Frank's been doin' her. She goes up to his house in Rye. He's right on Route 1A across the street from the ocean. It's cheap to rent up there in the winter. Anyway, he got scratch. He's movin' coke from Boston up to Maine."

"Did he kill Charlie's girl?"

"You can never say you heard it from me."

"A fuckin birdie tol' me. A woodpecka! Spit it out."

"Not personally. Destiny tol' me he paid this guy, Scully. He'd kill you for a few hundred and then go get a Big Mac. Scully is a fuckin' scary. He's ... what do they call 'em? A psychopath. Was a psychopath. He's dead, I hear. Charlie stole Frank's wife and then he killed his uncle, right? A'course Sago wanted to hurt him."

"An' he did."

Barnette looked at her expectantly, waiting for absolution for the theft of the dead man's ring. "Are we cool?" he asked. Grace was not ready to give absolution, yet. She wore a hard mask, blue eyes set in a pale expressionless face. "What house on Route 1A?"

Charlie had stopped at Fitzgibbons' old shop with a couple of coffees and a small cake from Olympos Bakery. "Happy Birthday, Fitzy!" he called as he pushed the door open with his shoulder. The notes of a classical-guitar piece wound their way through the clouds of smoke that rose from the seated figure of the old man.

"Come in, Charlie. Come in. Yeah, seventy-eight. I'm pretty sure that's old. I know that's old. I think it's time to quit working."

"You call this work?" Charlie pulled a chair up beside the desk.

"A wise guy. A *real* wise guy, eh? Well, it ain't digging ditches, that's true. Mainly puttering around, reading old poets, talking to people, making deals. I just picked up an original WWI US 6th Division Ammunition Train uniform with ID Tag, one Harold Nice. And a beautiful US Army World War I, 58th Regiment, 4th Infantry Machine Gunner uniform. No rips, holes or stains. Nobody died in that uniform."

"Cool stuff." Charlie eased the cake out of its bakery box, and from a Market Basket bag produced paper plates and plastic knives and forks. "I don't have seventy-eight candles. I got ten. You'll have to imagine the other sixty-eight you've lived."

"Oh, I do, Charlie. I do." Fitzgibbons squashed his cigarette into a bent tin ashtray. "I think I'd better give up the smokes, or I'll sure as shit never see another sixty-eight, right?"

Charlie laughed. "Probably not."

"Well, as the Bard said, 'To love that well which thou must leave 'ere long.'"

"The Bard said it all."

The old man blew out the candles in two breaths. They ate the cake and when the record ended, Fitzgibbons got up and put on another record. "There you go. Ella Fitzgerald. *Things Ain't What They Used to Be*. And that's a fact, my friend." He stooped before the bookcase by his desk and pulled out a blue volume.

"Remember this, Charlie?" He opened the book to a page marked with a pressed flower. "I read this to you and Foxy a long time ago.

> *Such clouds of nameless trouble cross*
> *All night below the darken'd eyes;*
> *With morning wakes the will, and cries,*
> *'Thou shalt not be the fool of loss'."*

He closed the book and set it down. "In life, loss is just guaranteed. Justice is not. Don't be the fool of loss, Charlie."

The younger man was quiet for a moment as the words sunk in. They meant so much more now than they had when he was a boy. "If her loss had been due to illness, a car accident, some natural cause, I could grieve and accept it as fate and move on. But I got her killed, Fitzy. She's dead because of what I did."

"You don't know that, and nothing you do can help her."

"Nothing anyone can do ever helps. The guys who wore your old uniforms in the World War . . . they died in the hundreds of thousands . . ."

"Yes. Millions."

"For what?"

Fitzgibbons sighed. "They called it duty. Useless carnage. An unnecessary war. And for you to try to go after this guy, it's useless, too. What would it accomplish? What good can it do for Laila? Or is it just for you?"

"Maybe it would be for me." He shook his head. "I just don't know. But isn't there such a thing as keeping faith with the dead? Do you think if I knew that someone killed you, and got away with it, that they would not have to face me?"

The old man nodded in understanding. "All I can say is, it's damned good to have you popping into the shop again, Charlie. I really hated visiting you in jail. Think hard. Don't do anything stupid."

"Well, you just said I was a *wise* guy."

The old man scoffed at that and said, "I'm reminded of John Donne: '*Who are a little wise? The best fools be.*'"

Anton's Cleaners, Molloy's Bar, George the Tailor, the City Barns. Not much had changed on Broadway, it seemed to Charlie. But he had changed. The dreams of youth. *Charlie Tumulty, the Olympian.* Those days were gone and would never come again. Mike Dineen had retired. When Charlie visited him, poor Mike told him the same story three times. He was losing it a little. He parked along the canal across the street and popped the trunk. Willie met him at the door, looking nervous. He told Charlie the story. "Shit. I have to go. Sophie is getting ready to move. Can you hold down the fort or do you want me to close the bar?"

"I can stay. Sorry, Charlie. She asked me . . ."

"That's all right. I know my mother. She does what she's gonna do."

He told Wille had to get his wallet, and went to the back office where he had stashed Eddie's pistol in the desk drawer. There was a dusty box of ammunition beside it. He put both in his jacket and headed out.

Barnette had decided not to open the door. Better to pretend he was not home. However, one well-placed kick and it flew open, nearly breaking the nose of the cowering man on the other side. With one hand cupped over his face, he told Charlie of Grace's visit.

"You gave my mother the address?"

"To give to you," Barnette said. "I know I fucked up with the ring."

"Forget the ring for now. Would you testify in court to what you told my mother?"

"No way, Charlie. You can beat the hell out of me if you want but I . . . I can't do that. I won't. You know I only . . ."

"Shut up, Barnette. You're useless. What's the address? Quickly."

Charlie pulled into Wally Drew's gas station, and while the tank filled, he heard Sago's voice in his head, "You're a fuckin' loser, Tumulty." He saw his arrogant figure the day that he had beaten Laila. He recalled the song and said aloud, "The time has come today, Frank." Too bad Grace had decided to muck things up. Her visit would be a warning. He would be armed and ready. Just let me get him, God, before he gets me. Wally came up, and Charlie handed him ten dollars and set off.

What would Grace do? Tell him we had a witness who would testify? Get herself killed? His hand slipped inside the jacket. Just please don't get in my way, Grace. He gripped the smooth walnut handle of the revolver. Old police issue, Eddie had said.

Laila was beside him, her body lambent now, being pure soul. Ghostly messenger. She watched him with mournful eyes. *Existing in memory and . . . anywhere else? What had she said? "Sometimes I believe in heaven." Sometimes. How can such a vital presence cease to exist? You're here, and then you're not. Fitzgibbons had said it. The world begins when you are born and it ends when you die.*

Yet he felt her with him now, somehow, and she spoke: *"Don't do it, Charlie."*

"In cold blood, he had you murdered, my poor Laila." He said the words aloud.

"Don't do it."

That's what she would say. She would never appear in a scarlet robe crying, "How soon will you avenge me?"

No, she would not understand. But how can I live my life content while this bloody bastard can sell his drugs and fuck his prostitutes and breathe the sea air? The cops can't do anything, they say. Maybe they won't be able to do anything after I kill him. No, Wayne Barnette would talk. I'd be the prime suspect. If I do it, I do it knowing the consequences. Farewell freedom, but farewell too, to the self-accusations that twist my heart through wakeful nights while Frank Sago enjoys his life after taking hers. Countless men have died for their convictions, for doing what they felt was right. Am I so much more of a coward? But maybe death is easier than life in a cage. Oh, but won't I sleep better, even in a cell, with that bastard dead.

Or I can disappear. Try a life like that hobo on the tracks long ago. Riding the rails and eating a can of beans on a dismal riverbank, a shadow in the railway yard, odd jobs for ready cash and no name.

His thoughts turned back to his mother. *What would she say, and how would Frank react? Would he attack her or just throw her out and prepare for Charlie's arrival? Call his friends? Would he ever kill her? He couldn't be that stupid. Jake Hutton said the cops were keeping an eye on him. But how could he be moving drugs if the cops really had an eye on him?*

He drove north along Route 1A, Ocean Boulevard. On his right, beyond a stone wall, endless blue. He spotted the house on a corner and took a left. The adrenalin began to kick in as soon as he saw his mother's car parked a little way down the street and a Toyota truck and a Harley in the unpaved lot behind the house. He pulled in beside her car and checked the gun. A big old Colt .38. He loaded six rounds into the cylinder and crept up the back steps. *The time has come today.*

The inner door was open. A simple screen door separated him from the interior and through it, he smelled something acrid. He heard no voices. He pulled the handle and the door opened quietly. He stepped into the kitchen and moved toward the adjoining room, heart pounding, gun raised.

He lowered it when he saw his mother sitting calmly on the couch thumbing through a magazine. There was a man lying on a blood-stained rug a few feet in front of her.

"Jesus, I thought you'd never get here," she said. "Bet you're glad now I never gave your father back his gun."

Charlie was speechless for a moment, and his mother continued. "So listen, I killed the two pieces of shit. That one is Frank Sago. I shot him dead no questions, and the other guy, the blond ugly one, he ran into the other room tryna get a pistol out of a drawer but I shot him before he could turn on me with it."

"You killed them both?"

"Sure. The other one's in there," she said, waving toward the next room. "After I shot him, he says, 'You crazy bitch!' I had to laugh. I said, 'You got that right you son of a bitch. You think you're the only ones who can shoot people? It's easy, believe me.' And I put him out of his fuckin' misery."

"How did you . . . why . . ."

"Why? You're not goin' to jail, Charlie, see? I'm goin' to jail. I told you I'd make up for it, didn't I? I told you I'd make up for bein' such a shit mother, an' I sure as hell did, didn't I? I'd kill twenty of these bums to keep you free. You already paid!"

He was stunned into silence as he took in the scene. He walked into the other room and returned with a look of disbelief. "Are . . . are you hurt?"

"No. But it wouldn't matter if I was. I got what they call the small-cell lung cancer, so I'll be checkin' out soon enough. You were right about the cigarettes. You were right about everything. But I finally did one good thing anyway, 'cause I do love you, Charlie. So I'm gonna call the cops. After you leave."

"I'll wait here with you."

Her eyes narrowed. "Are you gonna screw this whole plan up? The only thing that makes this good for me is that you're out of it, Charlie. I gotta die pretty soon, and I can die happy because I can say to myself, 'You dumb bitch, you screwed up everything in your life, but in the end you saved your boy.' You came in here with a gun! You know damn well you were gonna kill Sago. You're my boy. You're a Hurley! You don't let no murdering sons of a bitches just kill the people you love and go merrily on their way. No, no, no. It don't work that way. So, I did it for you. Death is comin' for me, but, goddammit, Grace came for them first. And I did it 'cause Laila *was* special, Charlie. There."

He looked around the room desperately. "Listen, Jack's old gun can't be registered. Maybe I can put it in Sago's hand and arrange it so it looks like they shot each other."

She laughed. "The cops ain't that dumb even up here in Cow Hampshire. You'd be the number one suspect." Her smile faded and she gripped his arm. "I already worked it out. Don't take this away from me, Charlie. Go. Go!"

He was in tears. "Jesus, Ma." As they embraced, Charlie saw that the eyes of the dead man who had been Frank Sago were open. An expression of shock lingered on his frozen features, shock that this haggard Fury had come to claim his life.

"You love me after all, right?" she asked.

"I always loved you."

"An' you forgive me, right? You gotta forgive me now."

"I never blamed you. You had it rough."

"And you forgive me."

"Yes, yes. I forgive you."

"Like you said, I coulda done better, no doubt. Now, go." She took the phone from the end table and put it on her lap. "I'll wait a bit before I call. If you touched that door handle on the way in, wipe it off. Oh, and Barnett passed the dead guy's ring to some bum named Skid hangs out at the Highland Tap. Now go, goddammit!"

"I love you, Ma."

"I love you, an' I'm proud of you, Charlie."

He stuck the gun in his waistband, wiped the door handle and left the house. He drove south and pulled into the Rye Harbor parking lot. The sea air was a tonic that began to clear his muddled head; he watched the fishermen in orange oilskins hauling boxes of fish up on a chain link pulley that hung from the pier above. In an irony that seemed to be devised for him, he saw that the name painted across the stern was "Parental Guidance." One of the men, with a great red beard and a knit cap that barely contained a wild mop of hair, clearly the entertainer of the crew, was singing "Young Girls Wanna Have Fun" with gusto as they slid the boxes across the deck and hooked them to the pulley chain. The others were laughing and shaking their heads.

This was life. The life of free-working men earning their living. It struck Charlie as something beautiful, and his heart ached at how close he had come to proving Hardie Bangs right by losing it all, and for Grace, who had lost what little of the world was left to her. Another irony, one that was both inexplicable and yet somehow logical, was that his mother was dying and facing prison, and he had never seen her so happy. Near the end, she had found a path to redemption. Her life had meaning because she had done what the best mothers do: she had sacrificed all for her son.

Charlie traced the curving stony shore to the jetty, a breakwater reaching an arm of granite blocks into the sea. Leaning into the chill Atlantic wind, he made his way to the end, where he flung the gun as far as he could into the gray water. He wanted no more of guns.

He heard sirens, and turning, saw three cruisers with blue lights flashing roaring up the coast road. He said a quiet prayer for Grace Tumulty.

Chapter 18

As soon as he arrived back in Lowell, Charlie drove to the Highland Tap.

Don, the bartender, saw him enter and called out, "Hey, cuz!" He was not Charlie's cousin; he called everyone 'cuz.' When Charlie asked him if he knew someone named Skid, he nodded discreetly toward a heavy guy in a leather coat holding a cue stick near the bumper pool table.

"Is he a fence?" Charlie asked quietly.

Don said nothing, but his eyelids lowered slowly for an instant. *Yes.* Never talk when you can nod. Never nod when you can wink, and so on.

Charlie approached the man as he leaned over the table for a shot. "Hey! Shit-for-brains." The guy in the leather coat looked up. His back straightened and his eyes got wide and round and Charlie could tell that he knew who he was.

"I need the ring you got from Wayne Barnett. He stole it from a dead man."

"Jesus, Charlie. I din' know that. Yeah, that ain't right."
"No, it ain't right."
"Thank God, I still got it."
"Thank God."

That night, near closing time, Charlie put on his jacket and ambled out of the piano bar, strolling along Market Street to the canal where he leaned on the railing and looked down at the dark water running between granite block walls. Irish immigrants had dug these canals in the 19th century to let the river's water flow through the raceways of countless mills and turn the belts of the clattering looms that made the city a textile center of the young country. There are people who build and people who can only tear down. And there are people who turn out all right. He recalled *The Great Gatsby*. Fitzgerald had written something like, "Gatsby was all right in the end." Yeah, and if he ever wrote the book that Miss Walker suggested he might write one day, he could say the same about his mother, "Grace was all right in the end." He would visit her the next day and that would be hard.

He heard voices in the direction from which he had come, and soon a young woman in a white denim jacket came up and leaned on the railing beside him. "What are you doin' Charlie?"

It was Alice Winter, a nice girl, a blonde who sometimes stopped in with college friends to share a pitcher or two of beer. They liked to sit at a table in the back and play *Trivial Pursuits*. "Don't jump!" she joked, grabbing his arm.

He smiled. "I'm just thinking."

"About the canal?"

He nodded, "About the canal . . . and other things. Been a long day."

She edged closer to him and asked, "Do you have a girl, Charlie?"

"I don't. Not anymore."

"Can I ask what kind of girl are you lookin' for?"

"I haven't really been looking." He shook his head, "My brain . . . God, it's been a crazy life so far." The streetlight caught her face as he turned toward her, and he was struck by her youth. "How old are you, Alice?"

She squinted apologetically. "Honestly? Nineteen."

"Drinking age is up to twenty now. Pretty soon it will go up again to twenty-one. Didn't I card you when you first came in?"

"I'm sorry. It was my sister's ID. Oops."

"You're gonna have to wait, Alice."

"I'm old enough for everything else, Charlie. You know."

"That's honestly very sweet and a very tempting suggestion. Not tonight, Alice. I'm just . . ."

"I understand. Long day."

"You have no idea, really." He walked her to her car and gave her a good night kiss on the cheek. "Come in with your real ID on your birthday. A free pitcher." He went back to the bar and helped Willie close up. After the young man left and he had locked the door, he poured himself a beer and sat at the empty bar for several minutes. *What kind of a girl are you looking for? You can't forever look for Laila at the mid-hour of night. Laila is gone and will never come again. Her killers are dead. I loved her, but she is no more. Can I keep going on alone? No, I can't. I can't. What kind of girl are you looking for? Are you looking, or have you found her?*

He sat in silence for a moment, like a man listening for a sound in another room. Then, he went behind the bar and lifted the receiver. *Are you sure? Yes. Yes, I'm sure.* He dialed a number and waited as with each ring the beat of his heart seemed to rise toward his throat and resound in his head.

"Hello?" A familiar voice, warm and low, not just from sleepiness; it was the undistracted calm that was the hallmark of her nature.

"Sophie? Listen, I'm sorry, I know it's late. But this is serious and I am . . . serious. As serious as I've ever been. Okay, see, I just realized, because I'm kind of slow, and I've been more than a little mixed up. But I do love you. I mean, listen Sophie, I want to marry you."

"Jesus, Charlie. Wait a minute. Let me get this guy out of here."

"Christ, I'm sorry, Sophie. You have every right . . ."

He heard that laugh of hers that suddenly was so dear to him. "I'm only kidding, but you're lucky. I never thought you would come around."

"I've been in kind of a daze. And I never imagined proposing over a telephone. It's really dumb, but will you marry me, Sophie? You can't see me, but I'm getting down on one knee, here." He took a knee beside the bar stool.

"Charlie, I've loved you for a long time. Yes, of course, I want to marry you. But my mother is expecting me to move up there to help her soon. I've promised her."

"We'll figure it out, I swear. I'll go with you. We have a lot to talk about. But I'm not giving you up to the anesthesiologist or to anyone else. So, is that a yes? Are we engaged?"

"Oh, my God. Sure, yes, but I'll need a ring. Doesn't have to be an expensive one, but a woman likes an engagement ring."

He rose, still trying to believe what had just happened, and wondering why he had not done it sooner. "We'll go together Saturday."

"You're not drunk or anything . . ."

"Have you ever seen me drunk? Sober as a judge. Sometimes you make a decision and then you immediately question it. But now that we're engaged, I feel really good. Like I've just come out of a bad dream. You're—I don't know how to say it, Sophie—you are what the old poets used to call, *constant*. You're solid. Not changeable. You're an anchor in the storm. I haven't let myself feel anything 'cause I thought I was going to meet Frank Sago and end up dead or back in jail. But that's over now. He's dead."

There was silence on the line. Then she asked, "Did you kill him, Charlie?"

"I wouldn't be asking you to marry me if I had. How could I? A lot of shit went down today."

"I heard a few things . . ."

"Grace killed him. You may hear it on the news. I'll tell you the whole story tomorrow, that is, like Paul Harvey says, *the rest of the story*. I'll tell you, but no one else. First, I have to find out if my mother is in the Portsmouth City Jail or if they're moving her to Rockingham County."

"Oh, poor Grace. She did it for you, Charlie. I'm sure."

"Yes, she did. To save me from going back. And the strange thing is, she's happier than I think I've ever seen her, facing prison and lung cancer."

"Oh, the poor doll. That's a mother's love."

"I believe it is, though I always doubted it. Anyway, I want to be with you, Sophie. I want to marry you."

"Charlie, come over. We can't say goodnight over the telephone, now. Stay with me tonight."

"I'm on my way. Just get rid of that other guy."

"There is no other guy. There never will be."

He turned off the lights and locked up, considering how one day can change everything. *Everything.*

The Piano Bar was for sale; he had helped Sophie move to Jonesport. A single U-Haul truck was all she needed, which he drove back to Lowell. He would join her as soon as he settled his affairs for the move. Grace had been held without bail at the Hillsborough County House of Corrections in Goffstown, New Hampshire. Due to the cramped and overcrowded conditions there, and her medical condition, she was transferred out of state to the Correctional Center in Windham, Maine, but before long she was transferred again, to the Maine Medical Center in Portland.

Charlie found a priest with her when he visited, and he was glad that she seemed to have taken some comfort from that visit. "It's hard, Charlie," she said. "Only to get harder before it ends." He put the flowers he had brought on a table near her bed and kissed her. "I love you, Grace."

It ended soon enough. He wondered if Jack would somehow manage to show up for the funeral or if he even knew. It was a small gathering: a few waitresses from the Pineview; Penny, her old drinking companion, whose mascara ran over her pallid cheeks as she sobbed, and of course, Charlie and Sophie.

On a gray Sunday in late March, Charlie visited St. Patrick's Cemetery, where Laila Grant was buried beside her mother. He was there to say goodbye and to tell her, as the poem said, that their love would be remembered. In the distance, a man pulled up on a motorcycle. He took off his helmet and walked to a grave where he stood, praying or thinking or speaking to another ghost in this city of the dead. Charlie stood at the grave for a while. From his pocket, he drew the stone he had picked up in the Groton woods and laid it on the headstone. A car pulled up behind his own, and he saw Joe Grant get out and walk toward him.

"Hello, Charlie. Sorry to hear about your mother."

"Hi, Joe. Thank you."

"Did we ever think, the last time we met, that we'd meet again in such a place?"

"No. Never."

The older man blessed himself and Charlie waited quietly while he prayed. Then he said, "Do you blame me, Joe? I often blame myself."

"You? No. We know where the guilt belongs. That son of a bitch would probably have gotten to her anyway, just because she left him. I blame myself."

"Why?"

"You remember I said I thought of shooting him, but I didn't want Laila visiting me in jail? I would happily have had Laila visiting me in jail rather than to be visiting her here. No, your mother had the right idea. I should have done it. I know some people will say it's not right, but here's the alternative." He held a hand out over the grave. "I won't shed a tear when cold killers get what they deserve. I've seen too many men die who never deserved it to worry about the fate of a bloody-minded man like Sago."

The sky had grown darker and a blustery wind rocked the boughs of the cemetery pines while a few crows descended through the still bare branches of the oaks, fitting inhabitants of this barren yard. "Strange," the old soldier said, "we got medals for killing the enemies of our country. And they put you, and then your mother, in jail for killing the enemies of all of us."

"I know. They'd say we can't have the wild west, though."

"I suppose. The killing has to be approved by the state. But you and I know we're better off without them. Well, Charlie, I hope you find someone else. It's not good to be alone. I know you'll never forget Laila."

"No. I never could. I'm moving up to Maine. What will you do?"

"I'll just go on. The living have to live all the appointed days. Yes, like the 'Book of Job' says, 'All the days of my appointed time will I wait, till my change come.'"

Charlie remembered that Laila had been able to recite the books of the Bible, and he guessed that book had seen this man through some difficult days. "I'll be going to a reunion of the 88th in Washington, D.C.," he continued. "Not as many as there used to be, but as Major General John Sloan once said: 'The glory of the colors will never be sullied, as long as one man of the 88th still lives.'"

The men embraced and Charlie said, "In my book, Joe, your colors will never be sullied."

A soft rain began to fall on St. Patrick's. It hurt both men to leave all that remained of Laila Grant in that place, but as Charlie drove the long darkening road between the name-graven headstones, he recalled Joe Grant's words: the living must live all the appointed days.

Dave McLaughlin, the lawyer who had visited Charlie in jail and who had done a good job for him in working with Brian McNamara to rehab the bar, was now acting as his lawyer in its sale, along with Paul Broulette, a real estate agent against whom Charlie occasionally played a losing game of pool at the Club Lafayette. On Monday morning, Charlie met with the two men at Tatsios's Diner. Broulette was expecting an offer on the property later that day or the next day. "Buyer wants to know if the piano comes with the property."

Charlie smiled, "Yeah, he can have the piano."

He returned to the bar, and after calling Sophie, prepared for what he hoped would be his last week in the business. Red, the wanderer of the streets, sometimes stopped in early, and Charlie had gotten him some clothes from Goodwill, and a coat from Birke's on Market Street. When he stopped in, Charlie gave him a coffee with a shot of Jameson and told him to go upstairs and take a shower. "There's a bit of a cloud around you, Red. And there's a bag of clothes and a coat hanging outside the bathroom."

"That's real good of you, Charlie."

"A parting gesture."

"Maine. They got a lot of lobsters up there."

"They sure do."

As he was heading upstairs, a thin man with a haggard face came in and asked apologetically if he could speak to Charlie Tumulty.

"I'm Charlie."

"Jack's son?"

"None other."

He nodded. "Listen," he said, "first let me hit the head. I been drivin' for a while." When he returned, he pulled himself onto the stool and said, "I'll have a draft."

Charlie pulled the long handle and poured a draft beer while the man looked about. "Nice place," he concluded. Charlie placed the beer in front of him, not without foreboding. The man took a long drink and wiped his mouth on his coat sleeve. "My name is Frank Wolfenden. I was in the 82nd Airborne with your father. So, when he got in trouble, he came to stay with me. I have an extra room."

"Where?"

"Up in Lebanon, New Hampshire. I'm afraid I got bad news, Charlie."

"Cut to the chase, Frank. Is he dead?"

A long sigh escaped the old man. "I'm afraid he is."

My parents are dead, Charlie thought. "What happened?" he asked.

"Well, Jack got a job. He was supposed to put a new roof on a rectory a few towns over, point the chimney, new copper in the valleys. Talked to the monsignor and convinced him he had a crack crew and they could do the job quickly. Start that day. He set up some ladders and asked for a check to go buy the supplies. It was a big check. He left the ladders up and cashed the check and never returned."

"That sounds like him," Charlie said, resignedly.

"Well, long story short, they caught up with him. He was in the county jail for a while, had to give back the money to the priest. The problem is, when his name got out on the police log, the guy he ripped off in Boston, something Boland, sent some guys up there. They tracked him down. Found his truck at a bar. He saw them and went out the back door. Now that bar, the Old Brick House, is on the Connecticut River. Jack jumped in. It was February, Charlie. I don't know if he was going to try to swim across or float for a while down the river, but they found his body two weeks later.

"He asked me once, if anything happened to him, if I would come down here and give you a message. I asked him to write it out, just in case, but he said he wasn't much of a writer. Anyway, I wrote it all down, what he said, so I'd remember it."

He pulled a piece of paper out of his shirt pocket. "Sorry I was such a disappointment as a father. You and your mother deserved better. I can't say I'd do it differently if I could do it again, 'cause I am what I am. I can't understand how Grace and I produced you. You're somethin', Charlie. I know you'll be out of jail soon an' I'm real glad. Be smart. Stay out of jail. You'll be all right. I love you kid even though I never showed it."

Charlie shook his head. "Thanks for coming down, Frank. I appreciate it. So ends a wild life."

"He was wild, all right. Couldn't accept any rules . . ."

"Oh, believe me, I know."

"There's one other thing." From the inside pocket of his jacket, he pulled a thick envelope. "When I cleaned up his room, I found this. He already paid back the church.

I think from what he said, this must be from another scam he pulled off in Boston. So, you're his son. This is yours."

Charlie peeked into the envelope. A thick wad of hundreds. "How much?"

"I don't know. Must be thousands. I didn't count it. The thing is that Jack, crazy as he was, he was my brother back in the day. We didn't think we were coming back. So, I gotta do right by him, come what may."

"All the way."

"That's right, Charlie. All the way."

Chapter 19

Charlie accepted the offer on the bar and the building, and the closing was set for the end of the week. Tuesday found him driving down Route 93 South. In less than an hour, he saw the sign, "Welcome to South Boston, Mayor Kevin H. White." He pulled up near a bar called Brooksie's and went in. The windows in the front were small, and inside, the bar was dark and made darker by the mahogany-colored tables and chairs. There were a few scattered tables at which men sat idly drinking. They all watched Charlie walk up to the bar. He ordered a beer and said quietly to the oversized bartender, "Would it be possible to see Neily Boland?"

The bartender leaned two meaty hands on his side of the bar. "And who the fuck are you?"

"I'm a guy from Lowell. I think he'll want to hear what I have to say."

"Really." He called out, "Denny!" beckoning one of the crowd of guys who were sitting at a table filling in Keno cards or watching the numbers that were displayed on a TV at the back. A guy got up and came toward Charlie. He was tall, slim, crew cut, wearing a Boston Celtics muscle shirt while everyone else in the bar had a sweater or jacket on. "Wants to see Neily," the bartender said.

Denny came up and kept coming. Charlie stood slowly, pushing his beer away. His nose was about an inch away from Charlie's, and Denny looked at him as if he smelled like Red McNulty on a hot summer day. Charlie took a step backward, fearing a head butt in the face.

"Says he has something to tell Neily," the bartender explained.

"Did he request an appointment?" Denny said in his face.

"Sorry, no." Charlie said. "Look, I'm not here to cause any trouble. I wouldn't do that in Neily's bar."

"I'll give you some fuckin' trouble." Denny shoved him against the bar and said, "You walk in off the street and say you wanna see Neily? Get the fuck out of here unless you wanna leave in an ambulance."

"Listen, I think Neily would wanna hear . . ."

He caught the sudden tension and the slight movement of Denny's right shoulder he had been expecting. He ducked and hit him with a right in the ribs, then moving left nailed him with a hard left. No further punches were necessary. Denny was on the floor. But two other guys were now moving toward him, and one charged. Charlie threw his beer in the guy's face, dropped the glass and nailed him with a right that sent him sprawling.

Three guys came running out of the back. Charlie was about to make a run for the door when one of them, Charlie's age, wearing glasses and a Fu Manchu moustache, shouted, "What the fuck is going on here?" Everyone in the bar stopped short, freezing in deference to the guy who must have been Neily Boland, and who now spoke to Charlie. "You come into my place causing trouble?"

"I was only asking to see you because I know you would want to hear what I have to say."

Neily looked at the bartender. "Gus?"

He nodded and admitted, "That is what he said, Neily."

"Then who started this shit?" The bartender looked at Denny, who was rising on wobbly legs while his friend stood rubbing his jaw. Neily shook his head and said, "I'll talk to *you* later . . . when you *recover*." He turned to the large man beside him and said, "George, pat this guy down and bring him in. We'll hear what he has to say." He glared around the bar and said, "In the future, *fuck-ups*, you let me know when someone wants to talk to me, and I'll decide if I see him or not."

He headed back to his office. George, a seemingly affable oaf, patted him down. He reached inside Charlie's coat and pulled out the thick envelope, then pointed toward the door.

Neily Boland sat at a table with a tall brunette in an Irish-knit sweater. George slapped the envelope down in front of his boss. Two other guys sat on a worn couch watching a small TV, on which horses were running at Suffolk Downs. Neily invited Charlie to take a seat at the table. He picked up the envelope and opened it, flicking the thick wad of cash with his thumb. His eyebrows rose. "Hmm," he said. "So, who are you? And what the fuck is this?"

"Okay, don't whack me, but I'm Charlie Tumulty."

"Tumulty. The boxer. You're the one killed the Beak. Did a good stretch for it."

"Malvert had it comin'," the brunette said.

"Don't get me goin'!" Neily said. "The receipts were always down. Son of a bitch would make a huge score and according to him he couldn't buy you a cup of coffee. I shoulda known, 'cause then we find out . . . well, never mind. You did us all a favor there, kid. Everything is smoother with the new crew. However, your father is or rather was not a well-liked figure among the locals."

The woman's snicker suggested that was an understatement.

"Right. My father was kind of an asshole. You won't get any argument from me, or anyone who knew him on that score. He's dead, as you know, and I won't say he didn't have it comin', too. He was living with an old Army buddy. I didn't know where he was. I was in jail when he pulled this shit and he never contacted me afterward. The guy, his Army buddy, found that cash in his room after he drowned.

He brought it down to me. I think it's yours in that he robbed your game. I'm bringing it back. End of story."

"How much is there?"

"The guy who found it didn't count it. He just gave it to me. I didn't count it. I'm giving it to you. Whatever it is, I don't want it."

Neily tossed the envelope to one of the men on the couch and said, "Count that, Jimmy."

"What *do* you want?"

"Don't tell me," the brunette said. "Now that ya shown us what a loyal, respectful guy you are, you want in on the Lowell area game. You wanna take action in your bar and you want Neily's protection, and then in five years we find out you're a rat. This is part one of infiltrating the organization, because . . ."

"No, really . . ."

"Don't interrupt my sister, Charlie, please."

"Sorry."

"Because nobody falls into a monster wad of cash and just turns it over out of the kindness of his heart."

Neily nodded at the woman, showing respect for her good sense. He turned to Charlie and said, "You may respond."

"Okay, maybe I'm stupid. I don't want to take action in my bar. I just sold my bar. I don't want to set myself up 'in the life,' as they say. I don't want anything from you. My father robbed you. I'm giving back what he had left. Nothing my father ever did turned out to be a good thing for me or my mother. I have his name, and I don't want to inherit anything else from him. *Nothing.* I guess the war messed him all up, and that's a damned shame, but he was no kind of husband and no kind of father, and really no kind of person I could respect. He was ripping off a church before he died, for God's sake. Any money I got from him that he stole from you or anyone—I need to set that right because I'm starting fresh, getting married to a good woman. I'm leaving Lowell. I just don't want to carry any of the *shit* of what remains of Jack Tumulty's fucked-up life with me. No good would ever come of it. So, it was your game. I came here to return the money to you, and I'm on my way."

"There's forty-eight hundred here, Neily," Jimmy said.

Neily whistled and stroked his moustache. His sister continued to watch Charlie silently. Neily lit a cigarette, still watching Charlie intently as he snapped the lighter shut. The clear blue eyes behind the glasses focused on him as the crime boss tried to puzzle out the strange calculation of the man called Charlie Tumulty. "What do you think, Molly?"

She remained quiet for a few seconds more, regarding Charlie as if he were some exotic new fish in a tank at the Boston Aquarium. "The nuns told us about some Greek guy who walked all around with a lantern tryin' to find an honest man. Pretty fuckin' tough job. But I gotta say, maybe we found one, Neily. I think we got a stand-up guy here."

"Does look that way," her brother agreed. "I remember the story now. He killed Beak because Beak had his friend whacked. Imagine that. Ten years he did for a dead pal. That is a stand-up guy. Then his mother," he continued, suppressing laughter, "his mother shot Beak's piece of shit nephew for good measure, wasn't that the story?"

"Yeah. Grace. She died not long after. Cancer."

"Fuckin' cancer," Molly said.

"So, listen, all of you," Neily added. "I'm inspired by this guy's honesty and all that. However, I never claimed to be such a model citizen. Now if memory serves, there were six guys playing the night the shit went down. So, if I split it up, that would be . . . Jimmy?"

"Ah . . . lemme see." He gazed at the ceiling while his lips moved for a few seconds. "Eight hundred apiece."

"Only who knows who was ahead, who was behind. We might open a can of worms trying to share out the dough. The other option is we could pretend we never heard a thing about it, what the hell, one guy is dead, we don't know who the other guy was, but if we ever find out he's dead, too. We can just split it amongst ourselves. Molly and I take three thousand, the rest of you split the eighteen hundred. That would be—even I can do that, three sixes are eighteen. That's six hundred each. I think this is the better option."

They all nodded. Big George said, "I'll call Dickie an' have him put it all on American Dream in the last race. Easy come, easy go, right?"

"Good luck, Georgie. Jimmy, give 'em their cash." He turned back to Charlie. "Now, the only thing is, obviously the recipients of the dough will shut up. We're not talking an Irish Lottery hit here, but still. So, Charlie, if you could not mention it to anyone, that would be helpful."

"In avoiding ill will," his sister added.

"Once I leave here, I'm done. I did what I wanted to do. What you do is your business, and I don't talk about other people's business. I'm starting fresh like I said. Putting the last ten years behind me."

"I fuckin' love the way this guy talks," Neily said to the others. Then he asked, "Where you goin'?"

"Down East. Way up the Maine coast."

"Well, that's nice, you know if you like fishing boats and cottages and shit. I mean we got the sea here. I love it. But I like buildings."

"I understand. You're a city guy. I'll be on my way, then," Charlie said, rising.

"Wait a minute," Neily said, "Can I buy you a drink or get you lunch?"

"I appreciate it, but I'm gonna head back. I would like to know one thing."

"What's that?" Molly asked.

"Can't matter much now. They're all dead. But my friend who was killed told me that Malvert told him he killed this kid Johnny Rivera because he was yakking to people about business deals that Malvert was involved in. That never made sense to me. What the hell would young Johnny Rivera know about Beak's business deals?"

Neily rose and said, "Let me walk you out." This time the crowd took no notice of Charlie as he passed with Neily through the bar and out the door. The sunlit air was welcome. Neily said, "Charlie, I'll answer your question from what I have heard. First of all, you ask what would that young kid know about Beak Malvert's business? Nothing. What is he gonna tell? This is what I understand actually happened. The kid, Rivera, was in a bar in Lowell . . ."

"The Star Lite?"

"No, some place called Pollard's, as I recall. Restaurant on one side, bar on the other. Not a mob hangout. Friendly place."

"Yeah, I know it."

"So, Beak's asshole nephew Sago is chatting up some chick at the bar. Laying the charm on her. Slick bastard. When she went to the Ladies, Rivera happened to see that Sago poured some powder in her drink and stirred it with the straw, you know? The woman comes back, and Rivera goes over and tells her don't drink that. This fuckin' guy just spiked your drink. Sago calls him a liar and throws the drink at him. Rivera slaps the shit out of him and kicks his ass out to the street. *Just desserts* as they say, right? I got no respect for a guy who drugs a woman."

"Who does? And that's how this whole miserable daisy chain started?"

"Frank and Malvert, they sic the goons on the kid, kill his father too, and your pal, and bring down all this shit on their heads, and on mine. I even had this cop from Lowell, Hutton, come down to talk to me. Of course, I couldn't say much of what I heard because it's safer to say nothing to cops, as you know. But if it's any consolation, I know a couple of Malvert's goons came to a bad end."

Charlie knew, from Sean Keenan, that the man he was speaking to had had those goons killed, but he said nothing.

Neily continued, "Yeah, Charlie, all of this shit went down 'cause one predatory cocksucker got humiliated by a good kid."

"I'm so glad my mother killed Sago and Catfish."

"Or you would have, right?"

Charlie nodded.

"That's a good mother you got there, Tumulty."

He felt his eyes welling up and put on his sunglasses. "Yeah," he said. "Grace was all right in the end."

"Again, I apologize for Denny and Johnny. It's always funny when guys who think they're tough 'cause they beat up schmucks on the street think they can take on a trained fighter. Like this big Mick says to me the other day, 'I think I could whip Joe DeNucci. I got some of the old warrior in me.' I said it don't matter what you got in you when you're knocked out in five seconds."

Charlie laughed. "A barroom fighter against DeNucci? Forget it. It's an art. A difficult skill you have to learn, and it takes time and everything you've got."

They shook hands, and Neily said, "Listen Charlie, if you ever need a favor, come see me. You'll be welcome here. I'll see to that."

"Thanks, Neily. I like you, but you'll never see me in Southie again."

Neily touched his forehead in a casual salute and said, "So long, then, champ. Take care of yourself."

As he walked back to his car, Charlie felt something dawning on him. It was a new feeling, as if he had been groping through a dark tunnel nearly full of water. He had been moving along in the darkness, snatching breaths of air between the water and the roof of the cave. Now, the cavern had widened; the ceiling rose, and he had found a way out. Before him stretched a vast sunlit bay. The tripledeckers around him faded; it was all white sand and blue sea. It was freedom, and the vast spaces no longer frightened him. Brilliant white against the blue, a pair of gulls cried. It sounded like freedom.

For the first time since the night Foxy McCrae had come to him with the story of Johnny Rivera's murder, he was free. Free to leave the past in the past, free to accept the assurances of Joe Grant that his daughter's death was not his fault, free to live, and to accept the hard reality that what might have been would never be. Free to give Sophie the love she deserved.

Chapter 20

Charlie was surprised at how little he had to pack. You learn in jail to live without a lot of things. Some books, an alarm clock, a few blankets, a photo of Grace. The old military bunk bed and its lumpy mattress, he had thrown out. He did bring his timeworn ring shoes, sparring gloves, bag gloves, boxing gloves, and headgear. He was not thinking of trying to reignite the career. That was over. But he thought at some point he might like to open a gym where young boxers could train and learn the right way, the way Mike Dineen had taught him. He'd been to see Mike, who had lost some of his old energy. His wife sat by in a sort of fond sadness.

"You really gave those judges hell in Worcester that night," Charlie told him.

Mike's expression showed he was still offended at the memory. "Sons of bitches," he said.

"Thanks for everything, Mike. I learned a lot from you. Not just about boxing." He'd given him a final heartfelt embrace. "You're a good man, Mike," he told him. "The best."

"Charlie," Mike said, "they put your picture up on the wall in the gym. Makes me proud to see it."

"Thanks to you, Mike." As he spoke, he realized that Mike's pride in him now meant more to him than being counted among the local boxing legends.

Once his car was packed, he took a drive through the old mill town. Fitzgibbons had gone to Newton to bid on an estate sale, but promised he would stay in touch with him and Sophie. Charlie was glad, in a way. That would have been the saddest goodbye of all.

He decided to take a last walk through the downtown, and grab a coffee on Palmer Street. Near St. Anne's Church, he spotted Red McNulty coming out of Lucy Larcom Park. He pulled over by Solomon's and caught up with him. "Red, I was looking for you. Listen, I don't have any Old Golds, but take this." He pushed a ten-dollar bill into his hand and said, "Buy a couple packs. I'm moving now, like I said. Up to Maine."

Red tucked the money in his pocket. "Thanks, Charlie. Can always use a sawbuck. Maine is nice. Cold though. Winter's a little longer up there."

"That's all right. Sophie and I are buying a diner in Jonesport. It's already called Flo's Diner, so we'll probably keep that name, but Flo is retiring. If you ever want to come up and work . . . doin' dishes, sweepin' up, clearing tables.

You could do that, right? Have to clean yourself up a bit, too, of course but there's a bathroom with a shower in the back."

"Jeez, I don't think so, Charlie. Thanks, but I like Lowell. I grew up here, and . . . I like it."

"I understand. It's hard to leave what you know. But the offer is there. Flo's Diner, Jonesport."

"Thanks a lot, Charlie. I'm real sorry to see you go."

"Well, good luck."

"Okay, Charlie." He started to walk down Merrimack Street but turned and called back, "The Pride of the Acre!"

Charlie shouted back, "The Acre will be just as proud without me."

Red went on his way, that uncomplaining wanderer of the streets, remembering how once he too had been young and danced the Lindy Hop until closing time at the Commodore Ballroom. Charlie stood still for a moment and took in the panorama of his hometown: the canal flowing through granite archways of the gatehouse, the stately bricks of the Yorick Club and the stolid Greek pillars of Masonic Hall. His gaze rose and took in the tremendous gray stone clock tower of City Hall, a reminder since 1893 to all the citizens that the hours were ever passing and that they must be about their business. The great golden eagle descended from an azure sky and was, forever, or as long as the City Hall stood, alighting on the tower's pinnacle.

He watched the people, his people, passing along the streets. They, or their ancestors, had come from every part of the globe, but they were all Lowellians now, a living part of the entity that was the city, as he would always be. He knew them. He knew their bakeries and restaurants, their neighborhoods and bars, their churches and temples, their gardens and grottos, and all the city's saints and sinners. The scene before him filled his heart, or maybe his soul, and he remembered the lines of the poet:

From terrace proud to alley base
I know thee as my mother's face.

My mother's face. He bought a coffee on Palmer Street and walked back to his car. As he drove down Dutton Street toward Rt. 495, he turned to take a last look down Market Street. The sun burnished the gold dome of Holy Trinity Church and sharpened the gothic spire of St. Patrick's Church beyond. He turned on the radio. The Allman Brothers—Blue Sky. The music, the morning, and he himself were all part of one thing, and he thought of Laila: *the kind of music that makes you believe in God.* He sipped the hot coffee, and he set his face to the road before him. Farewell to the Acre.

Envoi

Charlie and Sophie were married in the Holy Name Church in Machias, Maine. It was too far for Fitzgibbons to drive; his rusting Ford cargo van was well suited to convey a man who lived amid antiquities across moderate distances, but like its driver, unfit for a trip of such magnitude. The old man sent a vintage clock set in a brass ship's wheel, which he must have thought an apt timepiece to measure a life on the doorstep of the sea. Mornings, Charlie often ran along the shore, luxuriating in the grand and limitless space of it all, and recalling always, as the sun rose, the words of Homer, "When dawn spread out her fingertips of rose . . ."

Sometimes he lay in the darkness, sweating through vivid dreams, his heart pounding as his mind returned to a place where some C.O. herded him into a cell and slammed the door, but Sophie was there to wake him gently and stroke his brow and tell him it wasn't real, and those dreams visited him less frequently. Charlie would never be thankful for his time in jail. But cooking for hundreds of men made the work at Flo's Diner seem easy. In Sophie's mother, Wendy Stiles, Charlie saw what a mother could be, or should be. In the evenings, even when Sophie was busy, he liked to go and sit with her and watch reruns of *I Love Lucy*.

He wrote to Hardie Bangs to tell him that he would never be back, that his mind was no longer bent on vengeance, and to thank him for the friendship that had saved him through his sentence. A month later he got a letter from Concord. *"Hey Charlie, I ain't much of a letter writer as you know. I'm real glad you got a good woman and a life to live. Be out soon too, before summer, my brother got me a job lined up, custodian in an office building in Hartford. Maybe one of these days I ride up your way and kick your sorry ass in chess one more time. Love you, brother.*

Hardie."

He folded the letter into a notebook he kept; he had honored some unspoken promise to Miss Walker and to himself to write, and one night after Sophie had gone to bed, sitting at a table on a screened-in porch in the stillness of a summer night, he began. He wrote of a freezing boy walking through a snowstorm to find something to eat. When he had done, he put down the pen, listening to the crickets and blessing the power of the love that had saved him from a road that was taking him down to imprisonment or destruction; the immeasurable love of a mother and, as Hardie had said, *a good woman*. He trembled to consider the hard road he had evaded: to live like a caged animal with nothing but hate and the memory of a useless vengeance taken, however justified.

The following day, when the crowd at the diner had thinned after lunch, Charlie watched a four-month pregnant Sophie standing by the window looking out on the street and nibbling a cookie she had just taken from a pan fresh out of the oven. She felt his gaze and turned, smiling, still chewing the cookie. Such a small thing, as the poet said, to remember for years, but in that moment he felt as if the final piece of the puzzle had slipped into place, and he could see the whole picture. His life made sense. In spite of the lost years, the pain and the broken dreams, he had this life, and he would not be the fool of loss.

His wife moved toward him, her head slightly tilted, and asked, "What?"

He took her gently by the shoulders and whispered in her ear. "I love you," he said. "My God, I love you."

Acknowledgements

It's a bit tricky to write a piece of fiction that takes place in a real city such as Lowell. The writer may be forced to bend time and history, and even a bit of geography at times, as the fictional characters move about their world beside actual people who lived, loved and fought at that time.

Lowell has long been known as a tough city. Cliff Whalen, another legend of Lowell, explained to me that Lowell's reputation spread over the country during the Second World War. Soldiers from Fort Devens often took the train into the city, usually to visit the now long-vanished bars of Moody Street. Soldiers who got drunk and misbehaved in the bars found themselves in brawls with locals who, it turned out, were very often more than they could handle. As Cliff said, "Those soldiers came from all over the country, and when they went home, they told others, 'Don't ever pick a fight in Lowell, Massachusetts.'"

The glory days of boxing seem to have passed in Lowell. Most of the numerous boxing gyms have closed. Micky

Ward is still deservedly a local hero, and people remember the career of his half-brother Dicky Eklund and his famous ten-round match with Sugar Ray Leonard. Both men were portrayed in the award-winning movie *The Fighter*.

Beau Jaynes and the late Manny Freitas were two wonderful characters and well-known boxers. I interviewed them for a radio show about twenty-five years ago. God only knows where that tape has gone; I'd love to hear it again. It's dangerous to begin to name boxers, because inevitably I will leave someone out who should be mentioned, but during what would have been near Charlie Tumulty's day, the name that arises often is Larry Carney, often called "The Pride of the Acre." Like many another tough boxer, and great athletes such as Babe Ruth, he didn't take as much care of his health as he should have, and still won three New England Golden Gloves Championships as well as New England Middleweight and Light Heavyweight titles. The fictional Charlie Tumulty would certainly have been aware of Larry Carney and some of the other fighters I've mentioned during the time period of this book.

Other boxers of earlier generations whose names are familiar to Lowell boxing aficionados are listed in *K.O. Digest* by Editor-in-Chief Jeffrey Freeman; boxers such as Al Mello, Phinney Boyle, Paul Frechette, "the Blond Tiger," Billy Ryan, Danny Heath and Jackie Morrell.

My grandfather, Jack Leahy, originally of Youghal Harbor, Co. Cork, was Phinney Boyle's manager. I didn't know Billy Ryan, but his brother Mike, also a tough boxer and later, a well-respected referee, is a friend of mine. I have to say that all the time I was writing the novel, I had the image of Mike Ryan in my mind as I wrote the character of Mike Dineen.

I should give a well-earned nod to Bobby Christakos, yet another fighter from the Acre who was a five-time Golden Gloves Champion.

Of course, though the boxing world is the arena in which Charlie Tumulty seeks to prove himself, the novel is really about human relationships, about how family shapes our destiny, and how good mentors can save a young man whose family has little support to offer. It's also, like *The Count of Monte Cristo*, a story of love and vengeance. I leave it to the reader to decide whether that vengeance is just.

I'd like to thank my friend, the writer, David Daniel, for having read the manuscript and offered his valuable insights. I'd also like to thank my reliable readers, Terry Downes and Kevin Cavanaugh, two erudite gentlemen, and finally, Lewis Karabatsos for his editorial suggestions. Terry, a former clerk magistrate, also answered some legal questions for me. Though the prison scenes are infrequent, I'm indebted to Gary Boyle, former inmate and current good guy, for questions about prison life.

For some of the boxing details, I owe thanks to Tommy Lee, the sage of Charlie's Bar, whose knowledge of all things boxing is encyclopedic, and my cousin Charlie Gill for having introduced me to Tommy. Charlie himself is also a valuable source for any local story-teller. I must also thank former boxer Paul Leakeas. He once mentioned that as a child, he would run down to the Press Club, where his mother worked, to get some food. That scene first suggested this story. Andy Robinson was also kind enough to sit with me one night at the Old Court and recall his boxing days, as did Ronnie Lutkus at the Tavern on the Square.

The quote from *The Iliad* in Chapter 9 is taken from the Robert Fitzgerald translation.

Many thanks to John Boutselis for his fine cover image.

As always, thanks to my dear wife, Olga Maria, for her support.

www.ingramcontent.com/pod-product-compliance
Lightning Source LLC
LaVergne TN
LVHW011806060526
838200LV00053B/3681